In the middle of the night,

Jessie awakened to fear licking at her senses. The darkness settled over her like a heavy weight. She sat up in bed, her heart beating frantically. He was near. Breathing became work. She could feel him trying to get inside her thoughts and take them captive; strong, pulling her into his web; choking the life out of her. She fought, singing the song in her mind. When she grew weary, and her eyes closed, the shadows began to dance, and the voices mockingly sang *you will die, you will die*. Jessie got up and sat on the floor. *I will not let you in. I will live, I will live,* she repeatedly whispered until his power was broken and the night gave way to the gray light of dawn. Strange. She should still feel fear, but it wasn't there. Why?

I0526650

Praise for Iona Morrison

"Not only are her human characters charming and likeable...Iona calls our attention to serious ills of society in her books, and she gives us food for thought as well as entertaining us. This is a definite must read!"

~Shelley Cadwallader

~*~

"Her tales are hand wringers that make me want to yell at the characters to warn them when they are in danger. It is difficult to put her books down. Loved book number two and am looking forward to book number three."

~ReNae Bowman

~*~

"I highly recommend this tight, fast-paced romantic intrigue-paranormal-murder-mystery to anyone who loves a good book. I hope we see more of Jessie and Matt."

~Carol Ann Kauffman

The Game Changer

by

Iona Morrison

A Blue Cove Mystery

This is a work of fiction. Names, characters, places, and incidents are either the product of the author's imagination or are used fictitiously, and any resemblance to actual persons living or dead, business establishments, events, or locales, is entirely coincidental.

The Game Changer

COPYRIGHT © 2016 by Iona Morrison

All rights reserved. No part of this book may be used or reproduced in any manner whatsoever without written permission of the author or The Wild Rose Press, Inc. except in the case of brief quotations embodied in critical articles or reviews.
Contact Information: info@thewildrosepress.com

Cover Art by *Debbie Taylor*

The Wild Rose Press, Inc.
PO Box 708
Adams Basin, NY 14410-0708
Visit us at www.thewildrosepress.com

Publishing History
First Fantasy Rose Edition, 2016
Print ISBN 978-1-5092-0857-9
Digital ISBN 978-1-5092-0858-6

A Blue Cove Mystery
Published in the United States of America

Dedication

I dedicate this book to my nephew
Dennis Paul Hurst,
who has inspired me with his convictions,
humor, courage, and his strength.

Chapter 1

The front door pushed open with a creaky squeal. Jessie flinched, hitting her head on the edge of the counter. "Darn." Her fingers gingerly rubbed the spot. She had forgotten to lock it again. She stood and peered over the mountain of books stacked on the work surface at a pleasant-looking young man standing in the doorway. His uniform was pressed and tidy. Perhaps another delivery of books from a vendor, she mused. Sunglasses covered his eyes. Masculine hands brushed the snow off the sleeve of his jacket, as he appeared to search the interior of her store. Her pulse quickened. A strange sensation crept over her as he came closer to where she was standing. The cold chill started at her neck and spread like icy fingers down her back.

"Hello. Is anyone here? I have a delivery for you," he called.

"I'm over here, by the counter." She waved at him. Jessie stepped from behind the boxes and motioned again.

He took off his sunglasses and stared at her. His jaw dropped slightly. "It's another cold one this morning." He looked intently at her. "I wanted to make sure someone was here before I unloaded the boxes out of the truck." He didn't move from the spot where he stood.

"As you can see, I'm here." Jessie pressed her lips

together.

"Yes, yes, I can see that you are." He shook his head.

Jessie clutched her phone, moving toward him. "You said you have a delivery." She placed her free hand on her hip, stopping in front of him.

"Of course…" His voice trailed off. "Yes, I have a delivery for you." He turned his back and walked out the door. A few minutes later, he returned pushing a hand truck loaded with several boxes.

"You can set them in the corner over there." She pointed to the spot.

"Will do." He gave her a slight smile and got busy unloading the boxes. "Looks like you've got your work cut out for you." He rolled the hand truck over by the door.

"You mean this?" She motioned around the room at the stacks of boxes. "This isn't work, it's my next great adventure." She gave a tentative smile when he rolled his eyes. "All right, I admit it may be a wee bit of work."

He walked toward her. "I need you to sign off on the paperwork. I marked all the spots where the company requires a signature." He studied her face as he pointed to the first place on the page.

She shivered, suddenly uncomfortable with the way he kept looking at her. Where was Matt when she needed him? She handed back the signed papers.

He cleared his throat. "I'm sorry. You must think I'm rude. I don't mean to stare at you. It's just that you're the last person I expected to see here this morning." He shifted his weight back and forth.

"Excuse me? I'm not sure I understand. Have we

met before?"

"No. I know I'm making a mess of this. Maybe I should start over," he mumbled. "I'm not sure I know how to explain this to you, so I'll just say it. I saw you in a dream last night. A woman in my dream pointed you out to me. She told me you could help me find my wife." He bowed his head shoving his hand in his pocket.

"Who said I could help you?"

He shrugged his shoulders. "I don't know, just some woman. I heard her say you were the one. You must think I'm crazy. I can assure you I'm not. Nothing like this has ever happened to me before." He turned his face away.

Goosebumps spread up her arms. "Maybe you should start from the top." She went over to the table in the center of the room, shifted a few boxes, and motioned for him to join her. "If it's okay with you, I want to call a friend."

"Sure." He sat across from her. "I would appreciate any help I can get. No one else seems to be taking me seriously."

She touched Matt's number. "Matt, where are you?" she asked the minute he answered.

"I'm next door getting your morning coffee, sweetheart. I have some extra time to help you unpack. How does that sound?"

"Perfect, get another coffee and hurry over, would you. There's something I think you'll want to hear." The tingle of excitement was growing stronger.

The man leaned forward in his chair, his fingers massaging his temples. His foot kept an annoying rhythm as it repeatedly hit against the leg of the chair.

"I'm sorry I said anything," he muttered quietly.

"I know you must need to get back to work. My friend should be here any minute."

"I'm only going through the motions. I can't seem to concentrate, if you know what I mean." His voice was flat. "I almost gave this run to someone else this morning but decided against it at the last minute. I have no clue why, but I knew I needed to make this delivery, and now, here you are…" He pointed at her, his voice trailing off. "Excuse my manners, I'm Evan." He rubbed his forehead. "Evan Foster."

"Jessie Reynolds." She extended her hand, and he took it. "Can I get you anything?"

"No, I'm good, thanks." His foot kept the persistent tapping.

The bell above the door rang when the door opened. At least the darn bell worked this time. Matt walked toward them with three cups of coffee on a tray with a bag in the center. He was a handsome devil for sure, and he always remembered to get her a scone. The calories weren't needed, but the scones were always good. Jessie jumped up and walked toward him. "Good morning." She leaned close to him to speak. "I think maybe you should listen to this."

"Okay." He smiled and softened his voice. "I get it, you're feeling a little nervous, and you want me around."

She nodded at him. "Evan, this is Matt Parker. He's the police chief in Blue Cove. If anyone can help you, he can."

Matt shook Evan's hand and then placed his hand on her shoulder. "Jessie here is my partner and a damn good investigative reporter. We've worked a few cases together. If it is help you want, you've come to the right place."

His praise brought a tinge of pink to her cheeks. "Yes, he has."

Matt sat next to her. "Evan, what's up?"

"To tell you the truth, I'm not sure. I'm still as baffled by it as I was when I first walked in the door and saw her." He pointed at Jessie. "I don't know what to think."

"Why don't you start at the beginning, and we'll go from there." Matt encouraged him.

"My wife, Adriana, was on her way to Blue Cove a few weeks ago to see her best friend Kathy. She left early in the morning so that she could spend the day with her. She never made it. It was as if she just vanished. They found her car abandoned on the side of the road several miles out of town, but there was no sign of her. No one has heard from her or seen her since." He swiped at the tears forming in his eyes.

"Which police department is handling the case?" Matt asked taking his pen out of his pocket.

"It's the county sheriff. They found her car somewhere between here and Rocky Pointe."

"Is there anything else you can tell me? Was there any blood at the scene?" Matt studied Evan's face as he wrote a few notes in his notebook.

"No, there was nothing." Evan shook his head. "I'm the prime suspect, of course." He frowned, making the small lines on his forehead more pronounced. "I have a solid alibi, though. I was working with a partner on a run at the time."

"There're other ways to be a part of it. You could have hired someone. Are you involved?" Matt's voice hardened.

Evan straightened in his chair and looked Matt directly in the eyes. "No! Never! I loved my wife. She's expecting our first baby. We had just found out a few days before she went missing. It's eating me up inside."

"What is the sheriff saying?" Matt took a sip of his coffee and handed one to Jessie. He gave the other cup to Evan, never taking his sight off him.

"Besides thinking it's my fault somehow, his next theory is maybe she ran off." He hung his head.

"What do you think? Is it possible she left you?" Matt asked.

"No—we love each other—I would never believe it of her." He crossed his arms across his chest. Evan's eyes met Matt's. "Look, to be honest, I had started to wonder if she had run off. Up to now, Adriana has always let me know her whereabouts. I didn't want to believe it of her, but the longer I've gone without hearing from her my mind has imagined all kinds of crap." He leaned forward in his chair. "Then I had a dream. Adriana kept telling me to come and find her. She begged me to hurry." His voice got stronger as he rushed on. "The dream changed from Adriana to another woman. As weird as this all sounds, I heard in my dream that this woman," he pointed at Jessie, "could help me find Adriana."

"You heard that Jessie could help you?" Matt raised his brow.

"Yes! I know how this must sound to you. It sounds crazy to me, too. I wasn't going to work today, but at the last minute, I took this delivery—and here she is. Hell, I don't know what to think." He shook his head.

Matt smiled at Jessie. "Nope, it isn't strange at all when it comes to her. It's par for the course."

Jessie gave him a playful hit. "You'll have him thinking I'm weird." She frowned at Matt.

"You are weird, sweetheart." He grinned at her.

"I'll admit I've had a few unusual things happen to me, but only since I moved here and met you." She turned her attention back to Evan. "These circumstances are certainly different, though. I don't know what to think about what you've told me." His slumped form touched her heart. "I'm not sure how I can help you." As soon as the words left her mouth, she knew she had to try.

"I can't imagine how you can either." He rubbed the nape of his neck. "But I'm willing to do anything if it can help me get my wife back."

"Tell me about her." She sipped her coffee, looking over the top of the cup at Evan.

He pulled a picture of her from the papers on his clipboard. "This is a recent photo taken a few nights before she went missing."

Adriana had a sweet face and an infectious smile. She was tiny, barely reaching to her husband's shoulder. An attractive woman, she reminded Jessie of Katie. An image flashed through Jessie's mind, large hands wrapped around Adriana's mouth. Her body hung limp. Scooped up like dead weight, she was thrown over a man's shoulders. Another image quickly replaced the one of Adriana. Jessie shut her eyes trying to erase the impression. For another woman, it was too late. "Do you have extra photos so I can keep this one or would you like me to make a copy?" Her voice trembled as she asked Evan.

"You can have it. I have several." He pushed another copy of his wife's picture toward her.

Jessie handed a photo to Matt. "Did she work outside the home?" Jessie wrestled to get control of her emotions. Evan didn't need any more stress.

"She's the VP at Rocky Pointe First Bank. The bank president had promoted her to the position a few weeks ago." He wiped the tears running down his cheeks with the back of his hand. "She was so excited about her promotion and I was proud of her." Evan clasped his hands together in front of him. "Honestly, I've loved her from the first moment I laid eyes on her." His voice broke.

"She obviously had a lot of contact with the public. Working in a bank gave her lots of exposure. Did she have friends at the bank?" Jessie asked as she wrote Adriana's name on the back of the picture.

Evan nodded. "Everyone seemed to like her. She was always talking about her co-workers, especially her friend Kathy. I wish now I had paid closer attention to what she was telling me." He stretched his legs out, slouched forward in his chair.

"Did the investigating officer question her friend Kathy?" she asked.

"The deputy took her name and told me they were going to talk to her and Adriana's co-workers."

"Could you write her friend's address and number down for me?" Jessie pushed a pencil and a slip of paper toward him.

"Did she have any enemies that you know of?" Matt asked as he copied the information in his notebook.

"If she did, I never heard about them." Evan

fidgeted with the pencil, tapping it on the table "So what do you think? I mean I don't know what to do next."

"Give me your number. Jessie can start snooping around. I'll call and talk to the sheriff for you. I'll find out who is handling your case and see where they're at in the investigation. Here's my number." Matt handed his business card to Evan. "You can let us know if you hear anything and we'll see if anything comes up on this side. In the meantime, hang in there."

"I feel better talking to you. You listened to me, at least." Evan started to stand but sat back down when he heard Jessie's voice.

"I think she's still alive, Evan. She would call you if she could, and the dream was probably her way of trying to get through to you. Someone is restraining her." Jessie stood, reached across the table, and touched Evan's hand. "Watch for her in your dreams. She may leave little clues as to where she's at."

"Okay." He shifted in his chair,

"That's my girl." Matt patted Jessie's shoulder. "You never fail to surprise even me."

They talked a few more minutes. Jessie watched Matt talk to him out near his truck until Evan left to finish his route and she went back to unpacking the boxes behind the counter. The petite brunette woman with her smiling brown eyes would fill Jessie's thoughts the rest of the day. Hooked, intrigued, and ready to get started, her mind raced ahead to plot a strategy. Another case had found her.

Jessie bent to pick up a heavy box. "Here, let me get that." Matt playfully pushed her out of the way, picked it up with ease, and placed the box on the table when she pointed him there. "What are you thinking?"

"I want to help, and I hope I can." Gathering her hair, Jessie twisted it and clipped it up out of her face. "Matt, it was uncanny how he kept looking at me. That's why I called, and I wanted you here." She clasped her hands together. "I didn't see this coming. I think I can safely say, here we go again."

Matt smiled and gave her a kiss on the cheek. "I'll call the sheriff's office today to see what's going on. I wonder if they used a dog when Adriana first went missing."

"Police are getting better about calling in search and rescue dogs when they're available. But dogs and handlers aren't always easy to come by, especially for small towns." Jessie glanced at him. "So you believe his story, and you're going to help?"

He handed her a stack of books. "We'll see. The jury is still out on the believing part, but I'm going to dig around a little. I do believe in you, though, and I know you saw something when you were looking at her picture, didn't you?"

"I saw a quick flash in my mind, I know someone took her, and she's still alive. But I didn't see who it was or why. I saw enough to know another woman's body will show up at some point."

"Hell, not what I wanted to hear. I knew you had seen something, which changes everything for me." He touched her hand. "I'll see you later. Are you working at the church today?" He grabbed his coffee.

"No, I have a couple of weeks off to work on the store." She smiled, turning around, taking it all in. "My dream is becoming reality." She stopped in front of him.

"My view of it is about perfect." He watched her, his grin fading. His tone became serious. "Maybe you should lock the door, sweetheart." He lifted her chin and gazed into her eyes. "I don't want just anyone coming in here to stare at you."

"I guess I could, but I'm expecting a few more deliveries."

"Put a note on the door and tell them to knock if they have a delivery," he said, handing her a paper and pen. "I'll get back to you if I hear anything. Lock it!"

She walked with him to the door and taped a note to the glass. As soon as he went out, she clicked the lock. She stood there watching him get in the car and then unlocked it. There was always some man thinking she was helpless and telling her what to do. She waited until he waved at her and then locked it again. Jessie watched him drive away.

The snow had finally stopped falling, and the sun was peeking out from behind the clouds. The church looked like a postcard picture. Her gaze followed the movement of the trees blowing in the cemetery, sending the icy white flakes flying from their branches. In the shadow of the church building, the graveyard looked cold and foreboding. Only the tops of the headstones peeked out above the snowy cover blanketing the ground. She shuddered, rubbing her arms. It had been a strange morning.

Back to work! She turned away from the window. The smell of new books, fresh paint, and leather tickled her senses. Grabbing the stack of hardbacks off the counter, she carried them to the front of the store, arranging them on the display table in the front window. Jessie smiled as she picked up the new release from one of her favorite authors, clutching the book to her chest. Corinne Clark had promised to come opening day and sign books. How cool was that!

Her smile broadened. She had done it. She was officially an adult who owned her own business. The French doors between her store and Java Joe's coffee shop remained closed. Paper covered her side for now, but only until she was ready to unveil her new store. Jessie ran her hand over the wooden sign, which was the last thing that would go up on the outside of the building, and then she bent behind the counter to open another box.

After hours of unpacking boxes and putting books on their shelves, it was starting to take shape. Cozy reading corners, with chairs and small tables to place drinks, were in place. She hung several of the paintings that had arrived earlier in the month; they added vivid color against the exposed brick walls. Every day it looked at little more like the place she had dreamed about when she first saw that it was for sale. It was an excellent setting to pass a little idle time in, reading and drinking coffee.

She laughed at the text Matt left her mid-morning asking her if anyone else had come into her shop to stare at her. He had the power to make her feel weak in the knees. What was she going to do about him? He had been dropping hints about marriage, but she wasn't ready. Not that there was anyone else; she wanted to get her business off the ground and had a few other things on her to-do list before she settled down. Matt wouldn't wait forever, but her over-protective dad was a constant reminder of why she wasn't ready. After twenty-six years of being an only child, Jessie was still learning to cope with her dad's domineering ways. Her mom had given up trying to keep peace in the family years ago. Only Grams, bless her heart, was strong enough to give him a run for his money, and Jessie had learned from her. Every time she turned around, Dad was giving his unsolicited advice. He had made the holidays tense. Jessie frowned. She had to admit Matt upset her a few times, too, when he had agreed with her father. It hadn't scored any points in his favor. Still she couldn't hold it against him either. Dad had a way of making people agree with him against their better judgment.

****

She was about to rip open another box when she heard tapping at the door. Jessie wasn't surprised to see Reba standing outside after her morning. She unlocked the door and held it open.

"How's it going, my dear? I wanted to stop and check out your progress." Reba swept in, touching Jessie's arm as she passed her then turned around taking it all in. "I like the way it looks."

Jessie clicked the lock on the door. "I can hardly wait until my opening day. Why the frown?"

"I knew this morning when I woke up that things were active again and that you were being called upon to do something." Reba stopped at the table, her finger tracing the letters on the wooden sign. "Hmm, I like this. *Idle Time Books* is a perfect name" Reba clasped Jessie's hand. "This case, my dear, may take you a little farther away from home."

"I can't go anywhere right now. As you know, my store will keep me busy, and I'm working a couple of jobs." *No, please not now*. Jessie's mind raced ahead, but she knew she wasn't winning this one.

"Needs are seldom convenient; they just are. I could be wrong, but I rarely am. So I expect that you might want to keep a bag packed just in case you need to leave in a hurry." She patted Jessie's hand as she let it go. "Why don't you tell me what happened this morning."

Jessie motioned to the small table and chairs in the corner. Reba sat in the leather chair, crossing her legs at the ankles. Jessie gave Reba the details and sat back in her chair to wait for her wisdom. Reba was too quiet, which was unusual. Jessie's fingers tapped on the arm of the chair. Waiting wasn't one of her strengths. "So what do you think?"

Reba folded her hands on the table in front of her. "Well, it's a unique approach, I'll give you that, but I'm not sure what I think. You were in his dream, and he came into your store, what are the odds of that?"

"Almost improbable, I'm sure." Jessie pushed the picture of Adriana in front of Reba.

She stared at it a minute. "She's a lovely girl. Her smile is sweet, isn't it?" Reba held the photo up close. "It makes me wonder."

"What?" Jessie leaned forward closer to Reba.

"Maybe the person who abducted her doesn't want to hurt her but is obsessed with her. You know a stalker."

"I had the same thought cross my mind." Jessie leaned back in her chair. "How can you know for sure?"

"We'll know soon enough, I guess." Reba smiled and patted Jessie's hand. "I'm glad you bought the store. This building needed some tender loving care for a while. Tying it together with the coffee shop is pure genius." Reba pointed at the closed doors. "The customers will be dropping by in droves." She reached for her gloves on the table. "When is your grand opening?"

"The first week in March. Why?"

"That should give you plenty of time in case you're needed. You can't have the store open without the owner being present." Reba stood. "It's always good to see you, Jessie girl, but I need to get on my way. I have to do some grocery shopping so Lawrence will have dinner tonight. He's been very patient with his less than spectacular meals lately. I think he deserves a good one this evening."

"Be careful, don't slip." Jessie followed Reba to the door and let her out, locking it again behind her. *I'm not going anywhere. I want to be here, doing what I'm doing. Please, oh please, let her be somewhere nearby, so I don't have to leave Blue Cove right now.* She tilted her head heavenward.

Jessie worked the afternoon away. By the time five rolled around, she had unloaded, sorted, and shelved several boxes of books. Her mountain was declining slowly to a molehill. A few more days of hard work and her store would be ready.

She stepped into the back room to get her purse and jacket. Winter days meant it was getting dark early; the air was cold and crisp from the earlier snowstorm. She buttoned her coat, pulling the scarf around her face. Shutting off the lights in the store, she went to her car parked at the back entrance.

Jessie fumbled in her purse trying to reach her ringing phone. Why did it always seem to go missing? She shifted things around, finally reaching it on the fourth ring.

"Hi, Grams."

"Hi, how's my favorite granddaughter?"

"I'm your only granddaughter, and I'm okay. What's happening?" Jessie smiled. Sadie was up to something. She could hear it in her voice.

"When we were all together at Christmas, I noticed that you and Matt were having some trouble. I can talk to him if you want."

"That's okay, Grams, I'll handle him." Jessie grinned, knowing what Matt would think about that statement.

"I thought you could use a little time away from him. Absence makes the heart grow fonder as they say. I looked into some airline tickets for a vacation retreat. I want to take Katie and you. The whole week will be on me. To tell you the truth, I need time away from your father before I let him have it."

"When and where?" Reba's words raced back into Jessie's mind.

"When depends on you and how the store is coming along. The where is a surprise, but it'll be warmer than where we both are now."

"My first thought would be to say I'm too busy, but by the end of the week, I should almost be done. I have some vacation days, and it will still give me nearly three weeks until the store opens. You know, I think it sounds great. I'll talk to Katie and get back to you so you can book it."

The minute she hung up, Jessie called Katie. She explained Sadie's getaway idea.

"Oh, that would be wonderful. I can take the time since the holidays are over. Also, a spa—well now—

that sounds too divine. You can count me in for sure. It'll take a least until the end of this week to get things ready for Alisa to take over for a few days. Next week would be perfect, and any place would be delightful."

"How's Alisa working out?"

"She's great! I'm so glad I had the funds to hire and train her. Besides, I think Kip is sweet on her. He shows up for dinner at the Inn a lot since she started working here."

"She couldn't get a nicer guy than Kip. I hope she treats him right." Jessie laughed. "If not, she'll answer to me. If I had a brother, I would like him to be just like Kip."

"Sure, sure, or like Dylan, or Jeremy, Gary, or any other guy you've ever met besides Matt."

"Katie, you'd be wise not to start on me." Jessie ruined her firm tone by laughing.

"Why's that?" Jessie heard the laughter in Katie's voice. "I may be shorter than you but remember— dynamite comes in small packages." Katie's giggle punctuated the air.

"You're too much. I'll talk to you later, and I'll let you know when Grams gets everything settled date-wise." Jessie smiled as she disconnected the phone and smiled all the way home.

Jessie sat at her computer, turned it on, and jotted off a quick email to Sadie to let her know they would both be going with her. Excitement filled her, a surprise destination was perfect, and maybe Grams was right; time away from Matt might be good. Oh, she loved him all right, but he needed to give her credit for having some intelligence and being capable of making some decisions for herself. He might miss her too, which wouldn't be a bad thing. They could have a great reunion when she got back. Her face flushed just thinking about it.

Jessie looked at her computer screen. *What happened to you, Adriana? I'm going to keep looking until I find you.* Jessie dialed Adriana's friend.

Chapter 2

Matt had spent the better part of the afternoon on the phone with Sheriff Thompson. The whole case was an inept mess. No one seemed to know what was going on in regards to the investigation. He didn't want Jessie involved in this case, but telling her no wouldn't be easy. Their relationship was still recovering from their fight over the holidays. Why he had acted the way he did was a total mystery to him. Hell, he was jealous, plain and simple. His brothers kept hitting on her, the guy staying at the Inn wouldn't leave her alone, and like a chump he had agreed with her father when he lectured her about the bookstore. No wonder she hated when he lectured her. What was even worse, he didn't agree with what her father was saying. A case of nerves was his one and only plausible excuse. It wasn't a good one. His apology had better be fine-tuned. Maybe he should ask her not to get involved and not tell her. If he knew his girl, he was too late anyway.

He smiled when she answered the phone. "Hi, sweetheart. Can I take you to dinner or bring it to the house?"

"What do you have in mind?"

"How about I pick you up in twenty minutes and we'll figure it out. I'm getting ready to leave work now."

"Sounds good, I'll see you soon. It'll give me time

to fill you in on what I've found out about Adriana so far."

Matt groaned inwardly. "Sure, that would be great. See you in twenty."

Now what should he do? She was already involved. He was going to have to do some pretty fancy maneuvering on this one. There was more to the case as one of the deputies had suggested. Matt considered the conversation he had with the deputy earlier in the day.

"Ever since we started investigating this case," Deputy Johnson stammered. "Strange things have happened."

"Strange like how?"

"Well..." He hesitated. "All of our reports on her have disappeared. The legwork, interviews, and the man-hours we put in are gone. I'm not only talking about paper files, but our computer files on the case are wiped out."

"Are you sure you didn't just misplace them."

"Of course, I'm sure. They're flat out gone." Matt had heard the officer's exasperated sigh over the line.

"What else?"

"We've noticed strange things like—I don't know how to say it without sounding ridiculous—just your usual dolls with pins stuck in them, dead chickens, and basic vandalism using blood. It's hard to believe even for me, and I've seen all the crap. Hell, it's been chaos around here ever since we started the investigation. Every day we come across some other strange occurrence. The evidence suggests a cult ritual or voodoo. Whoever is messing with us, knows what he's doing." The deputy cleared his throat. "What I'm trying to say is this isn't kids stuff or a juvenile prank."

Matt had heard the fear in the deputy's voice. Johnson was afraid and cops rarely were. It made him wonder what Johnson wasn't telling him.

He pulled his car in beside hers. She was standing outside waiting. He smiled as she hopped back and forth trying to keep warm in the frigid night air. Bundled up from head to toe, she was a beautiful sight. Her gloved hand started waving the moment she saw him. He wanted to protect her, but he didn't have a clue what he was protecting her from or what they were dealing with yet. *Face reality, Matt, she doesn't need you to babysit her.*

She popped her head in the door. "Hi."

"You know you don't have to stand out in the cold. I'd be happy to come to the door for you."

"I know, but I was too excited to sit still and wait." She flashed him a smile. "Did you talk to the sheriff's department?"

"I did." Boy was he ever in trouble. At fault were those eyes and that smile. *Jeez, I could use a little help, here.* A diversionary tactic was in order. "Before we talk about the case, I want to say something to you."

"Sounds serious, what's up?" She pulled the seat belt across herself but held the buckle in her hand. "Did I do something wrong?"

He shook his head. "I owe you an apology."

"For what?"

"Some of the things I did while your family was here." He paused, taking her hand in his. "I didn't agree with what your father was saying about buying the bookstore. Any business is a risk, but you're a smart woman, and I knew you had considered it thoughtfully."

She looked puzzled. "For heaven's sakes, why would you agree with him? He still brings it up. He'll continue to use it against me."

"I have no real defense except to say, I was trying to fit in with your family and feeling nervous about it. The worst part is, I was jealous of my brothers and that other guy. Ah, hell, I have no good excuse, just bad judgment, and I'm sorry." He could see her shaking her head.

"You know your brothers were only flirting with me to bug you. They aren't interested in me, and the guy at the Inn was a little tipsy, that's all."

He winked at her. "Yeah, well you believe that if it makes you feel better. I know my brothers. I'm sorry, I shouldn't have let them get to me."

"Look, any guy who will say he's sorry is okay in my book. We're good, and I'll add the points back that I took away from you when you did it." She turned in her seat and clicked her seat belt.

He laughed. "I just knew you did something like that. I could feel you were upset with me, and that I wasn't living up to your expectations."

"It's all in the point system. Now drive, I'm hungry." She grinned and pointed at the steering wheel.

The Waterfront Grill was a nice quiet place for them to talk. The host took them to their table. Matt pulled her chair out for her.

"So what did the sheriff say?"

Matt sat back in his chair and was careful how he answered. "I can tell you right now, no one has a clue what's going on. It's a mess. They passed me from one person to another and shuffled me from department to department. There was no new information and no leads at all. What did you find out?" The server handed them each a menu and left them to look it over.

"Adriana grew up in Rocky Pointe but went to college at NYU. I found out that while she was in college, several times she had called the campus police about someone stalking her. There was no name given. She had also turned over a couple of bizarre, rambling love letters he had mailed to her. The campus police had no suspect and never made an arrest."

"That's interesting," Matt replied. "I wonder why Adriana didn't know who he was. Usually, a victim has some idea of who the stalker is or least a description."

"If she did, it wasn't in any of the reports I saw." Jessie took a sip of her water. "I thought it might be a good idea to visit the Rocky Pointe Bank and see if someone might have seen a strange person hanging around. What do you think?"

"Sounds like a good place to start." Matt cupped her hand in his. "I can't believe you found that all out today and the sheriff's office didn't have any of that information." Matt frowned. He decided to let her run with it and to not say anything for now. He would find a way to keep a watchful eye and be close if she needed him. "I can help you all weekend at the store. I have this one off. How's that sound?"

"Perfect," she said as she examined the menu. "Sadie called and asked me to go with her next week on vacation. I mean, all expenses paid, who could turn that down?" She gave the waitress her order.

Speaking of perfect, at least for the next week he wouldn't have to worry about her. He could look into a few things while she was gone. When the server left, he reached across the table and took her hand again. "So where is this vacation going to happen?"

"It's a surprise. Did I mention Katie is going, too?" He shook his head. "All Sadie would say is that it will be warmer than Blue Cove. At this point, I'm just happy to get away."

"I'm sure you'll have a great time."

"Anywhere will be delightful. It's always a great time with Katie and Grams." She took another sip of water. "Will you miss me, maybe just a little?" she asked with a flirtatious smile.

"What do you think? Who is the one that can't go a day without calling you or dropping in to see you? The question is, will you miss me?"

"I'll have to think about it. Since I've added all your points back for the apology, yeah, I'll miss you." She patted his hand. "I think you should know I don't really have a point system." She grinned at him.

The server set their food in front of them and then left. "What do you think about Adriana?" Matt asked, his tone serious. "I know you well enough to know you're already starting to formulate something in your mind."

"I learned a few things. I know what Evan told us, and I believe him. I also know she had a stalker in college who disappeared. I talked to her friend Kathy who had no new information, and she's struggling with Adriana's disappearance. She feels guilty for not reading between the lines when Adriana talked to her."

"Did you ask her about the Foster's relationship?"

"Of course I did." She rolled her eyes at him. "I learned all the right questions to ask in Investigative Reporting 101!"

Matt grinned at her. "Sorry, sweetheart."

"Kathy told me Adriana loved Evan. They seemed to have a healthy marriage. Adriana was excited about the baby and was already planning the nursery." Jessie grabbed her notes from her purse, giving them a quick glance. "She also told me that Adriana was coming here to talk to her about a problem she was having with another man, but she had no idea who he was. Adriana wouldn't talk over the phone about him. She was afraid someone might be listening. Kathy didn't press her and now she wishes she had."

"No other details, I take it."

"No, but Adriana had a stalker once." She pursed her lips, her fingers tapping on her cheek. "What's to say that he hasn't come back? Adriana's missing, but so far, there's no ransom note, which leads me to lean toward a stalker, someone infatuated with her. She's alive. I can feel it. She's scared, but I don't think he plans on hurting her, at least not yet."

"What do you mean by not yet?" His voice sounded gruff.

"You know better than anyone obsessive people are often irrational. It won't take much to send him out of control if she doesn't cooperate with his plans."

"That puts it in another light doesn't it?" He frowned, his body tensing. "Jess, I can't tell you what to do. I've learned that the hard way, but I wish you would stay out of this. If you're right, this man is obsessed with her and, therefore, dangerous. I know you're a strong woman. You were doing this kind of reporting before I met you, so I'll leave this up to you. As much as I want to protect you from everything, I know you can take care of yourself. Promise me that you'll be careful."

"I will. I know when I get involved in a case I can be stubborn and I'm not good at taking orders. Who knows, there might not be anything for me to do. I can't go anywhere if I don't know where I'm going, now can I? Besides, we're in this together." She held the warm cup of coffee in her hands before she took a sip.

The rest of the evening was pleasant. They parked at the Yacht Club and Marina. Repairs and renovations on the Marina had moved ahead in the weeks since the bombing, and Matt wanted to show it to her. He spent a little extra time kissing her after he took her home. His excuse was he wouldn't see her for a week. He kissed her once for each day she would be gone and for anything clever he could think of in the heat of the moment. Her response told him what he needed to know. She was into him and the sexy little groan she had made almost tipped him over the edge. It was getting harder to walk out the door and leave her. The truth was he couldn't seem to get enough of her. Reality and the cold air hit him when he stepped outside. Damn, he was going to miss her.

****

Jessie watched him walk away, slowly closing the door. The air outside was cold, but she felt downright hot. His lips did magical things to her. There was no one who came close to making her feel the way Matt did. He had better be a patient man. She sighed. It was probably a good thing to go away for a week. Otherwise she could forget her dreams. All rational thought disappeared when he kissed her.

Jessie took off her coat, hung it in the closet, and sat on the couch. There was something strange about this case. She found herself pulled into the vortex of it even though she hardly knew any details. The fact that Adriana was taken was only a small part of it, not to her husband, of course, but to the dark figure that Jessie had seen grab Adriana. Someone involved was very powerful, but not in a normal way. An elusive dark shadow crossed her mind whenever she thought about Adriana. He wanted to erase her and create someone new in her place. Jessie shivered at the thought. They had to find Adriana before he accomplished his goals and she was lost to Evan forever.

How long she sat there thinking, she didn't know. Finally, she shook her head and stood up. She got a glass of water and headed for bed. The first shiver hit. The temperature in the room said 68. She got in bed with her clothes on, pulling her blankets tight around her. The blanket couldn't warm her from the chill that reached deep in her, running along her spine until she shivered out of control. It was not a healthy feeling of cold. Jessie saw Adriana, deathly quiet and still. She went from cold to hot, in a moment, a smothering heat that stunned her. Panic seized her, pushing her not too gently toward the edge. Her heart raced at a frantic pace. Jessie knew Adriana was in the trunk of a car. She remembered all too well the fear she had felt. *Please, oh please. I need to see something.* Jessie took deep breaths trying to calm the panic she was feeling. Adriana's eyes flew open, and Jessie's body relaxed. As quickly as she had come, Adriana was gone, replaced by a dark shadow bending over the trunk. In her heart, Jessie knew it was more than a man. Something else was involved, but she couldn't begin to explain what it was.

Chapter 3

Jessie rolled over and turned on the lamp. She was wide-awake as her eyes adjusted to the light flooding the dark room. Sleep? No way. Not tonight. Jessie threw the covers off and slipped out of bed going over some of the cases she could remember. Nothing stood out.

Wow, did she ever need this vacation and the sooner, the better. She pushed her hair out of her eyes, sat down at the computer, and searched the web through her article archives hoping something would jog her memory. Her free hand tapped on the desk. She clicked back and forth between articles. She stared at the words on the screen, but her mind was blank. As far as she could see, Matt didn't need to worry. She couldn't get involved in a case when she didn't have any clues to go on. She checked her email, and there was one from Sadie.

Here are your printable tickets for the first part of your trip. You will fly out of JFK and meet me here at the airport. We'll then go on together to our final destination. I think you'll both be pleasantly surprised. Love you, sweetheart.

****

Matt gave up. Wide-awake he sat up in bed. He leaned his head back on his folded arms. Another mess. Jessie seemed to be at the heart of it again. His conversation with Johnson earlier still bothered him. Not that he believed black magic was real, most likely they staged it. He frowned. Of course, he hadn't thought much about ghosts either until Jessie came along, and Gina with her. Maybe he'd have to rethink this. He didn't like it, but he would stand by her decision. "Give her breathing room," Sadie once told him. At least for the next week she would be safe and out of the area. Why then did he have such a bad feeling about all of it? Matt looked at the clock, eleven-thirty. She was probably sleeping, or maybe she wasn't and was restless, too. He was willing to chance it. Letting the phone ring a couple of times, he was about to hang up when he heard her voice.

"It's a little late. Can't you sleep or something?"

"You could say that. Did I wake you?" He grinned, imagining the expression on her face.

"Nope, I had a visit from someone earlier which woke me up for the rest of the night."

He heard her sigh through the line. "Who came, and what kind of visit are we talking about?" His free hand clenched behind his head.

Jessie described what had happened to her earlier. "I relived in one moment all the panic I had felt in the trunk of Anderson's car."

"Damn!" He swung his legs over the side of the bed and sat on the edge. "Sorry, sweetheart. Hearing what you went through, I'm going to have to tell you about my conversation with the investigating officer. I didn't want you to know, but it seems it's on a need-to-know basis."

"I thought you said they had no new information, and the whole thing was a mess."

"I did and it is. But I left out a few details."

"I don't like the sound of that. We aren't talking about minor details are we?'

"Let's say I don't know what to make of them." Matt's hand rubbed his forehead as he talked.

"Start talking and please don't leave out any details. You know me." He heard her smile behind her words. "I need to know so I can have a plan."

Matt told her about the missing records, computer files, and interviews on Adriana. He also told her about what was happening at the station with the dead chickens, blood, and strange occurrences. "I think some of that might be staged. But, Johnson was scared. I could hear it in his voice when he told me about it."

"That's it."

"What's it?" He could hear the excitement in her voice.

"Computer files can easily be hacked and records missing. That could be an internal problem, but animal sacrifice, staged or otherwise, means someone from the outside. I've had a strange feeling every time I think of this case. I haven't been able to understand some of its twists. I mean the disappearance was strange in itself, but I kept thinking there was more. I wasn't getting the full picture. There is a powerful dark figure that shows up each time I see Adriana. The occult is a real possibility or maybe it's more about leading everyone off the real trail than the voodoo. I have lots of questions."

"Like what?" He reached over and turned on the lamp.

"I want to know how I ended up in Evan's dream. I mean, don't you think it's a little creepy that he came into my store and stared at me as if he saw a ghost? I have to admit that has me a little puzzled. The probability and odds of it happening are staggering."

He smiled. Her enthusiasm colored every word. He knew she was in it whether he liked it or not. "I can't answer that. You know me—when it comes to this part of your life, I'm just along for the ride. And damn, what a wild ride it's been. What other questions do you have?" He sat forward on the edge of the bed.

"Where's Adriana? I know she's in the trunk of a car but not the location. Has someone masterminded all of this? I mean, did he put me in Evan's dream to trap me. Or, am I supposed to be the one to find her? My mind keeps going around in circles. No matter what, I'm going to have to do a little investigating of my own. Do you want to go to Rocky Pointe to do a little leg work with me?"

"First of all, I don't like the whole trap idea. I hadn't thought of that." He raked a hand through his hair. "Hell, I don't like anything about this case, and I would like you to stay out of the whole damn thing." He groaned, wishing he had kept his mouth shut. He could almost hear her bristling over the phone.

"It's not like I went looking for it, now is it? So you can keep your opinion of what I should or shouldn't do to yourself."

"I didn't mean it the way it came out."

"Yes, you did. The least you can do is to be honest about it." He imagined her chin edging up with every word.

"You're right, I did mean it. I don't like where this case is heading. But, I do like you. And when it comes to legwork, I'll work with yours any day."

"Ha, ha..." The bristling turned into a chuckle. "Smooth recovery, but I think you overreached a little."

"Probably, but I do like your legs." He stood up and walked toward the kitchen. "Jess, I know you didn't purposely get involved in this mess. I'm concerned about its strangeness, so be careful, sweetheart. A person willing to steal the records from the police in their backyard is liable to be bold enough to do anything."

"Part of me is involved, but I can't do anything to find her if I have no clue what the next step is. All I can do is some investigative work for now."

He was relieved, but he wouldn't tell her. "I should let you get some sleep. Remember I'm yours for the weekend. I'll look into my schedule, and we'll go to Rocky Pointe one day this week."

"I'll keep you in the loop. I won't be reckless."

"That's good to know. I've waited a lifetime for you, and I'm hanging on."

"Don't let go," she said softly.

"Who me? I hold tight to the ones I love." He smiled. "Now get some sleep, and I'll see you tomorrow.

****

On Wednesday, Jessie was up early and waiting for Matt. A drive to Rocky Pointe to interview Adriana's co-workers was on for today. Jessie had already started to compile information on her. An article for Max at the local paper might trigger someone's memory. Evan's interview had put the human face on his wife. There were clues out there, and all they had to do was find people who saw them.

She straightened the magazines on the end table,

moving the lamp slightly and went to look out the window for the umpteenth time. Before she left on her mini vacation, she would have a good portion of the work at the store finished. A few pieces of artwork would need hanging when they finally arrived. A myriad of little details awaited her final touch the week of the opening. They would present themselves at that time and not a moment before.

Katie was catering the event, and Jessie knew it would be excellent. They had gone over the menu ideas for the appetizers and drinks last week. Katie had put together a great presentation. Jessie's excitement was building, especially with Corrine Clarke's appearance. It didn't get much better.

Jessie looked at her watch, then looked out the window again. Finally! She glanced at her watch as she closed the door behind her, thinking she could tell him he was late. He was on time.

"As I've told you before I'll come to get you at your door," Matt said, as she slid into the passenger's seat.

"I'm excited to get going," she said as she fastened her seatbelt. "I'm looking forward to finding out anything we can about Adriana." She waited until Matt backed out of the parking space and drove past the Inn. "I have to admit that spending a few hours with you might not be so bad either." His expression was priceless. She liked taking him by surprise.

"Sweetheart, you don't play fair. One of these days you're going to do that while I don't have my hands full with driving or something else, and the only one who will be in my hands will be you."

"Are you threatening me?" She flirted with him.

The flush on his neck gave her a small sense of power. She was getting to him, too.

"No, it's a promise. Do it again and I'll stop the car and show you." He grinned, glancing at her.

"Well, maybe someday I'll take up the challenge. It might be interesting to see how you'd react if I did."

"I know what I'd do. I'm just not sure what you'd do." He glanced at her. "Something tells me your dad had his hands full with you. Maybe that's why he's so protective."

"I think not." She feigned an innocent look. "I rarely flirted with guys. To tell you the truth, I think you're one of the first for me other than Katie's brother." She placed her hand over her heart giving him a coy look. "Most of the other guys I hung out with were more like brothers, or at least that's how I felt about them."

"When it comes to you, I doubt most of them were feeling brotherly." He grinned. "I sure as hell don't."

"Not to change the subject or anything." Her face felt hot. "I have to admit my store is looking sharp. I'm excited to get it opened."

"I never took you for a scaredy-cat. You face everything put in your path, but you're timid when it comes to me. Why is that, sweetheart?" He glanced at her.

"You want the truth?" She looked down at her hands in her lap.

"What do you think?"

"I can't control you, let alone my reaction to you."

"Damn right you can't control me, but the other part, well now, that's nice to know." He tapped the steering wheel and smiled.

She cleared her throat. "I like to control the situations in my life and there you have it. I'm a control freak and a tad on the stubborn side. It's best you know it now before you get in too deep." She laughed.

"I'm afraid it's already too late for me." He glanced at her. "I'm in over my head, but I'll die happy."

"Die happy, you'd better not even think about leaving me," she muttered. "Now do you mind if we change subjects for a while? Rocky Pointe is quite a drive yet." Her voice sounded shaky to her.

"Sure, what do you want to talk about?" He gave her a puzzled look.

"Why, this case, of course." The thought of a life without him was too much to consider. Love made her feel vulnerable.

****

Matt held the door open for Jessie and smiled when she walked past him. After a short wait, they were ushered into the office of the bank's president, Bob Sievers. He motioned for them to sit down. Matt showed him his badge.

"What can I do for you, officer?" Bob asked Matt.

"We're looking for any information you can give us on Adriana Foster. As I told you earlier when I called, my partner is an investigative reporter. She's doing a story on Adriana, trying to keep her face before the public, hoping someone can remember a little detail that could help law enforcement find Mrs. Foster."

"Adriana is a great young woman, and we'll cooperate in any way that we can. I'm holding her position open until she comes back, or we find out more. She was one of the best employees I've ever had." He opened his drawer and took out a notepad. "I took the liberty of writing down some pertinent facts about her after you called this morning."

Matt looked over the paper Bob handed him. "This is a great start." Not everyone's boss would be so helpful and work with the police. A lot of them saw any police interference as just that...interference.

"You're free to ask any one of her co-workers questions. Jayla Conner was one of her closest friends here at the bank. If you'd like, you can use the conference room, and I can send them in one at a time."

"I'd appreciate that, Mr. Sievers."

"Bob is fine. Let me show you to the conference room." Bob led them across the hall to a spacious room with a large table. Would you like some coffee or water?"

"A couple of bottles of water would be great." Matt pulled out a chair for Jessie. "I want you to ask any questions that you have. Interrupt me if you need to. You often see what I don't." He spoke softly in her ear, smelling the floral scent of her hair. "I like the way you smell."

"That's nice to know." She smiled up at him. "I do have a few questions I'd like to ask." Jessie pulled her list out of her purse and laid them on the table in front.

****

Most of the interviews were average with little information. Matt wasn't expecting to get much more out of the day by the time they were finished interviewing the employees. Adriana might have been friendly enough, but she apparently hadn't shared a lot of personal information with her co-workers.

A tall man in his early thirties walked into the

room next. His neat blond hair didn't have one hair out of place. In fact, there wasn't anything out of place. From the perfect crease of his suit and a shirt that didn't appear to have a wrinkle, it was almost obsessive. Matt watched the man sit in the chair, careful not to mess the crease in his pants. He hadn't even loosened his tie. Matt was tempted to do it for him. Average would best describe his looks but not his appearance. He was obviously a neat freak who couldn't take his eyes of Jessie. Matt schooled his features to hide his anger. He was simply staring, and simply rude.

"Randy Wallis." He extended his hand to Matt, barely looking at him.

"Randy." He stood and extended his hand. "This shouldn't take long." Matt took the cap off the bottled water and took a long swig. "How well did you know Adriana Foster, Randy?" It was quick, almost too fast to catch, but Matt saw the strange look flash across his face.

"I didn't know her well. I've had lunch with her and all the others that hang around her, a few times."

"Did that bother you?" Matt watched him carefully. "All the others who were hanging around her." He noticed Randy's puzzled look. "Did that bother you?" He asked him again.

"Not really, she was real popular that way. People just naturally liked her. Would I have liked to have had lunch just once without the whole groupie thing?" He gave a careful shrug. "Sure, it might have been nice."

"You do realize she was married and probably didn't want to eat alone with another man?" Jessie frowned at him.

"In this day and age, that means nothing. Adriana

was a looker, and the bottom line is girls like that don't hang with guys like me." He flicked a piece of lint from the sleeve of his jacket.

Was there a tender nerve under that casual statement? "What kind of guy are you? How would you describe yourself, Randy?" Matt jotted a few lines in his notebook.

"I'm a hard worker…" He straightened in the chair. "I don't mingle with a lot of people. I'm an introvert that hates small talk. I figured out early on that Adriana was not for me. As smart as she was, she was messy and a bit scatterbrained. Her desk wasn't very neat." His lip curled just a hair. "He still promoted her to VP, though."

"Did that bother you?" Matt watched Randy strain to see what he was writing.

"Sure it did. I'm the one who should have had the job. I've been here longer. I'm much more organized." His voice rose. "She was flighty, but he was fooled by her just like everybody else was."

"Who was fooled by her? Do you mean Bob Sievers?" Matt asked.

"Who else! She fascinated me, but I was taken in. And if you think to pin her disappearance on me you can forget about it." A faint tinge of red showed on his face. "I have an alibi and she wasn't worth ruining my life over."

"No one was suggesting that you had anything to do with her disappearance, but we will need to verify your alibi. I'm sure you understand." Matt gave him a neutral smile. "That's how we rule people out."

"Sure, whatever." He waved his hand.

"So what's your theory about what happened to

Adriana?" Jessie made eye contact with him. "You must have been thinking about it like everyone else."

"Of course I have. I mean it's a terrible thing that she's gone." Randy had visibly relaxed when Jessie asked her question, Matt noticed. "There's a guy who comes in here every week. He wants change for a twenty every single time. While he waits for the teller, he watches her. When he gets his money, he watches her. And he watches her until he leaves the bank."

"Did he ever try to talk to her or anything?" Matt quizzed him.

"Not that I ever noticed. I think that he's a strange one, though. He's a small man, I mean he's not very tall. Not exactly what you'd call handsome. Eccentric would be my description of him." He examined his nails.

"Could you describe him to a sketch artist?"

"Yes, I never forget a face." Randy ran his hand over his suit jacket, smoothing it out.

"You've been extremely helpful, Mr. Wallis. If I think of anything else would it be okay with you if I call?" Jessie glanced at him and then at her notes.

"Of course, I want to help any way that I can." He smiled at her.

As soon as Randy left the room, Matt looked at her. "What did you think of him?"

"He was odd and a bit of a cold fish. There's something else, he's too uptight." Jessie made a face.

Matt nodded at Jessie wanting to say more, but the clicking of high heels alerted him that the next interviewee was on her way. Her auburn hair swung loose around her shoulders, a pair of brown glasses framed her hazel eyes, and a pair of dimples made her face memorable. Her voice was the real stand out.

"Hi, y'all. Bob told me to hurry right on in here and answer any questions y'all might have. I'm Jayla by the way, and just so you know, I'm an implant from Georgia. I thought I would tell y'all because everyone is always asking me. They say I have an accent. To my way of thinking, you Yankees are the one with the accent. I sound normal to me." She smiled at them and sat down in the chair across from Jessie. "My, oh my, you're sure a pretty one. It would take a lot of work to get me looking as good as you do, sugar." Her bracelets banged on the table.

Matt had to agree with her. "Bob told us you were good friends with Adriana. Can you tell us anything about the last few times you saw her? Was she worried about anything or give any indication that she was?"

Jayla frowned in concentration. "Well now, let me think. Adriana was the best. A real sweetheart, you know what I mean." She looked at Matt. "She was excited about her promotion. She earned it—contrary to a few rumblings around here. The customers loved her; most everyone else did except for maybe one or two here or there." She took a deep breath. "She was just the sweetest little thing, and her husband adored her. Whenever he was in the area, he would come and take her to lunch. Once a week like clockwork, he sent her flowers." Her face scrunched, turning her lips down at the corners.

"Do you remember something?" Jessie asked her.

"A few days before she disappeared she got another flower arrangement with a strange note. She took them right out to the dumpster and threw them away. I remember because they were the prettiest red roses I'd ever seen, and so fragrant. I hated to see those beautiful flowers tossed in the trash like rubbish. But, they weren't from her husband." Jayla's bracelets clanked the table.

"Do you remember anything about the note?" Matt pressed her.

"Of course I didn't read it, but I do remember she was scared. Terrified! She was worried that death had found her again. My heart broke for the poor little thing. She seemed to be real jumpy after that." Jayla leaned forward in the chair, her elbows on the table.

"Did you say she was worried that death had found her again?" Jessie wrote on her notepad.

"As strange as it sounds to me now when I say it, those were her exact words. When I asked her about, she tried to laugh it off and said 'I meant to say it's death to my freedom again.' It didn't ring true, and she knew that I knew it. She kept trying to reassure me, but I could tell it was eating at her."

"How could you tell?" Matt watched her as she answered.

"Adriana became withdrawn and quiet. She came to work, but it was as if the fun-loving, sweet Adriana was far away. She was real skittish. She was constantly watching the door and anyone who came in it." Jayla looked at her watch. "Are you finished with me? I have a couple coming in for a house loan in a few minutes. I need to skedaddle."

"Just about, I have one last question. Did you ever see a strange patron around who cashed a twenty and always watched Adriana?" Jessie smiled as she asked her.

"Let me just guess, sugar, who told you that.

Randy was jealous of our little Adriana." She tossed her head, clicking her long red nails on the table. "The man who cashed the twenty has been in every week since as long as I can remember. He still comes in here. That's how he gets his tip money. He liked looking at her, but he'd never hurt a fly. She was kind to him and always made him smile. He's simple if you know what I mean, but he wouldn't hurt a fly."

"Thank you, Jayla. If you think of anything else, even if it's small, give me a call." Jessie handed her a business card.

"I sure enough will." She left the way she came with the staccato rhythm of her heels clicking on the floor.

Matt stood and stretched. "Let's get out of here so we can talk. While you gather your notes, I'll let Bob know that we've finished up here and thank him."

****

As soon as Matt left the room, Jessie put her notes in her purse. She was sifting through what she had heard in the last two interviews. Randy was bitter about the promotion. Jayla didn't like him. Why not? What was it about Randy that was such a put-off? It gave her something to think about, but nothing stood out yet.

"Excuse me." A deep voice startled her. "I was out earlier, and I was told to come in and talk to you." He walked into the room as if he owned it. He was good looking, extremely so, and Jessie could tell he knew it.

"Please have a seat." She motioned to the chair across from her. She didn't want him next to her.

He sat looking her over insolently. "So what's this all about, sweetheart?"

Before she could reply, Matt spoke from behind

her. "She's not your sweetheart, but she is my partner." He pulled out the chair by Jessie. "I'm Matt Parker." He showed him his badge. "My partner is Jessie Reynolds. We'd like to ask you a few questions about Adriana Foster."

Jessie hadn't heard Matt walk in, but she was happy to hear his voice. "How well did you know Adriana?" She watched the two of them size each other up and dig in their heels.

"Let's just say not well enough. She was liked by everyone but didn't give me the time of day." His handsome face was stony.

"I might be guessing at this, but it might be the way you treat women that turns them off." Matt's face was expressionless except for the flash of anger in his eyes.

"How in the hell would you know how I treat a woman?" His back stiffened in the chair.

"I don't!" Matt leaned forward in his chair. "But your little display with my partner gives me a picture, and I didn't like what I saw. I doubt Adriana's husband would have either. So let's begin this again, shall we? You can start by telling us your name."

He nodded. "I'm Jordon Daniels. I'm one of the loan officers here at the bank."

"That's better, Jordon. How well did you know Adriana?"

"I talked to her. I mean, she was a sweet little package, but like I said, she didn't give me the time of day."

"Did that bother you?"

"Yeah, sure." He jerked his shoulders irritably. "I've never had any trouble talking to women, but she

43

was a different story."

"Did it make you mad enough to do something?" Matt frowned and leaned forward in his chair.

"I don't like what you're insinuating." Daniels scowled. "I didn't hurt her if that's what you mean. Do I need a lawyer?"

"I don't know." Matt kept his voice even. "Do you need one?"

"No, and I'm not hanging around to listen to this crap." He stood. "If and when you have some real evidence to tie me to this case, you know where to find me."

Matt stood to block his exit. "If I do, you can guarantee I'll be back. I'd be more than happy to put your sorry ass in jail."

Jessie watched the two men, equal in height, square off. Jordon was the first one to back down and left the room. "What was that? There was enough testosterone in this room to start a war."

"That guy was a jerk. I didn't like how he was hitting on you or treating you. I didn't like him period." Matt's eyes were simmering. "Let's get out of here before I give in to the urge to punch him because it would make me feel good."

Chapter 4

They stopped at a small diner that overlooked the rocky cliffs for lunch before heading back to Blue Cove. The place was hopping so they took a seat at the counter where they could see all the action of the food preparation. It was too loud to talk seriously, which was okay. Matt was thoughtfully quiet. It gave Jessie time to watch the endless moments of entertainment. Written on the menu was a blurb about the café's history. The owner was also a teacher at one of the culinary schools in the area. Several students from the school who were studying elements of the food industry worked there along with some of their professors.

Jessie loved watching their efficiency as they worked as a team. The restaurant advertised organic food made with fresh ingredients that were locally grown. Each student worked several elements from the grill to garnishing. The teacher had to give final approval of the food presentation on each plate before the server brought it out. The owner had found her niche; The Early Bird had gotten an excellent write-up by the food critic Howard Hill. Jessie fully understood why. Her chicken salad on raisin bread was good, and so was her salad tossed with a raspberry vinaigrette. She glanced over at Matt, who was still frowning.

Watching the students carry on as they prepared the food was a show in itself. There was more heat in that small kitchen than the stove. Jessie chuckled, watching the bantering and flirting going on between the students. A few towel slaps and pinches made for an enjoyable lunch.

"Are you enjoying yourself?" Matt heard her chuckle.

"I am." She ate the last bite of her sandwich. "The students are extremely entertaining." She watched him place the tip on the counter as he stood up to leave.

He held the door open for her, and she glanced his way as she swept by him. "Thanks, I enjoyed the whole experience. My meal was excellent."

"It's pretty good. I stop here a lot when I'm in the area. It's probably not the best place to talk, but we'll have time on the ride home."

"I found the students' interaction diverting." She smiled.

"I think a few of those boys were trying to impress you." He unlocked the car for her.

"I doubt that. There were some attractive girls their own age which was reason enough for them to show off." Jessie clenched her mouth to keep from laughing at his expression. "It was fun watching them work and flirt. You know, Matt, not every guy is looking at me. There are lots of other women around." She slid in the car when he opened the door. "Have you cooled down yet? I think Jordon Daniels made you angry."

"That obvious, huh?" He grinned at her. "I could put my fist in his face a couple of times and probably feel a whole lot better."

"Why? He wasn't that bad." She watched him get in the car. "I've had guys treat me worse."

"Not in front of me you haven't. Some men think

they can say and act any way they want to a woman, and I was reminding him that he couldn't. That's all."

"I think it was more than that. Do you care to elaborate?" She watched his stony face, and he watched the road. "Maybe not, hmm, okay, that subject is closed." Her voice was at a near whisper.

"It's not that I don't want to. I'm trying to figure out my response. I intensely disliked him the minute I heard how he was talking to you. I know men can be sexist and obnoxious jerks at times, but there was something more. When I figure it out, I'll let you know."

"Fair enough." She looked out the side window, her lips turned up at the corner. "So, what was your take away from the interviews?" She turned in her seat so she could see him when he talked.

"I think Randy Wallis is an interesting character and his anger over Adriana's promotion could be the motive." He turned to look before he pulled onto the highway. "But he's way too fussy to get his hands dirty, so if he's involved, someone else would have to do the dirty work."

"I agree. He might hand her over to someone. I don't think he'd do anything himself, although, there could be a scenario where he might. I remember something from my Psych class. I'd have to do some research on the subject though. It's been awhile. Do you think he's so fastidious about everything he does?"

"I know he is. I checked out his workspace. It was almost scary how neat it was. I wouldn't be able to find anything in a space that neat." He put on his signal and passed a car moving too slowly. "He was always wiping up with an anti-bacterial solution in the kitchen.

He used it on his hands after he touched anything. I know. I watched him for a little while."

"When did you see all that? I was with you most of the time and never saw it." She frowned and pulled out her notes.

"From the time we walked into the bank and waited, I was watching them at work. It's what I do." He smiled as she glared. "What?"

"I don't think I want to know what you've observed about me. Although, I do remember wondering what made you glare at me the first time we met."

"I've never looked at you as a suspect, so you don't have to worry about my observations. Most of them are honorable, and the others are fantasy. The first time we met." He grinned. "Let's just say you unhinged me. We'll leave it at that."

She felt the familiar heat creep up around her neck and face. "What did you think about Jayla?" Her voice sounded strange even to her ears. She watched him smile.

"Jayla was interesting. Too much makeup, way too many bangles, but a pleasant smile. It was hard to figure out what to look at first. Her drawl and dimples were memorable, though. I loved how she called you sugar. I think she's probably harmless, but you never know."

"Are you being serious? I can't tell." She scrunched her face, and he laughed.

"Of course. All I'm saying is Jayla is an intriguing character. She's a colorful personality, a visual contradiction."

"I didn't see her that way, but then I'm a woman

looking at another woman. I just wondered why she wasn't more broken up about the loss of her so-called close friend. She gave us some good information, especially the bit about death finding Adriana again. Her story about the man and Randy's version are entirely different, though. So who's telling the truth? I find the part about Adriana interacting with the man strange when Randy said he never noticed any interaction."

"And that's the reason I want you along whenever I do any interview. I observe details, but you get to the heart of it."

"Dare I ask what you thought about Jordon Daniels?" She flipped the page over to find her notes on Jordon.

"You mean besides him being a pompous ass?" He watched her shake her head. "Honestly, I don't know what to think. He was extremely defensive, but so was I. It could be the whole male thing, or I observed something in him that I didn't like."

"I think," she said softly, "that he's arrogant, that he doesn't like you, but that he's also hiding something. It was there in his eyes. What it is, I'm not sure. Maybe he knows more than he's letting on."

"I plan on doing a little snooping around while you're gone. We can pick up where we left off when you get back. I might have to give your friend Jeremy a call." Matt glanced quickly at her.

"That's a splendid idea. I know he'd be happy to get involved. He loves research but after being here for the last case he considers himself something of a super sleuth now." She giggled. "We may have created a super alter ego. Only time will tell."

He drove off the highway and slowed down. "You're fun. I've laughed more in the last few months than I have in a while. I like hanging out with you, Miss Reynolds."

"You're not half bad either. I think I can tolerate it for a while."

"Do you think you might expand that *while* to cover a lifetime?" Matt's lips turned up at the corner.

"I'll take it under advisement." She smiled at him when he stopped in front of her store. She reached for the door and then stopped. "Thank you, Matt." She reached across the seat and brushed a kiss across his lips.

She heard his growl of pleasure, and he intensified the kiss. He pulled away first. "For what, sweetheart?"

Her heart was still racing. "For being you." She opened the car door. "I'll work here the rest of the day, but don't forget, I don't have a car, and you'll have to pick me up."

He gave her his lopsided grin. "Pickup is such a loaded word. I'll be here."

****

Jessie unlocked the door, walked in, and paused briefly to take it all in. She loved everything about her store; from the artwork on the walls to the pendant lights, it was all hers and the bank's, which held the mortgage, of course. She walked into the back room and hung up her coat. Where to begin? She eyed the room and headed back toward the front door.

Matt was handsome, caring, and maybe a bit overbearing at times, but she was hooked. Fanning her face, she picked up the stack of mail that had come through the mail slot and randomly began to open it.

Most were invoices, which she put on the counter. One was a plain white envelope addressed to her but had no return address. She put the letter opener inside the flap and slit the envelope open.

She answered her ringing phone. "Hi, Katie."

"Hey, Jessie. Did Sadie tell you where we're going yet?"

"No, Grams said she would tell us when we get there on Monday. She has the tickets for the next flights."

"I can't wait, but I don't know what to take. Will it be hot or cold?"

"Sadie said she wanted warm, but how warm is any place in February? Still I think it will be warmer than here."

"I'll pack a light jacket and maybe a sweatshirt. That should cover it if I need it."

"Sounds good to me. Are you packed already?" Jessie slipped the paper from the envelope and opened it. Her name was in bold black letters at the top. "Hey, Katie, can I call you back. I need to take care of something at the store."

"Sure, I'm so excited to get away for a few days. I'll talk to you later." Katie squealed and hung up.

What was this? Jessie's eyes got huge the farther she read. It was happening again to her. She read the letter another time and then re-read it.

Dear Jessie,

I've been watching you.

A chill went down her back, and she looked around the store and then again at the paper in her hands.

You've come a long way from those first days in New York, but how good I have yet to determine. I've decided to find out. We are going to play a game together, Jessie. If you're good, you'll find the clues. Here is the first few, a freebie of sorts.

I've looked and looked for the perfect wife, a few choice candidates to become my fantasy bride. One by one, they failed me in turn. So I got rid of them, which I've grown to like. You're too smart not to know what I mean. All of these were only in practice for my ultimate queen. Let's see if you can find us before she fails me, too. I'm going to enjoying playing these mind games with you.

Jessie sat down in the nearest chair, shaking. What kind of a sick game was this? Matt would know what to do. She handed the note to him the minute he walked into the store a while later.

"What's this?" He took the paper from her hand barely glancing at it.

"I found this note mixed in with my mail that I thought you should read." She watched understanding hit him as he read.

His hands fisted, and his eyes flashed with anger. "What the hell!" He started pacing. "Where's the envelope? Handle it carefully in case there are fingerprints on it."

"I doubt that there are, except for mine and the mail handler's when he pushed it through with the letters." She grabbed his hand hoping to calm him.

"Do you understand now why I didn't want you involved?" He pulled her into his chest, locking his arms around her. "Tell me how can I keep you safe from this?"

"You're not responsible for my safety. You've trained me to take care of myself." She took a step back to look up at his face.

"Jess, we're not going there. I brought you into this partnership. I watch your back, and you watch mine. I would do the same for Dylan, Kip, or any of my officers."

"Okay, I get it." She stood in the circle of his arms glancing up at him. "He had to know me from my articles or New York when I worked there. I need to think about some of the reports I did over the years. He has Adriana. She's his queen. I know that much." She shuddered, and he pulled her close again. "Somehow we have been tied together. I don't remember any connection, but I have to think about it. I did take a couple of classes at NYU. Somehow our worlds crossed paths, and he has connected us."

He rubbed his hand up and down her back. "What else stood out to you about this note?"

She shuddered again. "He's done this before and then killed them, hasn't he? It has to be the woman I saw." She pulled back in his arms, a thoughtful look on her face. "He's gotten the taste for it, hasn't he?"

He nodded and pulled her back close to him. "So it would seem."

Chapter 5

Matt drove Jessie home. He didn't want to leave. There were times he felt like the deck was stacked against them ever having a life together. She must have stirred up a hornet's nest in New York. It wasn't as if she was easy to ignore. He had given it his best shot and had no luck. He surrendered. He was just happy she liked him, too.

She wasn't afraid to tackle anything. The old saying 'fools rush in where angels fear to tread' would fit her to a tee, but she was no fool. No wonder she wanted a quiet life. How had this happened again? What connected Jessie and Adriana? It had to be simple, but right now, it didn't seem so. He figured out everything logically—eventually.

Think, Matt, think. He pulled into the garage, grabbed his phone, and made a call. If anyone could tell him, maybe Jeremy could.

"Jeremy, Matt here."

"Hey, Matt, what's up?"

"I need to ask you some questions about Jessie."

"Are you two having trouble?"

Matt made a face. "No, it's nothing like that. Jessie's in the middle of something that has me concerned. I need you to do some thinking for me from your days in New York with her. And, some research if necessary."

"Okay, fire away."

Matt sat in his truck for the next ten minutes telling Jeremy about the case. He read the note that Jessie had received then got out of his truck and walked into his house. "Can you think of any case that Jessie was in on or anything that she did over the years where their lives might have intersected?"

"Not off the top of my head, but I'll think about it. I'll go through some of our old research together."

"Thanks, Jeremy."

"You know, Matt, your guy sounds a little squirrelly to me. Have you checked her store for a video camera or a bug?"

"I haven't, but that sounds like a good idea to me. I'll do that first thing next week. Maybe I should check her house, too."

"I think it would be smart. How's she dealing with it?"

"She's working on a plan, which seems to calm her."

"And you, how are you dealing with it?" Matt could hear the laughter in his voice.

Matt winced. "I'd like to lock her up and put a guard around her twenty-four seven, but since that will never happen, I'll make a plan, too. Then maybe I'll be able to smash a few faces. One good thing about it is she's going away on a mini-vacation with Sadie and Katie for a week. So that will give us time to figure some of it out."

"I'll stay in touch, and I'll start this as soon as I hang up. Is there anything else?"

Matt thought for a moment. "Jeremy, could you try to find some information about a Randy Wallis and a

Jordon Daniels who work at Rocky Pointe Bank? Thanks, we'll talk soon."

Matt's shoulders finally relaxed. He sank into his easy chair, grabbed the remote, and turned on ESPN.

He stared at the screen but his mind wasn't on the show. All he could think about was some sick bastard out there that had grown to like killing the women he had chosen when they didn't 'measure up.' What made a guy like this tick? He needed a criminal profiler to look over this note and tell him more about a possible suspect. He also wanted—no, he *needed*—Sadie to be aware of this and keep an eye on Jessie for him.

He smiled and wondered if Jess knew how often he called her grandmother. "Hi, Sadie, this is Matt." He muted the TV.

"Is everything okay with Jessie?" He could hear the concern in her voice.

"She's fine, but we have a little incident going on which has me concerned," he explained it all to her.

"That doesn't sound good." Her voice was laced with concern. "I'm glad we are getting her out of there."

"Me too. It will give me a chance to do a little snooping around while she's gone." He sat forward in his chair.

"She told me you apologized. That was a smart move. I told her I thought you were a keeper."

"Having you on my side is good." Matt grinned. "I know how much you mean to her. So I'll try to live up to your faith in me."

"You'd better!" Sadie said with a slight laugh. "You love her, don't you?"

"I sure do." The words had popped out before he

had time to think about it.

"That's all that matters. She'll understand that soon enough." Her words became firm. "Now, tell me what you are going to do about this guy."

"I have a few ideas, but I wanted to make sure you keep an eye on her. Don't let her go off by herself. If you get worried, call me, Sadie, and I'll be on the next plane. Promise me!" He frowned and combed through his hair with his hand.

"I will, Matt. You sound concerned about this. Are you worried he'll come after her?"

"I don't know what he'll do because I'm not sure what we're dealing with. He may be toying with her to get her off Adriana's trail, or he could be using Adriana as bait to get to her." He stood up and paced. "I've got Jeremy, Jessie's friend, checking to see if there's something that connects the two of them from Jessie's reporting days in New York. I hope to know more in the next few days. In the meantime, I know she's looking forward to this trip."

"So am I. I need to get away from her father. My son drives me nuts some days, but then, I'm not too easy to handle either."

Matt chuckled. He imagined Sadie could be a handful. "Where are you headed?"

"I wanted to surprise them. I'm taking them to Palm Springs and the West Coast. I think they'll love it."

"I'm sure they will."

"I never tell her much up front. She analyzes everything and it would ruin the surprise." He heard Sadie laugh.

"Sadie, I like your style!" Matt laughed aloud.

"It's difficult to pull anything over on her, so I do the best that I can." She sounded pleased with herself.

"I'm not going to worry Jessie with any of this. I am asking you to be my eyes and ears while you're with her, though. Like I said before, if you are concerned at all, call me, and I'll get there."

"I will, Matt. Before you hang up, I have a question for you."

"What's that?" He stopped pacing.

"How's her store coming along? Will this trip set her back? She'll do anything to please me even if it puts her out."

"She'll have plenty of help all weekend; it'll be ready for opening day. I wish you could see how her face lights up every time she's there. She loves it. She's done an excellent job, and it looks terrific." He smiled, picturing her standing there among her books.

"The store has always been her dream. If she's happy, I'm happy."

"You know, Sadie, I feel exactly the same way."

Sadie chuckled. "That's good to know. Stop agreeing with her dad and you should be okay."

"Yes, ma'am. Call me if you need me."

Sadie made him smile. Jessie was like her in so many ways. He would spend as much time with Jessie as he could over the next few days. Besides wanting to be with her, he needed to see if any new clues came out in their conversations.

Matt sat back down in the chair. They still had to unravel the facts of the case. One could only hope whoever it was would overplay his hand and give him something to go on. The note told Matt the man had a big ego. Their suspect wanted them to know he was watching them and that it was a game to him. Matt hoped he would keep it up.

He leaned back in the chair and closed his eyes. Tomorrow he would brief Dylan, talk to Jeremy, and, of course, see Jess. He could picture her standing there among the boxes, smiling and happy. Content, his body relaxed, and sleep claimed him.

****

He could see her through the store window. The sunlight skimming across her hair made it look like spun gold. She waved when she saw him, her face lighting up with a smile. She walked over and unlocked the door, letting him in. "Hi, I wasn't expecting you yet."

"Are you about ready for a little break?" He came in carrying a pizza and placed it on the table. He put a paper bag there as well, slipped off his coat, and watched her, intrigued by this side of her.

"Yes," She turned around in a circle gesturing with her hands. "It looks good, doesn't it? I mean it looks really good."

"You've done wonders with the place." He walked toward her and pulled her into his arms, locking them around her. He leaned his chin down, resting it on the top of her head and breathed in the scent of her. Feelings exploded within him. He had to keep her safe and would do anything to do it. He nuzzled her ear. "We fit well together. I'm going to miss you, Jess. Do you know that?"

"I'll miss you too!" She felt him shudder. "Are you okay? It'll be fine, you wait and see."

"I know," he whispered in her ear. Slowly he lifted her face and gazed into her eyes. A heated looked passed between them, and he claimed her lips in a tender kiss.

"Anything else unusual happen today?" He rested his chin on her head once again.

"No." She pulled back just enough to see his face. "Nothing unusual, but I've been wondering about that letter—that he's been watching me. Do you think there's a camera hidden in here somewhere?"

"We're going to check it out while you're gone."

"I love how you're always one step ahead of me." She rested her head against his chest. "Thank you for thinking about me."

"Like, I could stop." He grinned at her. "Let's eat before this gets cold. I'm yours for the rest of the night. Put me to work!" He unlocked his arms and gave her a playful push toward the table. "Dylan and Kip are going to help us on Saturday and Sunday."

"That sounds good. I think I can get it all done with a little help." She took the plates, napkins, and drinks from the bag. Matt pulled out her chair.

"By the way, tomorrow night you'll have the night off, so I'm taking you out." He noticed her shaking her head. "This topic isn't open for discussion. You've been working hard the last several days, and you could use it. Okay?"

She grinned at him over her slice of pizza. "Okay, if you say so. I think I can live with it."

"I say so." He took a bite of his pizza. "I need it just as much as you do."

Chapter 6

Jessie's bags were packed and waiting at the door. Katie had already called to let her know she was ready to go, too. All they needed now was Matt and a cup of coffee from Joe's to fortify them for the trip. It was a cold morning. Matt had called her earlier and told her to wait in the house. He would come to the door and get her. She smiled. That had been her plan all along so that Matt could carry her suitcases.

What a fun weekend. Dylan, Kip, and Kenny had helped her at the store along with Katie and Molly. The store looked great and was full of laughter as they worked. It was just as she had envisioned it would be every time she dreamed of owning a bookstore.

The highlight of the weekend was her date with Matt on Friday night. He had arrived with a bouquet of red roses and treated her to a special evening at the Chowder House. He had managed to secure the best table in the restaurant, one with a beautiful view of the cove. They sipped wine as the evening sun slowly set and fuchsia tinted with orange light sparkled on the water. A moonlight ocean drive followed their meal, and they parked near the beach and talked. After a few memorable kisses—she could still feel the heat of them just thinking about it—he brought her home, and they sat on the couch. They spent the next few hours watching an old movie together, huddled under a comfy throw. If he'd asked her to marry him then, she would have forgotten her resolve and said yes. She scrunched her face. She didn't know how much longer she could hold out against his charm campaign.

The light tapping on the door startled her. "Good morning." She smiled up at him.

"Are you ready?" The condensation of his breath rose like fog in the chilly morning air.

"I'm packed and ready, sir." She smiled at him and saluted.

He went to get her suitcase as she grabbed her laptop. "You're only going for a week, right? What do you have in this thing?" He grimaced as he picked it up.

"I only have clothes and a few necessities." She laughed when she saw his puzzled look. "Oh, and a few books of course."

"I knew it had to be more than clothes." He opened the door for her and followed her out.

"I'm taking Grams some books from the store and naturally I have to have some reading material." Jessie gave him a guilty smile. Matt would find out soon enough Katie's suitcase was heavier than hers.

****

The trip into JFK went fast. Katie chatted the entire way. Before they went through security, Matt pulled Jessie aside.

"Keep your eyes and ears open, sweetheart. If you need me, call." He held her close and spoke softly.

"It's just a simple vacation, Matt."

"Honey, nothing is simple when it comes to you." He looked at her expression and laughed. "You know it's not, so just do what I told you."

Her eyebrows arched. "How would you like a few

of those imaginary points I added taken off again?"

"If it keeps you safe, I don't care."

"Come on, Jessie, just give him a goodbye kiss, and let's get going." Katie was tapping her foot, letting a few people get in front of her in line.

Jessie looked at Matt. "I need to go. I'll keep my eyes open." She turned to leave, pulling out of his hold, but he held fast to her hand.

"That's good enough. Hey, where's my goodbye kiss?" He brought her back close.

"You mean right here, now?" She bit her lip to keep from laughing.

"I sure do. Katie told you to give me one." He kissed her soundly. "I'll be here to pick you up on Sunday night."

"Thanks." She waved at him and got into the security line with Katie.

"Where do you think Sadie is taking us?" Katie edged her suitcase along as the line progressed.

"I have no idea. She hasn't let any details slip. I have a feeling Matt knows but he's not giving anything away. He always seems to be one step ahead of me." Jessie removed her shoes placing them in the tray.

****

Matt had arranged to meet Jeremy in the city at Mike's Delicatessen for lunch. With Jessie safely on her way, it was time for him to get to work. Matt ordered the hot pastrami on rye and Jeremy had the corned beef.

"Did you find anything for me?" Matt took a bite of his sandwich.

"I looked back over the archives of Jessie's stories. A couple of things stood out to me." Jeremy scrolled on his phone to his notepad. "Jessie did a series of articles on the subject of living with mental illness. One of the reports was on notorious crimes committed by people in society with compulsive tendencies and those with a sociopathic personality disorder. They were folks who appeared normal but weren't. I've copied a few of those articles to read. She interviewed a few who seemed to function well in society, but ultimately, they used people for their own ends."

"And this is a problem? Why?" Matt looked over the articles Jeremy handed him.

"The articles weren't a problem, but what happened afterward was. It exposed a man who had been abusing people on the job. His co-workers were afraid to turn him in out of fear of losing their jobs. He was their supervisor. Jessie received a few threats after he lost his employment." Jeremy looked over his notes. "Don't get me wrong, she found a lot of people functioning well in society with mental illness. It was more that society itself didn't know how to deal with the problem or to treat the mentally ill. Needless to say, many don't get the help they need."

"There's no doubt about it. Most people in the field will tell you the same thing." Matt took a bite out of his pickle. "Mental health is an issue we sweep under the rug."

"You'll find that the article on the sociopath tells a different story. Reading over the traits and symptoms that she wrote about reminded me of the words he wrote. This guy, whoever he is, seems to fit it to a tee." Jeremy took a bite of his sandwich.

"Not what I wanted to hear. I'm far more concerned about this than she seems to be." Matt studied the article in front of him as he ate the rest of his sandwich. "This looks informative. It could be our suspect was angry over this article, but how does it tie her to Adriana?" Matt frowned in concentration.

"Jessie was interviewing one of the professors at NYU on this subject at the time when Adriana had the problem with a stalker. The professor quoted one of his favorite studies in one of her articles. It centered on the traits which a sociopath and a stalker have in common. They often have a narcissistic personality."

"It's difficult to see that as a big enough issue to create a problem."

"You need to read the whole article. I think you'll see what I did." Jeremy finished the last bite of his sandwich. "I'll put together what I found out about the two men who you told me to look into and send it all over to you. I'm still waiting for some information."

"I appreciate you doing this for me, Jeremy. My gut tells me it started in New York somewhere, and it's just catching up to her now. It doesn't make sense otherwise."

"I'll keep digging. We'll find it while she's gone. Do you think she'll be okay?"

"I'm hoping so. I want to believe getting her out of Blue Cove is the answer."

"But?" Jeremy's brow rose.

"If he's watching her then he knows she's gone, doesn't he?"

"Hell, I didn't need to hear that. I think I need to bring her back to New York to live." He gave Matt a crooked smile. "She was safer here."

"Give it up, Jeremy. You know I'm never going to let that happen." Matt shook his head and wiped his fingers on his napkin. "I'm going to do everything I can to keep her safe, though, that's for damn sure."

"I'll be right there with you—and many others I'm sure. Jessie has a way of stealing your heart while driving you crazy at the same time. Is it too soon to ask what you're thinking about this so far?"

"It's in the early stages, but I believe they are linked. Adriana's abduction and Jessie overlap. She's either the bait to get Jessie involved or a way of throwing her off the trail. The one who sent the note knows them both, and he probably is a sociopath. There are others involved as well. I think one of those men at the bank may have given information willingly or unknowingly to the suspect. Also, someone knows enough about voodoo to scare some deputies in their precinct. That's what I know so far, but before this week is over, I hope to know a whole lot more."

"Wow. That's a lot to digest in a few days." Jeremy looked thoughtful. "What are we going to do?"

"We? Does that mean you're going to help?" Matt watched Jeremy's face as he answered.

"Damn right I am. When do you want me in Blue Cove?"

"Just as soon as you can get there," Matt answered him.

"I'll be there the first thing tomorrow."

"Thanks, Jeremy. The more heads we have to think on this, the better, as far as I can see. It wasn't my case until Jessie received that note. It was out of my jurisdiction, but not anymore."

"I'm going to check out a few things tonight. I hope to have some more answers for you tomorrow when I get to Blue Cove. Not to change the subject, but did the girls get on their way okay?" Jeremy sent a text off.

"They were just going through security when I left them. They should be in the air by now." Matt scrolled through his messages on his phone.

"They are. Katie just responded to my text saying that they were somewhere over Ohio. Do you have any idea of their destination?"

"Palm Springs is what Sadie told me. They'll find out as soon as they meet up with her. She gave me the resort name and number last night. It's a beauty." Matt gathered up his stuff and stood up. "I guess I had better head back to the Cove. I've got some small petty stuff the guys are working on, and Gary's checking the store for any bugs or video equipment." They talked as they walked out of Mike's together.

"Do you know the guy who owns Joe's? Have you ever met him?"

"No, why?" Matt's eyebrow arched.

"Jessie had to deal with him when she was buying the store. I remember her telling me he was from New York. I was just wondering if you should check along the wall that connects with his store. At least it's something to think about."

"He's from New York. What are the odds of that? I'll see you tomorrow then." Matt shook Jeremy's hand and drove back to Blue Cove.

Chapter 7

Jessie looked at her book without reading a single word on the page. She tried not to think at all, but it wasn't working. How long could she get away with pretending to read? She could hear Katie's foot tapping under the seat; see her glances now and then, out of the corner of her eye. The quiet was blissful, but it wouldn't last long if Katie's looks were any indication. Jessie prepared herself for the onslaught.

Katie pinched her arm. "You didn't hear a word that I said, did you?" Her foot tapped faster against the floor under the seat.

"Ouch." Jessie frowned.

"Are you going to sit with your nose in a book the whole flight?" Katie's fingers drummed the armrest in time with her feet.

Jessie shook her head. "I'm sorry. I have a lot on my mind. Let me bookmark this and we can talk." Jessie sighed and turned to face Katie. "What's up?"

"I just got a text from Jeremy. He wanted to know if we got off all right. That was sweet, don't you think?" Katie waved her phone in front of Jessie's face.

Jessie smiled. "Jeremy is nice."

"Did you know he was having lunch with Matt today?" Katie's voice sounded irritated. "You never tell me anything."

"I didn't know." Jessie clamped her mouth shut.

"Matt said he was going to contact Jeremy about some questions he had. He must have decided to meet him while he was in the city." Jessie frowned. "Jeez, Katie, don't get so snippy. He doesn't tell me everything he's going to do, you know. I don't make him check in with me to okay his plans."

"I know." Katie looked away from her for a moment. "Jeremy is on his way to Blue Cove to help Matt. I hope this isn't what I think it is." Katie's brows furrowed, her lips turning down at the corners. "Please tell me you aren't working another case. You are, aren't you? What is it this time? Do I need to be worried about things happening like last time? I don't want to say the words aloud because we're on a plane." Her frown deepened. "It won't be anything simple, you know. It's going to affect this trip. I know it! I just know it, and then I'm going to be mad." She paused to take a breath.

"Give it a rest, Katie. You're such a drama queen." Jessie picked up her book hoping Katie would take the hint.

"And you have no feelings at all."

"That's not true, and you know it." Jessie frowned at her. "I'll tell you everything that's happened so far if you'll give me half a chance. Matt is trying to get some answers for me. It's no big deal." Jessie explained to her about Evan and the note.

"No, big deal? Who are you kidding?" Katie threw her hand in the air, her voice rising.

Jessie put her finger to her lips. "Take it down a notch, Katie. People are starting to stare at us."

"Don't you dare shush me." Her voice slowly quieted when she saw the turned heads. "You can't tell me that you don't find all this a little strange. I've always thought of you as normal, but I don't know what to think anymore."

"Listen to me, Katie. I didn't go looking for any of this, but it's still happening, so I'm dealing with it the best that I can." Jessie's hand clenched the armrest.

"I know. It's just that I was looking forward to time alone with my best friend. I don't want you preoccupied with all this stuff." Katie pouted and sighed. "I want to have fun and not have to be looking over my shoulder for who knows what."

"We're not in Blue Cove. We should be fine. Depending on our destination, all I'm thinking about is a massage, sightseeing, shopping, and some wonderful food. If it's warm enough, we could even do some swimming." Jessie leaned her head back and started to close her eyes.

Katie nudged her arm and frowned at her. "I just know that wherever you go trouble follows. So I won't hold my breath."

"The least we can do is to give it our best, don't you think? I don't want to worry Sadie. She paid a lot of money for this trip." Jessie took her book out of the seat back. "I intend to enjoy myself and I think you should try to do the same." She opened her book and flipped to her bookmark. "Maybe we should change the subject."

"You know what bugs me?"

"No, what?" Jessie closed the book again and got comfortable in her seat.

"Jeremy is going to be in town, and I'm not going to be there. Man, do I like that guy. He's scrumptious. I could think of a lot of things that a girl could do with a guy like that." Katie fanned herself with the magazine.

"You're funny, do you know that?" Jessie chuckled. "Anytime I'm with you, it's a good time. You'll see! We'll have a great time." Jessie put down her tray and placed her book on it. "The other stuff isn't going anywhere. It will be waiting for me when I get back. Unless, of course, Matt solves the mystery before I return. Technically, it isn't his case." She frowned, deep in thought. "I'm not sure, but I think the threatening note brings him in on it since it happened in Blue Cove."

"Who cares? He won't let anything happen to you even if he has to go after the guy single-handedly."

"This isn't the Old West, Katie. There are laws that even cops have to obey."

"You know what I mean." She winked. "He loves you, Jessie. He'll do everything he can to keep you safe." She put her hands to her face. "Oh, no, I just thought of it; he's not going to be around to keep you safe. I sure hope this guy doesn't know where we're going."

"How could he? *We* don't even know where we're going." Jessie smiled at her.

"That's true! Okay then, I can relax now." Katie giggled.

****

"Flight attendants, prepare the cabin for landing." The Captain's voice came over the intercom. "Ladies and gentlemen, we will be making our descent into O'Hare shortly. There are a few planes ahead of us. Please remain seated for the remainder of the flight until the aircraft comes to a full stop. Thank you for flying with us this morning."

Jessie was relieved for the interruption since it shut

Katie up for a minute. She had talked the entire flight. Jessie needed a break. Katie was great, but when she got on a subject, she was tenacious and wouldn't let go. She had come up with every worst-case scenario possible, going over them repeatedly for most of the flight, Jessie was about ready to turn around and fly back to Blue Cove. Almost. She might enjoy sending Katie back on the next flight, though. The man would have to be superhuman to do all the things Katie had suggested he might try. She sighed and closed her eyes. She needed a few minutes alone to clear her head. She had to get rid of all the awful stuff Katie had suggested. Some of it hit too close to home.

The plane touched down safely after circling several times around the city. One more dip of the plane up or down and Jessie thought she would scream. She was more than ready to see Sadie and let *her* deal with Katie on the next flight. She couldn't help it. Katie had one vivid imagination.

Sadie was waiting for them by the baggage carousel, right where she'd told them she'd be. She took one look at Jessie's face and put her arms around her. "Is everything, okay? You didn't have a rough flight, did you?"

Jessie waited until Katie stepped away to search for her luggage. "Let's just say Katie was extremely talkative, and my head is still spinning."

Sadie laughed. "That girl can talk, that's for sure. How about I sit between the two of you and let her chat with me?"

"I was hoping you'd volunteer." Jessie turned, spotted her bags, and went to get them. She showed the attendant her luggage tickets and returned to stand by

Sadie.

"Sadie, I can't take the suspense another minute. Where are we headed?" Katie dumped her suitcase by her feet as she joined them.

"We're on our way to Palm Springs for a few days and then on to San Diego so you girls can see the Pacific. How does that sound? It's been a mild winter there, and I'm looking forward to the warmth."

Katie grabbed Sadie and let out a squeal, turning several heads.

"Wow, it sounds perfect." Jessie smiled. "You were good at keeping it secret."

"I wanted to surprise you."

"You did."

Sadie grabbed her hand. "I'm so happy to spend some time with you, girls. I think it will be great fun. Wait until you see the resort in Palm Springs. It's a five-star beauty. Each suite has a hot tub and private courtyard. I think you're going to enjoy it, and your dad, bless his heart, will probably explode when he sees the bill—even though it's my money."

"I think you might enjoy that the most." Jessie laughed and pulled her bags behind her.

After they had checked their luggage, they made their way through security and finally arrived at their departure gate. Sadie pulled out the brochures so they could look at all the amenities the resort had.

"This place is amazing," Katie squealed. "I've never been anywhere so beautiful before."

"What do you mean; you live in a place with a five-star rating." Jessie couldn't help herself. It was Katie's turn to be bothered.

"It's not the same. You know what I mean." Katie

scowled at her.

"Sure, but the Blue Iris Inn is beautiful, you have to admit."

"Of course, but I don't have to work at *this* place. They are going to serve me, and boy, oh boy, am I going to enjoy it." Katie bounced from one foot to the other. "What should we do first?"

"Get there." Jessie winced as Katie pinched her arm again.

"What's up with you?" Katie got in her face. "Are you going to be this disagreeable the whole way?"

"I'll try not to be if you promise not to dredge up any more of your scary scenarios. Fair enough?" Jessie glared right back at Katie.

Katie nodded. "Okay, I can see how that might have bothered you. I promise. Now, can we plan some of the things we want to do during our stay?"

Jessie listened half-heartedly to Katie and Sadie as they made plans. Some of the things Katie had brought up were troubling her. The possibility that he could follow them or know where they were going had never crossed her mind until Katie carried on about it. She began the text.

—*Hi, Matt, I was wondering if you found out anything yet.*—

His response was immediate.

—*Gary's checking your store now, and I'll call you later after I know more. Were you surprised?*—

—*Yes, how did you know?*—

—*I talked to Sadie a few nights ago, and she told me about where she was taking you. I like the idea of taking you by surprise.*—

—*Don't get any bright ideas. The resort looks*

amazing. Katie and Sadie are planning things now.—

—Why aren't you involved in the planning?—

—I have to admit my mind is a little preoccupied.—

—If you need me, you know I'll come.—

—I'm sure it'll be okay, but Katie filled my head with scary scenarios that I need to get rid of somehow. I'll wait to hear from you. They're starting to board the plane.—

—Talk to you later.—

****

Matt didn't want to worry her. He paced a little, and frowned a lot, then paced some more. Maybe he should put Dylan in charge and take the first flight out to Palm Springs. He would wait. It wasn't what he wanted to do, but he would hold on, at least until he heard from Gary, and Jeremy had arrived. After that, all bets were off. He tapped his pencil on the desk. When it came to Jessie, he didn't know whether it was his instinct as a cop or whether he was overprotective. Possibly both! He would wait. No, he was a damn good cop, and his gut told him to be concerned—so he would go with his instinct. He made a quick call to the Palm Springs Police.

He turned his chair to look out the window. He had pored over her reports. He could see where someone might object to some of the conclusions, especially those doctors who sometimes dispensed meds without the proper follow-up. Could it be a doctor or a patient who was behind this? He scowled. Who knew? Her premise that the nation didn't know how to deal with mental health issues was spot on, and it could upset a few folks. He knew all too well that many people who needed help ended up in the prison system. They didn't

75

belong there, but no one, including himself, knew what to do about it. He scanned another page for something, anything at all that might be helpful. Matt knew firsthand how the criminal system found itself burnt too, by an unwarranted insanity plea. No trust or cooperation makes for a broken system. All good stuff but nothing earth shattering, and he still couldn't see any connection. Something had to be there. He turned his chair back around and kept reading.

It could be any one of the many people she had interviewed. How was he supposed to narrow it down? He stretched his arms over his head. Damn but he wished he could find a little clue.

"Matt," Dylan popped his head in the door. "Joe told me to tell you there's a call for you on line two."

"Thanks. Come back in a few minutes, will you? I want to talk to you."

"Will do." Dylan walked toward his office.

"Hey, Matt, this is Gary. I think you need to get over here quick. I want you to see this for yourself. I think we may need a search warrant for Java Joe's."

"I'll be right there." Matt grabbed his coat and headed out of his office. He turned around in the middle of the hall and walked toward Dylan's office. "Dylan, I think you need to come along on this. I'll fill you in on the way."

"Collins, we'll be out for a while. You can reach us on my phone," Matt told him as they passed his desk."

"All right." He nodded. "I'll hold down the fort."

Matt brought Dylan up to speed with all the details and handed him a copy of the note to read. "Gary has been combing over Jessie's store to see if he could find a bug or a video camera, without letting the guy know we're on to him. He just called and sounded like he'd found what he was looking for."

"Bizarre. I don't know how she deals with this crap." Dylan frowned. "I sure as hell couldn't. And now this." He held up the note. "This guy is just toying with her and sounds like an arrogant SOB if you ask me."

"I hope we can keep his delusion intact. People tend to make mistakes when they think they are outsmarting everyone. I don't know if our suspect is in town or if he's from her days in New York. Jeremy will be here in the morning, and he's going to work on this alongside us. He knows about her research in New York. He worked with her often." Matt pulled the car into the parking space in front of Jessie's store.

Dylan got out and knocked on the shop door. The door swung open. "What'd you find?" Dylan walked in first.

Gary led the way up the stairs to the attic space. "I turned the sound off for now so that we could talk. Look at this." He pointed to some wires and several small devices along the ceiling looking directly into Jessie's store below. If you track all the wires, they're coming from Java Joe's next door. Her phone has no service as of yet, but I found a bug in it. I also found a couple of other listening devices among these."

Dylan squatted down to look at the equipment. "Whoever it is knows his tech stuff. There're some sophisticated items here. He could be miles away or sitting in front of the store, and he'd hear what was going on." Dylan picked up what resembled a small lens. "The serial numbers have been filed off." He frowned. Matt squatted down beside him to look. "Do you think Jessie is the target, or is it Adriana?" Dylan asked.

"It's possible it's Jessie, or it could be both, with more than one person involved." Matt stood up. "Either way Jessie is in the center of it somehow. I hope to know more when Jeremy gets here in the morning." Matt followed one of the wires to where it came through the wall. "Let's leave it all for now. I'll talk to the judge and see about a search warrant. We'll have to locate the owner of Joe's to talk to him. He's a possible suspect. The realtor who sold Jessie the place should know how to get a hold of him." Matt raked his hand through his hair. "Damn, I don't like the looks of this."

"If I could offer another piece to the puzzle..." Gary followed them down the stairs. "Somewhere, somebody with some pretty sophisticated monitoring equipment has been watching our girl. I'm heading over to check on her house. He might have come in disguised as a contractor putting in a phone line or the electrician who hung her pendant lights. In other words, he's been around her up close and personal."

"I don't like the sound of that." Dylan looked at Gary.

Matt clenched his fist. "Let me know what you find at her house."

"I will. I'll check for prints or any identifying numbers. I think there won't be any.

Matt frowned. "He may be careful, but it doesn't mean he's invincible."

Gary locked the door and walked out with them. "I'm headed to her place now and I'll call you just as soon as I check it all out." Gary started to walk away and then came back. "You might want to tell her to put a piece of duct tape over the camera lens on her

78

computer to be safe. It's fairly simple to hack into a computer and watch someone."

"No wonder you're feeling edgy." Dylan opened the car door. "It's never anything simple with her."

"You're telling me. It's changing how I think. These guys are getting more sophisticated all the time, and I guess we'd better get there too, or we won't be catching them."

Chapter 8

The sweetest words Jessie heard in a while were that of the captain of the plane telling them that Palm Springs was having a warmer than usual winter with temperatures reaching into the high seventies and low eighties. They could shed their coats and do a little sunbathing. She smiled in anticipation.

The car from the resort turned into the grounds. Everywhere Jessie looked she saw landscaped gardens full of palm trees, colorful bougainvillea flowers, flowering cactus, and passionflower vines. The grounds were lovely, and so was the resort; their luxury home away from home for a few days, complete with staff working overtime to provide for their comfort. Sadie arranged for their rental car through the resort. A new red convertible was waiting for them in front of their suite.

Jessie opened the door to a beautifully appointed suite of rooms. The interior was an outstanding mix of new and traditional furnishings with beautiful fabrics and rich textures in soft yellows and blues. A vibrant red and dark blue in the vases and pillows added a pop of color. It was a feast for the eyes, from the paintings on the walls, to the fresh flowers that filled the vases. A bottle of California wine with cheese and crackers placed artfully on the table gave them a delicious welcome. It would be a few glorious days and a small taste of the high life.

"Oh look, there's even a small kitchen, with a well-stocked mini-fridge." Katie held up a water bottle and showed them.

Jessie smiled as Katie gushed on about their accommodations. She had to admit they were wonderful. A private entrance from the outdoors and a secluded courtyard with a hot tub made it the perfect place to relax. She could get used to this.

"Well, girls, what do you think?" Sadie grinned, looking around her.

"I think I can handle it." Jessie hugged Sadie and then stretched out on the couch. "I mean it's only for a few days." She laughed. "Grams, it's perfect."

"I second that." Katie plopped down in the floral chair. "What do you say we dress for dinner and then later have a nice soak in the hot tub before we turn in?"

"It sounds like the perfect end to a day of traveling to me. I'm going to shower." She closed the door to her room.

****

Showered and dressed, they entered the resort's famous five-star restaurant. They were ready for the great food they had read about in all the brochures. Looking over the menu, they made their choices. Sadie wanted the filet medallions; Katie ordered the lobster, and Jessie ordered a Blackened Grilled Salmon on a bed of greens. A Riesling rounded out their meal followed by an incredible chocolate mousse and coffee.

"The lobster was wonderful and the mousse was unbelievable." Katie licked her spoon one more time. "I would love the mousse recipe for the Inn. My guests would enjoy it. I wonder if I talked to the chef and told him I would put his name on it if he'd share it with me. I'm going to give it a try." Katie got up and went to talk to the maître d'. Jessie watched her friend charm her way back into the kitchen for a conversation with the head pastry chef.

"I believe that girl could talk her way into almost anything." Sadie smiled at Jessie. "Or out of it, depending on the circumstances. She's something. I can see why you two have been friends so long. You complement one another." Sadie shook her head at the waiter when he offered her more coffee. "I believe I've had enough."

"I'm good, too." Jessie placed her hand over her cup.

Jessie watched Katie coming out of the kitchen with a big smile on her face and a paper in her hand. She gave them a thumbs up.

"He gave it to me." She was slightly breathless. "He said since I had a five star inn, and it was in the East, he would let me have it. Of course, I had to butter him up more than a little and stroke his male ego. But it's in my hot little hands now, with only minimal groveling on my part, and soon my guests will be enjoying it." Katie sat down and showed them the recipe with the chef's signature on it.

"I, for one, am impressed, Katie." Sadie smiled at her. "I doubt just anyone could have gotten it."

"Katie could talk a man out of his last dollar and convince him it was his idea to give it to her." Jessie watched Sadie sign the receipt, charging the dinner to their room. "Shall we head back?" Jessie opened the door for Sadie. They walked out into a beautiful starry night. The temperature was still mild, and they opted to take a leisurely stroll around the grounds. Jessie inhaled the fragrance of the evening air. She didn't miss the cold of Blue Cove.

"The vegetation around this place is beautiful, especially the passion flower vines." Sadie pointed out certain plants they passed along the lighted walkway. "Look over there. I think that's a butterfly bush."

Jessie let her eyes follow Sadie's finger. She shivered, a sense of panic growing in her. He was watching her. She could feel his eyes on her. How? Where? Her eyes darted back and forth, searching all the places where he could hide. Jessie grabbed Sadie's arm linking hers through it. Stop it, she told herself. It was just Katie's constant chatter on the plane affecting her. Shaking her head, she mocked herself for letting Katie's words affect her so. She shivered. He was nearby.

"What are we doing tomorrow?" Katie grabbed Sadie's other arm.

"We are scheduled for a massage and a facial to be followed by manicures and pedicures." Sadie looked from one face to the other. She smiled as Katie cried with delight. "Here we are, girls. Be sure to shut that gate so it locks. You have to have one of these to open it." She held up the card in her hand. "Get your suits on; the hot tub is calling to us."

****

Jessie grabbed her towel and was on her way to the courtyard when her phone rang. "Grams, I'll be there in a few. I need to take this call." She thumbed her phone. "Hi, Matt, what's up?"

"Are you enjoying yourself so far?"

Jessie told him all about the resort—every little

detail. She followed that with what they had for dinner and their conversation. She ended with how Katie now had the recipe from the chef and how she had obtained it.

"Is everything okay?" He sounded concerned. "I've never heard you talk so much or so fast."

"I think I'm trying to put off the inevitable." She groaned. "What's the news?"

"He's been watching you, both in your store and your house."

"When you say watching me, what exactly are we talking about?" She sighed.

"In every way you can imagine but don't. You'll be better off if you don't think about it."

She sat down on the chair clutching the towel to her chest. Her stomach turned, she suddenly felt sick. "How am I supposed to not think about it? Are we talking about the bedroom or what?"

"I'll be honest with you, he's probably seen you in all states of dress and undress if our perp was monitoring you."

Jessie's hand clutched the towel tighter.

"How?" She sucked in a shallow breath. "Why? Who is this creep? Just knowing he was watching me freaks me out."

"It'll be okay, Jess. We'll get him. Gary has taken all of the equipment out of your house."

"I don't know what I'm going to do. How did he get in?" Tears filled her eyes.

"We're working on that right now. It looks like some of the wires in the store come in from the coffee shop. He could have been someone who came to wire your lights or hook up your phone. It had to be someone who had to go up into your attic to do some of the work. You need to think. You do have a surveillance video, so we'll check out the tape, but he seems to be aware of things like that. I doubt he'll be on it. Can you think of anybody who fits that description?"

"Not really, I wasn't paying attention."

"If you think of anyone, let me know."

"Sure, you know I will, but there were several people who had to go up there. No one stands out to me. No wonder I felt like he was watching me." She shuddered. "He was."

"It'll be okay, Jess. You're safe now, and he doesn't know where you are."

"Of course, you're right. He can't know, could he? I mean we didn't even know so how could he. Right?" Her hand clutched the towel, closing it tighter around her.

"Jess, Gary mentioned that you should put a piece of duct tape over the camera lens on your computer. He said it would be easy to hack into and watch you from there,"

"Matt, could you ask Gary something for me?"

"Sure, what do you want me to ask him?"

She frowned, pursing her lips. "Ask him how easy it would be to trace my cell phone to know where I am?" She could hear his intake of breath and his muttered curse.

"Hell, Jess, I didn't think about that. He knows where you are, doesn't he?"

"I'm pretty sure that's an affirmative, but I doubt he'll try anything with the others around." She closed her eyes and shivered.

"You're probably right, but just as soon as Jeremy

gets here tomorrow, we'll be on a plane headed west. We'll be close if you need us, but try to let you have a vacation without interference."

"I don't think it's necessary. I can't imagine anything happening when I'm with the others and in this well-patrolled resort," Her voice softened. "I wouldn't mind if you wanted to come, though."

"I'm coming. Stay close to them! Do you hear me? Don't go running by yourself, don't go *anywhere* by yourself. As soon as I have the details, I'll let you know when I'll be there."

"Okay." She felt relieved.

"Remember, Jess, he could be anyone, the guy bringing room service, a waiter, or someone who tends the gardens. Be careful who you talk to and keep your eyes open."

"Now you sound like Katie."

"Who sounds like me?" Katie walked in the room. "What are you doing in here talking when you could be in the hot tub? Sadie sent me to get you."

"I need to go, Matt. I'll talk to you later."

"Jess, promise me you'll be careful. You're smart, and you need to use your head."

"I will." She hung up.

****

The warm water felt good on her body but did nothing to soothe her mind. What had made her think of asking about the cell phone? Matt would come. If someone was watching her, he would know when Matt arrived. Was it possible they could lose their chance to help Adriana? She let the water swirl around her, closing her eyes as Sadie and Katie talked. She was afraid and knew what she felt each time she sensed him.

She was the one who could help find Adriana. Without her, Adriana didn't stand a chance. Still she was happy he was coming.

"Are you sleeping?" Katie nudged her foot.

"No, just relaxing." Jessie opened her eyes.

"I think we should turn in early. We have an action-packed day tomorrow starting at eight a.m." Sadie stood up and grabbed a towel.

Jessie helped her grandmother out of the hot tub. "I think you're right, Grams. Are you coming, Katie?"

"Yes, you don't think I want to stay out here by myself, do you?"

Sadie went to bed. After talking with Katie for a while, Jessie double-checked the locks and went to call Matt. He had made it clear that he would come sooner rather than later because that's what partners do. She was happy he would be nearby. Jessie shut off the light and climbed into bed. She listened in the darkness, straining to hear any noise, but there was only silence. The sheets wrapped and bunched around her in knots before she finally went to sleep.

Chapter 9

Matt looked at the clock. He got Tom's answering service and left him a message. He arranged for airline tickets for Palm Springs and talked to Dylan. Matt arranged to meet Jeremy at the airport instead of him driving to the Cove. Tom's return call came a little after midnight.

"What's up, Matt?" A tired voice asked him. "You sounded like it was an emergency."

"I think it is," Matt explained it all in detail.

"Someone in our office is handling the Foster kidnapping case. I'll fill him in on what you've told me about the note. Can you email me a copy of it?"

"I'll do it when we hang up." Matt made a mental note.

"You think the guy has Adriana in California. Why?"

"Jessie feels he's there and you know how that works. It's possible he's listening in on conversations, but this guy seems to be one-step ahead of us. He must have another source."

"I'll call the West Coast office and get you set up to work with them. Since we worked together on the last case, I think they'll be willing to bring you in especially with the note and surveillance equipment involved. If he gives her any more clues or approaches her, let me know."

"I will and thanks, Tom."

"Did you call Palm Springs PD to introduce yourself?"

"I did."

"You'll need to stop in when you first get there and meet them up close and personal. I'll call and give the chief a heads up about it," Tom told him.

"Thanks, Tom."

"And, Matt, keep your eyes and ears open. I know this much, some weird stuff has happened to the investigating deputy and even in our department. There's more here than meets the eye."

"Would you ask them if they'd be open to us bringing the tracking dog? If we find that our man is in the area, it may be Adriana's best chance of being found."

"Okay, I can personally vouch for the dog. I'll call you back as soon as I have it set up."

****

Matt met Jeremy at the departure gate. As soon as they took their seats on the plane, Jeremy opened his backpack and handed Matt several sheets of paper.

"What do you have for me?" Matt grabbed them.

"Look these over and we can talk once we're up in the air." Jeremy handed him a yellow highlighter too. "Mark the things that stand out to you. I have another set that I've marked in red. We'll talk once you've had a chance to read them." He put his laptop in the seat back so he could grab it when needed.

Matt read and marked places on the page. "She doesn't have any fear when it comes to writing does she? She'd take them all on."

"Jessie was a great reporter and was on her way up.

I think that's why her dad got so upset with her." Jeremy rearranged the pages. "People were surprised when she left."

"Sometimes people just need a change. I'm glad she did." He was proud of her and the more he read, the more those feelings grew.

The plane gave a small lurch as it moved away from the gate. The flight attendant came down the aisle, checking to see if the seatbacks were in the upright position. She took a few pillows from the overhead bins, handed them out to passengers, and smiled at him as she passed. Matt had the old familiar knot in his stomach. He was what he liked to call a white-knuckle flyer. He hated the take-offs, landings, and everything in between that wasn't smooth. He had done enough of it over the years. If he was ever going to get used to flying, it should have happened by now. He tried not to let anyone see it, but he was always happy when the plane had reached its destination and he was once again safely on the ground. Jeremy started talking about the same time the plane started down the runway. Maybe he was nervous, too.

"Did you get a chance to mark those first two articles?"

Matt nodded. "I saw a few things of interest."

"Some of what the professor was saying sounded a little flaky to me. I think he has his own issues." Jeremy had circled it in red. "And, on page three, look how Jessie questions him and her conclusions make the guy look like the jerk that he was being." Jeremy pointed to the paragraph he had marked. "Irwin was a Professor of Religious Studies and Native Cultures at the University when Jessie interviewed him. He had just given a lecture on the role that narcissism plays in fanatical fundamentalism."

"I marked many of those same areas." Matt looked at Jeremy's red marks.

Jeremy handed Matt a few other papers and a tape recorder. "Listen to this and then read the article. I told you about him the other day when we talked. I think you'll hear that this guy mirrors what you read in the note." He handed him some earphones.

Matt listened, put his glasses on, and began to read. He had a sick feeling by the time he was done. Jessie wrote the piece after her interview with Professor Irwin. A man in the crowd asked several questions during a question and answer session for students following the professor's lecture. He kept asking about the stalker at the school and became more belligerent and furious with each of Irwin's answers. His constant interruptions caused the professor to call him out in anger. The professor took it one step too far, to Matt's way of thinking, when he ridiculed the man in front of the crowd. Matt could hear the irritation in the tone of his voice.

Jeremy interrupted Matt's reading. "The guy grabbed Jessie at the end of the interview while the tape was still on and the camera was rolling. He told her his name was Brett Peters. His language was intimidating, threatening to the professor, and hateful. It was after this interview the man lost his job, as several co-workers came forward to say he had bullied them on the job. I thought you should know. At the time, Brett was the head of maintenance at NYU."

"So what happened after this article appeared and he lost his job?"

"It wasn't just an article—it was aired live on TV. The cameraman with her caught him in action. You can imagine how that went over. Jessie got a threatening note. When the police checked it out, they found that the University had determined that Brett wasn't his real name. He left, and no one knew where he had gone or who he was."

"Hell, that's not good. He was trying to impress her then, just like he is now in his sick way." Matt scowled. "Why didn't she tell me about this?"

"To tell you the truth, I think the way Jessie survived in that atmosphere was to forget. There's a lot of ugly stuff that goes on in the city and she was threatened more than once, believe me."

"We could get a look at the guy if they still have the footage."

"They do, and I did." Jeremy pulled out his computer and turned it on. "Here he is in living color."

Matt watched the clip run. "He's a big man. Jess is tall, but she looks little next to him."

"I also found several aliases he's used since Brett Peters, but who knows what it is now. His last known address was a dead-end, but the town is familiar."

Matt was impressed Jeremy had done his research. "Where?" Matt turned in his seat to ask Jeremy.

"Rocky Pointe. Don't get your hopes up. He disappeared from there a few weeks ago. I find the timing interesting, though, and he's still paying his rent."

"It can't be that simple. Next thing you'll tell me he knew the two clowns from the bank."

"Not yet, but I'm working on it. Remember what the conclusion in the article said? If you apply it to

Brett, we'll call him that for now, he wouldn't be hiding. He would want to throw it in our faces. He's been in plain sight all along; right under our noses so to speak, even if he has to stage it."

"I get you!" Matt raked his hand through his hair. He wondered if Jessie could remember what Brett looked like. Tired, he leaned back in his seat and closed his eyes.

The next thing he heard was the Captain's voice. "We have been cleared to land. Thank you for flying with us today."

****

Jessie kicked her shoes off as she came in the door after their spa appointment. "Grams, what a glorious day, I feel like a new woman." She gave Sadie a hug. "How can I ever thank you? This day alone would be worth the whole trip. I haven't felt this relaxed in months."

"My skin hasn't felt this good since who knows when." Katie stroked her arms and then her face. "I think I could get used to this lifestyle."

"I believe you girls enjoyed being pampered." Sadie smiled at them. "I asked the lady who did my nails for a good local restaurant. I know where we're going tonight. It's casual so dress accordingly. I'm relaxed. All I want now is a little nap, and then I'll be ready to go."

Katie headed to the small kitchen to get a drink. "Can I get you anything?" she asked Jessie.

"Not right now, I'm fine."

Katie came back carrying a bottle of tea and a glass filled with ice. I'm going to watch TV. Do you want to join me?" She sat on the couch, grabbing the remote.

"No, I think I'll work on my article for Max."

"Do you ever stop working?" Katie sighed. "I feel too good to work or even think about it." She stretched out on the couch. "You should try and relax. It would do you good."

Jessie noticed an envelope on the lamp table as she stood. "I stop sometimes, but I want to get the information about Adriana out there. The sooner I do it the better. I'll rest as soon as I'm finished."

"Are you sure you're all right? You look pale to me."

"I'm fine." She grabbed the envelope before anyone else found it. Funny, she didn't remember seeing it there this morning. When she turned it over, there was her name written in dark black letters across the front. A wave of nausea swept over her... she was clammy and then hot. She wanted to read it, but then again she didn't want to. He must have been in their room, but how did he get in? She looked around for some sign, any sign. Jessie ripped the envelope open on her way to her room, where she closed the door. She sat on the edge of the bed, paused for a moment, took a deep breath, and began to read.

Jessie,

I hope you don't think that I've been neglecting you. Surely not! I've come to give you your first clue. I'm anxious to see how well you'll do. (Don't fret how I left this little treat for you. I have my ways you know.)

I've tucked my queen in nice and tight. You'll never take her without a fight. Just a few days are all you'll have to find the place where she now lays. She may be hot, but the place is not. It's neither close nor far away. Another clue will come to you soon under the shadow of the moon. Ta-ta for now.

Jessie's mind went to work. She needed Jeremy's brain to help her with this. She could understand a little bit of it already or least she thought she could.

She called Jeremy.

"Hey, Jessie, what's up?"

"Can you talk for a minute? Is Matt with you, and are you in town yet? You can tell him if you think you should. I don't want him to feel he needs to run over here. I know he has enough to do."

"Slow down, Jessie, we're here. What's up? After I hear what you have to say, I'll decide what to do. If I think it's necessary, I'll drive him over there myself."

"Fair enough." She sighed at his sober tone. "I'm typing a note that I found in our suite when we got back. I'll send it to your email. I figure two heads are better than one. It's my first clue on how to find Adriana. I think I can see a few things in it but not everything. Get back with me as soon as you have a chance to mull it over."

"I will."

****

"What did she want?" Matt's eyes narrowed.

"She told me I could tell you, but she doesn't want us to run right over there." Jeremy looked sober. "Your instincts were right. He can't be too far away. Our friend left a note in her room. She's sending it to me in an email now. She wants us to mull it over and get back to her."

"That does it!" Matt bolted to his feet. "If he entered her room, then I'm headed there too."

"You're not thinking straight."

"The hell I'm not!" Matt's hand curled into a fist at

his side.

"Look, Matt, we are in the perfect place. She'll let me know what's happening, and we can stake out the area and keep an eye on her. We can do all that without interfering with her vacation."

"Okay." Matt conceded, not liking it at all, even if Jeremy was making sense. "Get her on the phone and let's have a look at that note; I'll watch from here for now." He pulled up a chair beside Jeremy.

"Hey, sunshine, Matt's beside me, and we're in agreement. We can watch you from a distance, but we're close enough to get to you if you need us. Let's go over this."

"Hi, Matt. Did I tell you I'm happy you're here?"

He smiled. "Okay, Jess, let's hear it."

They went over the note line by line. "Tucked in nice and tight, tells me she's tied up or she can't get away. What do you think, Matt?"

"Sounds feasible to me, anything to add, Jeremy?" Matt looked at Jeremy with a frown. He hated these cat and mouse games, but he would go along with it for now. "What about the next line?"

"She'll never be taken without a fight, tells me she's being guarded."

"I'll buy that, but by what?" Matt jotted down some notes. "Are we talking about people, animals, or is the place booby trapped? All things we need to consider."

"It doesn't look like you'll have much time to find her, so what do you want to do?" Jeremy asked.

"Of course the local authorities need to be notified."

"I've done that, Jess. You wouldn't be here without

protection. The minute you asked if he could track your phone, I knew I needed to talk to them and did."

"Thank you." He could barely hear her soft voice.

"You're welcome, sweetheart. What else are you thinking?"

"I'm going to need Frank and Radar."

"I agree. Tom is setting it up with the authorities here. I took care of getting an article of clothing belonging to Adriana the day we met Evan, just in case. Let's finish this note."

"Well, even though this is a desert and it's warm, she's not, so he's caring for her. She's not near or far so she must be somewhere in between here and wherever. There's not much to go on, other than I'll be getting another clue."

"I don't agree. He's telling us about himself in this note. Jeremy and I are going to work on this, and I'll get back to you later. What's a good time?"

"How about between nine and ten? Will that work for you?"

"That works for me. I'll take care of the rest of the details." He circled Frank's name on his notes. "Where are you headed tonight?"

"We're going somewhere in town for dinner. I had a perfectly glorious day until I found the note. I have to admit I'm worried about how he got in here."

"I'll take a look around your place when you leave. Maybe I can figure out how he got in. Do you want me to come now?"

"No, but I'm glad you're in town. You're my partner after all, and you should be in on this." Her voice softened again.

"Okay, sweetheart, I'll be watching your back

tonight and I'm only a call or text away." Matt smiled as he hung up.

"You look happy." Jeremy's voice was flat.

"I am happy. We've gone toe to toe over this before. The fact that she recognizes that she needs help means we're making progress. Every good investigator knows you never work without a backup." He slapped Jeremy on the back. "Now let's get to work and tell me what you think. We have a stake-out to do."

Chapter 10

After Jessie had put her phone down, she lay on her bed staring at her laptop. The ugly gray tape across the camera lens was a reminder of her present situation and the things she didn't want to remember. Her forehead creased. She started scrolling through her article archives. She wondered how she'd had the guts to do any of those stories. After reading a few it hit her, she could have made many powerful enemies. Why hadn't that registered with her at the time? She was just doing her job, but somewhere in the back of her mind, she must have known it was dangerous. No wonder she had jumped at the chance to leave it all behind and head for Blue Cove. She wasn't a bit tempted by the possibility of a significant promotion, but the thought of a quiet life had intrigued her. She frowned again. Like that had worked. She tapped her finger against her head. *Look at the mess you're in now, girl,* she scolded herself. *You're still doing the same thing only this time with real bullets and bombs for special effects.*

There was a knock on the door followed by Sadie's voice. "Jessie, are you awake?"

"Come in." Jessie closed the program she was in and sat up on the bed.

"Are you okay?" Her faded blue eyes looked worried. "Matt told me a few days ago about the note. He wanted me to be aware and call him if there was any trouble."

"I wish he hadn't told you. I don't want you to worry."

Sadie grabbed her hand as she sat down beside her. "I'm a big girl, Jessie. I would do anything I could to keep you safe. At my age, it may not be as much as in my younger days, but I still have a few tricks up my sleeve."

"Oh, Grams, I love you." She hugged Sadie. "I wouldn't have come if I had thought I would put your life or Katie's in jeopardy. I didn't think someone could follow me if *I* didn't know where I was going."

"Like a baby playing peek-a-boo." Sadie placed her hands over Jessie's eyes. "They close their eyes and think you can't see them because they can't see you." She removed her hand. "Honey, you know better than me that we live in a high-tech world. You always have to be one step ahead of those who are plotting against you."

"I know…You're right."

"I don't want to be right." Sadie patted her knee. "I just want you safe. You think he's here, don't you? I could tell that last night. I knew exactly the moment you felt it when we were walking back here after dinner. I don't think Katie has a clue, but you and I must put our heads together. I think I need to call Matt and tell him." Sadie took her hand.

"I already told him, and he's here in town, but he wants to give us space." Jessie handed her the piece of paper.

"That's good; I feel better knowing he's in town." Sadie took the note and read it. "Oh, my! I hope Matt's close." Sadie turned the piece of paper and then she read it again. "I wonder if there is more than one person involved."

"Why?"

"One person can't be in two places at once. I'm thinking a person here and one back in Blue Cove sounds more likely."

"You could be right."

"I believe we should notify the local authorities. It would be the smart thing to do, dear."

"Matt already notified them, so they're aware. The police are willing to work with him. The FBI became involved when Adriana was abducted and moved across state lines. I can call either of them for help because they know about the case." Jessie clasped her hands in front of her.

"Maybe you and I should pay them a little visit tomorrow. That way they'll know who you are. I have to admit this note intrigues me. He's sounds like he's playing games, but maybe he's giving you a chance to find this other girl." Sadie stood. "Let's put it out of our minds for now and we'll talk a little later. Why don't you get dressed for dinner? Maybe that'll help." She paused before walking out the door and smiled. "I think a quiet dinner is just what the doctor ordered."

Jessie knew her grandmother. If she didn't miss her guess, Sadie was in her room calling Matt right now to make sure he was in Palm Springs.

When Jessie walked out of her room, Sadie was all smiles and Katie was talking a mile a minute. "I hope you weren't waiting too long."

"Only a few minutes, dear." Sadie smiled at her.

"I'm starved. Let's go." Katie stood and pulled Jessie toward the door.

"Wait for me. I'm a little hungry myself." Sadie placed her hand on Jessie's arm.

****

Matt examined the doors when he first got there. The guy had to have a key. There was no sign of forced entry. He had also checked the surrounding area to make sure she didn't have company hiding in the vicinity. Matt would follow her. Officer Carter and a rookie from the local police were keeping an eye on their suite while Jeremy and Taylor went to the restaurant to stake it out. Matt got his first view of Jessie as she left the room, sandwiched between Sadie and Katie. He felt the familiar catch in his throat. He loved the gentle sway of her hips as she walked, and the way her hair bounced against her shoulders. It always felt like silk running through his fingers. She was sexy without even trying. His grin broadened as she laughed with Katie. He could imagine her eyes lighting up. Those damn blue eyes were a major distraction. A man could get lost in them. He had. On more than one occasion. 'Please,' she would say softly, and turn them on him, complete with dimples and he melted like butter. He'd be a mess with a daughter. After waiting for them to pass, he started his engine and followed. So far so good. A moment's relief gave way to anger, as he thought of anyone trying to hurt her.

Matt heard static and then Jeremy's voice came across the line. "Hey, Matt, I wanted to check the radio to make sure it works."

"I hear you loud and clear." Matt smiled. Jessie was right. Jeremy was getting into playing cop. Matt could appreciate his love of his tech toys and willingness to help.

"We're in place with eyes on the front and the back of the restaurant. Where are you?"

"I'm following them. It's all quiet so far." Matt signaled, changing lanes.

"Did Sadie say how Jessie's doing?"

"She told me that Jessie was handling it all admirably and taking it in stride. According to Sadie, she's more intrigued by what the guy is doing and trying to anticipate his next move than thinking about what he could do to her."

"Sounds like our girl to me. Once she's drawn into a story, she'll follow it with no concern for herself until afterward."

"I remember that about her. In our last case, when she saved my life, she faced Booker fearlessly, shot him, and promptly walked into my arms falling apart." Matt hung back and pulled into on open parking space where he could see the restaurant's entry.

"It's like I told you—she has a way of tuning it out. When she sees injustice, she'll go after it like a mother bear protecting her cub; not one thought for her safety. After it's over, you'd never know she met any resistance—except for all the tears. All in all, that's what makes her an attractive package. That and being one beautiful looking lady." Matt could hear Jeremy's laugh in the background.

"You won't get any disagreement from me. She's an attractive package all right."

"I guess I better start doing my job. I'll check back in later on. Over and out. I know it's corny, but I've always wanted to say that." Jeremy chuckled.

"We'll talk later. Keep your eyes open." Matt took a swig of his coffee and unwrapped his sandwich.

He watched the people coming and going. He could see the trio sitting by the front window. The waiter, a young man, was falling all over himself trying to impress them. Boy, did he know the feeling. She looked stunning, and Katie did too. Matt took a bite of his sandwich.

He glanced at his watch. It had been about forty-five minutes since they went in. He still had time. Katie's hand was gesturing as she spoke, Jessie and Sadie were laughing. His grin broadened. She had brought laughter back into his life. Even his brothers had noticed.

"Matt, are you there? Come in, Matt, come in." Jeremy's excited voice came across the line.

"What's up, Jeremy?"

"I've been trying to reach Carter, and I'm getting no reply. Should we go check on him?"

"Stay where you are." Matt sent a quick text to Sadie. "You keep watch here. I'll go check on Carter."

"Will Jessie be okay? Maybe the suspect is setting a trap." Jeremy sounded breathless.

"She should be fine. You need to stay here. I told Sadie to stay put in the restaurant. She assured me they would be there for a while, she'd make sure."

Matt called the police station, to get officer backup. A patrol car was there when he arrived back at the resort. Two officers went one way and searched. Matt and the rookie went the other way toward the front of the unit. They looked through the bushes and foliage. They found Carter shoved behind a clump of bushes, slumped over, face down. He radioed the others as he felt for a pulse.

"His pulse is faint." Matt stood up from his

crouched position as the two officers approached. "I don't see a visible mark on him, but he's in a bad way." One called dispatch for an ambulance. Within fifteen minutes, Carter was on his way to the hospital. Matt searched the unit and walked the grounds with the other officers.

They found nothing, but Matt knew this little drama was all part of the game. He talked to Jeremy on the radio. "The suspect apparently knows we're here. He staged this scene for our benefit, a little welcome present." Matt pulled out his phone and texted Sadie. *It's all clear for you to come back. Jeremy and Officer Taylor will follow you back.*

"You're probably right." Jeremy's voice came over the radio.

"He'll want her to know how he bested us." Matt walked around to the side of their unit.

"How's Carter?" Jeremy asked.

"Let me check." Matt turned to one of the officers and asked about Carter. He put the phone on speaker.

"He's struggling to breathe, but there are no visible signs of injury. His vitals are starting to improve. We almost lost him." The officer looked grim. "The hospital will call when we can question him."

"Do you mind if we sit in with you when you question him?" Matt asked.

"I'm sure it will be okay. I'll run it by the chief first."

"Did you hear, Jeremy?"

"I did. I'll catch you later. They're coming out of the restaurant."

Matt turned off his phone. He checked again to make sure the lock on the door was secure. He walked around the suite one more time, not sure what he was looking for. Troubled by what had happened to Carter, he was searching for anything that showed how their suspect could have taken him completely by surprise. Something glimmered on the ground in the beam of his flashlight—crimson red smeared upon a pile of rocks with some odd-looking feathers and fetishes. There were makeshift altars at several spots around their unit. They were uniform in placement and in appearance. Matt squatted down to get a closer look. When he reached his hand forward with a stick to lift one of the feathers, a strange sensation went up his arm. A jolt propelled him onto his backside. "What the hell!" he yelled out.

"Is everything okay?" The rookie called out to him.

"Yeah, but before you leave I want to show you something I noticed as I searched the perimeter." Matt pointed out several small pools of blood around the unit. He left them untouched. "Look at this." They walked to each altar he had found. Matt couldn't shake the strange sensation that he felt.

"It looks like some religious symbol." The rookie crouched down next to Matt to see where he pointed.

"I talked to the Sheriff's department in charge of Adriana's disappearance and they found similar things at the station. We'll need to keep this in mind during our investigation." Matt looked at the other officers from his crouched position.

The rookie reached his hand forward with a small tool on his pocketknife to scoop up some of the blood to have it analyzed.

Matt grabbed his hand. "I wouldn't do that if I were you. I had to pick myself up off the ground when I attempted it."

"You're kidding, right?"

"I'm serious. There is something strange going on here." Matt felt almost foolish saying it, but he knew what had just happened to him. He still didn't feel quite right. "Let's try again in the daylight."

"Sounds good to me," one of the other officers said. "We'll be able to better see what we're dealing with. I think we'll head back on patrol. To tell you the truth I don't know how to handle this in my report."

"I've heard from two other agencies that strange things have happened since they started investigating this case. I'm now inclined to believe them. Carter was almost dead with no visible signs of injury." Matt shook his head. "None of this makes any sense. He walked to the cruiser with them. "I'm going to hang out here until we tuck the ladies in nice and tight. Will you call me when you head over to the hospital?" Matt shook hands with the officers who had helped.

"Sure thing, I'll call you as soon as we hear." The officer lifted a hand. "See you later."

Chapter 11

Against the wall, hidden by the bushes, was the perfect vantage point to watch. The man pulled his dark hood tightly around his head moving deeper into the shadows. It was too damn hot for the hoodie. Sweat was already forming on his forehead. A branch whipped across his face when the breeze caught it, leaving a stinging welt. The place was crawling with cops. Except for the one who was out of commission—he wasn't moving. A bit of hocus pocus and—bam—there was one less cop. Laughter rolled through him in silent waves. Boy, they were dumb. The boss put one of them to sleep right under their noses, and they hadn't seen a thing. Surprise, surprise. The cop would have one hell of a headache if he survived. Stupid cops! They had to play by the rules, but not him. He was the game changer and the game changer made the rules. A smile spread across his face when the ambulance rolled up.

Those damn altars had worked. Unbelievable! The cop was picking himself up off the ground. The Game Changer rocked back and forth, his grin broadening with each motion. Another check of his watch. Almost showtime. This was going to be fun. Jessie was smart, but no match for the boss's skill. "Be patient, all you have to do now is be patient." He knew his boss was close by. A shudder racked his body. He could almost feel the darkness swirling around him.

****

Jeremy joined Matt after following the women safely back. They hid in a place where they could watch the area for a while.

The night was quiet except for the chirping of a few crickets. The air was warm enough to be outside and enjoy the moonlight. Matt looked over at Jeremy. "How long have you known Jessie?

"Several years. I first met her when she set up a meeting with me. I was doing research on banking fraud in the housing industry, and she was doing a story on it at the time. She walked in, and it was all over for me." He grinned. "I could hardly hold an intelligent conversation with her. I don't know how, but somehow I managed to hold it together. We worked together several times after that." Jeremy got quiet and then smiled. "It took a while, but eventually I realized she saw me as a brother and nothing more. I nursed my broken heart, and we became great friends. That's what we are now."

"How long did that take?" Matt asked him.

"Let's just say long enough. How did you meet her?" Jeremy stretched out his arms behind his back.

"I met her right after she moved to Blue Cove. It was the first day of her arrival. She was at Angelo's with Katie. I tried to play it cool, but one look and she hooked me. We both fought the attraction for a while. I was a jerk." Matt's grin broadened. "I wonder if I'll ever escape the need to slug every guy who comes along and looks at her."

"Once I got over I wasn't the guy for her, I watched her reaction to those who came on to her. She seemed to take it all in stride and put them in their place fast if they crossed a particular line with her. She had to handle some sticky situations with co-workers and people she interviewed. She did it with class, but she still put them in their place with little doubt about how she felt about their actions." Jeremy slapped Matt on the back. "That's why I can say she's different with you. Lots of guys have fallen for her, but she always kept her distance." He shook his head. "Not so much with you."

"That's good to know." Matt's grin vanished. "Do you think it's possible this guy is one on the long list of those who she's discouraged? Are we looking at a disgruntled would-be suitor who is unstable, or a stalker?"

"That's an angle to consider. Maybe Adriana's stalker became hers, and maybe he's setting it all up because Jessie's the ultimate prize."

"Hell, we could be dealing with someone's obsession. We'd better dig deep and see if we can find anything." Matt's jaw flexed.

"I don't know how you can stand the waiting." Jeremy strained to see what had moved the bush on the other side.

"Let's just say I can't. I was never good at it." Matt moved out of their hiding place. "I think we should call it a night."

****

Jessie was restless. Sadie was asleep and so was Katie, but she was wide-awake. She remembered Reba's words about being the gatekeeper of her mind and she shouldn't let anyone into her thoughts who didn't belong. Maybe Adriana would try to get in touch with her or maybe the dark figure who had been standing over Adriana would try to force his way into her thoughts. The resort staff had already turned down the bed and left a piece of chocolate on the pillow. She opened it, popped in her mouth, and let it melt slowly, savoring its goodness.

Shutting off the light, Jessie lay across the cool silky sheets, but sleep still evaded her. Adriana had been too quiet. Why? Drugged perhaps. Jessie didn't want to consider the other possibilities. Her mind raced on. Is that what the note meant when it said *tucked in tight*? Talk to me, Adriana. Jessie rolled onto her side, the blankets bunching around her legs. Boy, another piece of that chocolate sounded good. She could still taste its smooth rich flavor.

She took a deep breath in through her nose, held it for eight seconds, and released it through her mouth. Whoever had told her breathing this way was supposed to relax you had it all wrong. It wasn't working. The loud ticking of the clock shifted her attention. The numbers moved ever so slowly. One, one-fifteen, one-thirty, and then two. Jessie tossed and turned in rhythm with the ticks of clock. It was at five minutes after two when everything began to change.

The room came alive with dancing shadows and snake-like creatures with eyes that glowed in the darkness; hypnotic, hissing creatures spinning ever closer to the bed. Covers flew one way and Jessie rolled the other direction trying to distract them. Tightness settled across her chest. She gasped for air. Drums beat in the night. Had anyone else heard them? A quick peek out the window showed only a quiet night. No shadows, nothing. It was getting harder to breath. The curtain slipped from her fingers, and she crouched in the corner of the room in fear. "You're the gatekeeper, don't let them in," Jessie repeated the words in a panic. The creatures stopped to stare at her with hideous glowing eyes.

Jessie started humming a song remembered from her Sunday school days as a child. The words came flowing back and she found herself singing it aloud with gusto. Her mind closed tight to the one who was trying to infiltrate it. The drums beat on, the creatures danced into a frenzy, whirling about the room. As long has she sang her song, they didn't come near her.

The bedroom door flew open, and the light snapped on. Sadie burst through followed by Katie. They joined her on the floor and sang along with her until the sun peeked up over the horizon, and the darkness slunk away, taking the fear of the night with it.

****

"What happened?" He screamed at his boss standing beside him. "You didn't do what you said." He pulled his dark hood tighter. "You promised it would work if I did everything that you told me to do."

The man mumbled under his breath. "She fought us. I've never seen this strength before." He wiped the sweat from his brow. "She wouldn't let us in. Let me worry about getting her ready for you."

"I won't give up, do you hear me? I've waited too long for this. You told me it would be easy for you to take care of." He shoved his hands in his pocket. "I'll do it myself."

"You can try, but you'll make mess of it. You always do," his boss said, poking him in the chest. "Do what I tell you. Get back to Adriana and let me worry about Jessie. You don't want a visit from my friends do you?" He got in his car and drove away.

Out of control, he lashed out in anger. The trashcan careened across the sidewalk, emptying its contents along the way. It was time to find a new place, a way to change the game. His racing heart slowed, the anger subsided, his breath returned to normal. Round one went to Jessie, but that's the last one he'd give her or anyone else.

Chapter 12

"Jessie, what was that?" Katie's voice trembled as it sliced through the thick air that still permeated the room in spite of the growing dawn light. "What just happened? I can't stop shaking." Katie hugged her middle tightly with her arms.

Jessie remained huddled in the corner, grateful for the wall's solid support. "I don't know—it was unlike anything I've ever experienced before. Dark...evil." She shivered. "I was balanced on a fine line between sanity and insanity. It...it took all I had to hold it together. I thought for a moment that I would lose it." Tears filled her eyes. "That's why I started humming the first thing that came into my head and then singing it. It seemed to help me focus." She shivered again.

"What are we going to do?" Katie grabbed the chair to pull herself to her feet and stretch her legs. "It felt real. I wonder who or what it was?" She frowned. "Didn't it feel a little weird how it just sort of went away with the light of day? At least I hope it did." She plopped down in the chair.

"My, sweet girls." Sadie put her arm around Jessie and patted Katie's knee. "We'll be okay, but no more dilly-dallying. I think we need to let Matt know what happened, immediately. I'm going to call him." Sadie tried to stretch her cramped legs, and then groaned as she rolled over onto all fours and held on to the chair to stand. Katie held out her hand to help her.

"He said he'd come if we need him. I hate to bother him and bring him running over now." Jessie winced at Sadie's slow progress. Her grandmother didn't deserve this. She felt a pang. Her fault, she'd brought this danger with them.

Sadie shook her head. "We need him! The other man is here, and we need Matt." Sadie frowned as Jessie's chin started to lift.

"Okay, call him, but I don't think he could have done anything to help us last night." Jessie stretched her legs out in front of her. She shivered.

"Whoa! Back up. Did I miss something? *Who's* here?" Katie grabbed Sadie's arm. "You mean the guy who's been writing those notes?" Katie stood up with her hands on her hips. "I told you he'd follow you, didn't I? Now, what are we going to do?" She glared at Jessie. "Don't listen to her, Sadie. Call Matt, and get him here now. I'm scared."

"Matt flew in to help but wanted you girls to enjoy your vacation. You, my dear girl, can remove that stubborn look on your face." Sadie wagged her finger at Jessie. "He wants to be here. He's your partner. The case is here now, and so is he."

"I hate that he forever has to come to my rescue." Jessie shrugged her shoulders.

"I'm glad he does, with all the weird stuff happening to you and anyone else near you." Katie sniffed.

"First things first, girls. We need to shower, get dressed, and we'll have a lovely breakfast. We are going to be rational and sane about this. The three of us need to put our heads together and think." Sadie stretched her arms and walked about a little bit. "Boy, it's been a long time since I sat on the floor. I'm going to pay for it."

"Are you okay, Grams?" Jessie bit her lip.

"Yes, it's nothing that a nice hot shower and time in the hot tub can't cure." She held her hand out to Jessie as she stood. Sadie sat down on the bed. She patted the open space, but Jessie shook her head.

"I think I'll get dressed." Katie walked out of the room. "Call him," she called over her shoulder.

Sadie nodded. "What do you think it was?" Sadie looked at Jessie as she asked it.

Jessie began to pace. "I don't know. Matt had mentioned that the deputy in charge of Adriana's case said strange things happened at their station when they started investigating her case."

"What kind of strange things?" Sadie glanced at Jessie when she asked her.

"All the paper files, all the interviews from their legwork in the case went missing. Computer files were erased. They found blood and several small fetishes. Matt told me the deputy had sounded fearful."

"It sounds a little like voodoo, but most voodoo rituals aren't for evil purposes." Sadie frowned. "Although, it seems, I read once that there was a dark side of voodoo, with practitioners who did curses and cast spells for a fee. They believed it could bring the dead to life again. That's where the idea of the zombie originated. Who do you know that would be mixed up in that?" She looked thoughtful.

"I have no idea, but if their intent was to scare me, they did a good job." Jessie pushed her hair behind her ears and started pacing again.

"You must've been up against a cultic ritual of some sort last night." Sadie nodded. "It's probably best if we don't mention it to Katie."

"I agree. All I know is that right before it all started happening, Reba's words about me being the gatekeeper came back to me, and I knew I didn't want to let anyone into my head. I focused on keeping them out." Jessie stopped pacing and looked at Sadie. "I don't know if they were real or only in my mind. Ugly and dark is how I would describe them."

"You did well, girl." Sadie stood. "Make yourself presentable, and I'm going to call Matt. I'll speak to him about what happened last night and tell him we want him here. I'm doing this for me, as much as for you."

Sadie had won! Jessie knew her grandmother was worried, and she was right. Matt needed to be here. She was in over her head.

She headed for the bathroom and turned on the shower. Stepping into the warm water, she let it wash over her, taking away for a moment the stress and fear of the night, sending it swirling down the drain. Again, Jessie hummed the song, feeling her spirits rise. She had survived to fight another day. *Adriana, talk to me. I'm not giving up on finding you. You're fighting this alone. I can't imagine the fear you must be feeling.*

****

Matt grabbed his phone off the table when it rang. "Hey, Sadie, what's up?"

"Matt, I think you need to get over here tonight. We had an incident last night and I think it's more than the three of us can handle."

"You mean other than the one I was in on?"

"Yes." He heard her exhale a deep breath.

"What kind of incident are we talking about?" Matt cursed under his breath as Sadie explained it. "How is she?"

"She's decent, considering, but I think whatever it was wore her out. And, Matt, we're all glad that you're here."

"That's nice to know." Matt raked his free hand through his hair. "While we were checking things out last night we found some fetishes and these little altars sprinkled with blood placed around your suite. Whoever it was must have prepared the area for some ritual. Are you sure she's fine? I should have stayed in the area through the night." He knew what he had felt and the strength of whatever it was that knocked him to the ground.

"I don't think you could have done anything, and Jessie is fine. She fought it like a trouper. It was scary. Even Katie felt it. When the sun came up, it was gone."

"It seems when it comes to Jessie, every wacko comes out of the woodwork. Does she come by it naturally?" He jotted a thought on the pad.

"I admit similar things happened to me when I was younger, and my mother was the same. I never had the strength I saw in Jessie last night." Sadie sighed. "I'm proud of my girl, but I think we need to put our heads together to make sure we can keep her safe while finding Adriana."

"We'll come right now if you want."

"Unless I call you back, around dinnertime will be soon enough. We can all eat dinner together. You might want to consider checking out of your room. I'm glad you followed your instinct to come. We need you!"

Sadie's last statement both heartened and worried Matt. Sadie was seldom concerned, but she was now. He woke Jeremy up and told him what happened. "You need to look up any practitioners of voodoo in the area. I'm not sure you'll find anything here. He might have hired someone from outside the area."

"Man, nothing is easy when it comes to Jessie." Jeremy sat up on the bed rubbing his eyes.

"No, it's not, and we need to hit the ground running. We didn't learn much from Carter that was useful. He didn't know what hit him. He did mention he couldn't catch his breath, that hands were strangling him, but no one was there. Strange, he was afraid still." Matt pulled his shirt on. "I plan to check out of here later this afternoon before we meet them for dinner." Jeremy nodded and headed to the shower. Matt grabbed his phone and called the station. "Dylan, how's it going back there?"

"You know, just the usual petty stuff. With Jessie out of town, it's our quiet community again." Matt could hear Dylan chuckle. "Gary and I checked out the information you wanted. We learned some interesting things yesterday."

"Let's have it." Matt frowned.

"The owner of Joe's is out of the country. His name is Joel Cummings. He's the brother of Jason, our past infamous mayor, now living in prison."

"I forgot Jason had a brother. I didn't know he bought the coffee shop."

"It's a small world, as they say."

"Yes, it is. I'd say it's damn convenient for him to be out of the country right at this time." Matt looked at his watch. They'd have to leave soon to make their meeting.

"It would be too convenient if he's actually out of the country."

"Did anyone know about the wires coming into Jessie's place from Joe's?" Matt asked.

"Cumming's Enterprises had a work request and permit on record. Access was given to pull wires and install electricity into Jessie's store through Java Joe's. What I found interesting is Joel and Jason are partners in the company."

"Who requested the access?"

"The company name given was Idle Time Books. I'm sure Jessie's signature was forged. I doubt she requested the extra work. She thought she was paying technicians to install her lights only. The secretary couldn't give us any other information."

"I'll ask Jessie about it, Dylan. Joel or Jason probably ordered it but covered their tracks. What else do you have?"

"We went through the security camera footage at the coffee shop and Molly pointed out the man she remembered. Gary has isolated the frame and is blowing it up to send it to you as we speak."

"I doubt it will be any good. It seems like he might be working for our perp." Matt grabbed his laptop off the bed.

"How's it going out there?" Dylan asked him.

Matt filled Dylan in on the details. "That's where we stand right now. Jeremy and I are working to find some link that can tie the two cases together, but who knows if they're related."

"Gary said you can expect that photo in about ten minutes. He'll send it to your email so you can have it on your phone. Is there anything else you need?"

"See if you can find Joel Cummings. I'd be willing to bet he's still in the country." Matt put his gun in the holster.

"Okay, I'll look into it for you. We'll handle things from this end."

"I want you to look at a file for me and see if you see anything. I'll email it to you." He opened it on his computer and sent it to Dylan's email.

"What am I looking for?" Dylan asked.

"Anything that seems to stand out to you or that might tie these two cases together. I feel like I'm missing something." Matt put his badge in his pocket. "You know how to reach me." Jeremy walked into the room, ready to go.

"I'll read through it. Do you want me to see if Joel has signed in at the prison to see his brother in recent days?"

"Good idea." He should have thought of that. "They keep a log of all visitors."

"I'll get back to you, Matt, if I find anything."

"Same here." Matt hung up and emailed Dylan and Tom Maxwell a copy of the second note, then called Frank Wagner.

"What's up?" Jeremy asked as soon as Matt was through talking to Frank.

"We should be getting a photo of the man who installed the equipment in Jessie's store. It could be our guy or someone he hired to do it. I hope it will be good enough quality to see the guy's face."

"I've been thinking. What if Adriana's stalker and Jessie's worked together to help each other out? Maybe they hatched this little plan together or had the help of a few friends?"

"What made you think that?"

"I was checking on the guys from the bank like you asked, and some things just don't add up."

"Like what?" Matt's brows lifted slightly.

"They all belonged to the same health club, which could be a coincidence, and they all lived in the same apartment building. Two of them went to NYU, and one of them had just started at the bank a few months ago."

"Which one is new at the bank?" Matt asked, but he already knew the answer. "Jordon Daniels!"

"Yeah, how did you know?"

"I knew the moment I met him I wanted to punch him. Now I might have probable cause. One can hope." Matt grinned. "Who else went to NYU?"

"Randy Wallis. Another point of interest, which may or may not mean anything is Professor Irwin quit his job not long after the interview, which is unusual for a tenured professor. He'd had several death threats, and he seemed just to drop off the planet. Irwin's wife had mysteriously vanished the year before and was never found."

"Interesting. We may need to locate a living relative." Matt looked at Jeremy. "What else do you have for me? Damn, you're good at information gathering. I could use you on my team."

"Brett Peters' real name is William Mallory and he served a couple of years in prison. He was released six months ago, and that's when he moved to Rocky Pointe. I'm trying to find out who he associated with while he served time."

"Good work." Matt grabbed his files and keys.

"Guess who owns Java Joe's?"

"Not, a clue."

"Joel Cummings, Jason Cummings' brother. Do you remember Jason?"

"I sure do. He's serving time, isn't he?" Jeremy whistled softly. "I'll have to check it out. Where are we headed?"

"Tom has everything set up with the West Coast Office. I had a call from the Palm Springs PD to check in with Chief Balasco this morning. Agent Henderson will be there too." He printed another copy of the second note to give to them. "Let's get going."

Matt backed the car out of the parking space. "I would stake a lot on the idea that there's more than one guy in on this. The logistics alone dictate it."

"How so?" Jeremy clicked his seatbelt.

"Adriana was taken near Blue Cove. Jessie lives there, and they found bugs in her house and shop. They brought Adriana across the country to the desert of California, and someone placed a note in Jessie's store after Adriana was abducted." Matt looked in his mirror and changed lanes. "Jessie and I usually talk these things out together and we help each other think outside the box. If you have anything, lay it on me." Matt frowned. "It doesn't make sense. We're missing an important piece in this case..."

"The guys at the bank could be in on it."

"They could be, or they could have been inadvertently used to get information and set the abduction up."

"I'll try to find out who Mallory's friends are."

"I'd be surprised if you find any. Men like him don't have friends. They tend to use people or be used by them. He might have met someone in prison he tried to impress. We also can't forget the voodoo angle either, and how it might play into it." Matt turned in to the station. "From what Sadie said, it was pretty scary. I can agree with her assessment."

Just as Matt pulled into the parking space, his phone chimed an incoming email. He opened it up and saw a poor quality photo.

"This is the guy." He handed his phone to Jeremy.

"You can barely see his face. Jeez, I was hoping for someone that stood out, but he just looks ordinary." Jeremy handed the phone back to Matt.

"He was probably paid to install the equipment. I'll have Gary send a copy to Tom to see if the Bureau's technicians can clean it up a little. It would be great to find out who he is and who hired him."

"If he was a hire, there might be fingerprints." Jeremy grabbed his computer case off the floor when he opened the door. "I mean, if he's not in on this he wouldn't be worried about prints, would he?"

"I don't think I'd get my hopes up in that department." Matt opened his car door and got out with his case files in hand.

****

The sergeant ushered them into Tony Balasco's office. Tony stood up from his desk and reached over to shake Matt and Jeremy's hands. "We'll get started in a minute as soon as Agent Henderson gets here. Help yourself to some coffee." He pointed to the small alcove across from his office.

Matt stepped out to get a cup. The first thing Matt had noticed was that Balasco was a short, but a solidly built man with a thick Eastern accent. He had a firm handshake and a smile that reached his eyes. Matt liked him. He liked him even more when he heard him laugh at something Jeremy had said.

Matt sat down in the chair and opened his files. "You sound like a New Yorker." He smiled at the chief as he said it.

"I am, or I should say, I was." He briefly closed his eyes. "I bet you're wondering how I got here."

Matt nodded and took a sip of his coffee.

"I was a young cop working a beat the day the Trade Center Towers came down. I was several blocks away but saw the first plane hit the tower." His eyes fixed on Matt. "My first thought was that it was an accident until I saw the second plane do the same thing. Sirens were screaming all over the city. I tried to make my way there, but as you can imagine, there was a lot of panic on the streets. I got close enough to see people hanging out windows and jumping to their deaths. I was never close enough to get inside the building. Too many people running from the building needed help." He cleared his throat.

"I can imagine. As a kid, I watched the news coverage alongside my parents." Matt remembered it well.

"It still affects me." Tony's eyes were misty. "When the first tower fell, it was like being swallowed up in the gray mist of hell. God only knows what swirled around the city. You could hardly see or breathe. I tried to help people, but I knew with every step I took that a lot of people had died. It was the worst thing I've ever been near." He closed his eyes for a moment. "I lost a lot of good friends that day. I still have dreams that haunt me. After all the funerals, I knew I needed to get out of there and make a fresh start."

"This is pretty far from there." Jeremy sat forward in his chair.

"I put in for jobs as far away from the sad memories of that day as I could get. You have to admit this little place is an oasis in the desert and just about as different from New York as I can get. I don't regret it, not even for a moment."

"Being from New York, I can understand." Jeremy looked away briefly. "I was a kid, but everyone you talk to can remember where they were when the towers came down."

Tony cleared his throat again. "Before I forget to mention it, Jessie Reynolds will be here this afternoon to introduce herself. Her grandmother wanted us to know what she looked like, just in case."

"That sounds like Sadie." Matt grinned.

"Tom Maxwell filled me in on some of the details and I would like to get the rest from you." Balasco watched Jeremy stand up. "Decided on some coffee after all?" Jeremy nodded.

Tony looked at Matt. "Between you and me, I wish we didn't have to include Agent Henderson. He's somewhat of a control freak. He likes to micromanage things. He's trying to make a name for himself, I guess. On the fast track if you know what I mean." Tony stood abruptly. "Speak of the devil, here he comes. Prepare yourself."

A tall man with blond hair walked into the office as if he owned it. His broad shoulders filled the doorway as he paused to stare at Matt. "I see we get the honor of working with each other again, Balasco." He shook

Tony's hand, but his eyes returned to Matt.

"Agent Henderson, this is Chief Matt Parker."

Matt shook his hand and tipped his head. "Thanks for letting us work with you."

Henderson barely acknowledged Matt. "I'll be running this operation. You both need to go through me. I don't want any Lone Ranger messing up my case. If you're on to something, you fill me in. You got it?" Henderson looked directly at Matt when he said it.

"I sure do," Matt's answer was brief, his features schooled. If this were the avenue to get what he needed for Jessie, he would just have to suck it up and take whatever this fella dished out. And he was sure Henderson would dish it out.

"Okay then, let's get down to business." His cold gaze swept them. "I have what Tom sent me and I want to see what you have for me." He reached for the notes and files Matt had for him.

Chapter 13

Jessie walked into the small kitchen, checking her phone for messages.

"You look lovely. That pink shirt gives a little color to your cheeks." Sadie smiled at her.

"Thanks." She bent and whispered in Sadie's ear, "I love you, Grams."

"I love you, too." Sadie patted the chair next to her. "Sit down, dear." She took a cup and poured her some coffee. "I think we're all going to need this to get through the day."

Jessie held the cup between her hands. "You know, Grams, I'm ready to fight. If we were scared last night, can you imagine how Adriana is feeling? There were three of us, but she's all alone." Jessie's eyes flashed with anger. "They abducted her several weeks ago and there's no telling what they've done to her. I get sick thinking about it. If it were me, I would want Matt to move heaven and earth to find me."

"Have you heard anything from her or seen her in your dreams?" Sadie took a blueberry muffin from the basket and passed the basket to Jessie.

"No, and that makes this case harder. I think they might have sedated her. She's not dreaming, so I don't know. I would think she'd be hallucinating or something. I haven't seen her since the night I saw her in the trunk of the car and the dark figure bent over her." Jessie grabbed a sesame bagel.

"I hope her baby will be okay." Sadie pinched off a piece of her muffin popping it in her mouth.

"Who's sedated?" Katie walked into the kitchen.

Sadie smiled at her. "We're talking about Adriana, dear."

"Let's hope so. How else could she remain calm in an endless nightmare?" Katie sat across from Jessie.

"You're right, Katie." Jessie handed her a cup of steaming hot coffee. "I think you hit the nail on the head. She's sedated and out of it altogether." Jessie glanced at Katie "Sometimes you surprise me with your astuteness."

"Yeah, whatever that means." Katie rolled her eyes at Jessie.

"You know what it means. You always play dumb, but you're an intelligent woman." Jessie gave Katie a playful slap.

"Of course I am, but a smart woman is a threat to men. You're a prime example. You scare them off in droves."

"Any man who is threatened by a woman's intelligence isn't much of a man in my book." Sadie adjusted her glasses on her nose. "*Some* men love to talk things out with a woman who can think for herself."

"Oh my gosh, Sadie, you're cute." She blew her a kiss. "What man? Give me an example!"

"Matt, for one." Sadie grinned at Jessie.

"It's true." Jessie eyed Sadie's smug smile. "We do seem to work well together, bouncing ideas off of each other, but it wasn't always that way. We fought a lot in the beginning."

"Okay, so there's one, but it doesn't mean much. Matt loves Jessie. There aren't very many others." Katie took a muffin from the basket.

"I'm glad he'll be here soon." Sadie looked over her glasses at Jessie.

"Me too! He'll know what the next step is." "And you know, Katie, you're wrong. There are others."

"Like who?" Katie's eyes lit up.

"Like Jeremy." Jessie's eyes sparkled with mischief.

"Now there's a guy I could get used to talking to." She winked at Sadie.

"You'd better start practicing." Sadie laughed. "He's here in Palm Springs and will be coming tonight with Matt."

"Did you say Jeremy is here?" Katie jumped up and did her happy dance around the room. She grabbed Sadie and tried to get her to dance. Sadie shook her head no. "Oh, that's the best news I've heard all day."

"It's the only news you've heard. It's still early yet." Jessie laughed, and Katie gave her a playful slap.

"Party pooper." Katie sat again. "I have to do my hair and makeup. I wonder what I should wear."

"Settle down. You'll have plenty of time to get yourself ready. Matt and Jeremy won't be here until around dinnertime. Do you think we should order in tonight?" Sadie looked at the dark circles under her granddaughter's eyes. "You seem a little tired." Sadie saw Jessie's chin edge up.

Jessie shook her head. "If it's all the same to you, Grams, I think we should all go out. I think it would be good to get out of this room for a while tonight." She sipped her coffee.

"That's okay with me. You know, I was thinking, girls, instead of moving on to San Diego, how about we just stay here. I checked, and we can have this suite for a few more nights. There's an open street fair on Thursday that I thought would be great fun to see."

"I think you read my mind, Grams. It's perfect." Jessie took a bite of her bagel. It's not the right time to move."

"It's fine with me as long as whatever happened last night stays away." Katie shuddered. "If Jeremy's here, I'm not going anywhere." Katie took a sip of her coffee. "What's on the agenda for today?"

"We need to stop by the police station for a few minutes. I want them to meet Jessie. Then I think we should do a little shopping. I want to buy you both new outfits. How does that sound, girls?"

Katie smiled. "I'm always up for a new outfit." Katie spread some butter on her muffin and took a bite. "Oh my, this tastes wonderful. I guess I was hungry."

"I'll just give Matt a text and let him know we are planning to go out for dinner." She smiled at Katie's exuberance. "Finish up; we need to get on our way."

****

Jessie shut the door behind her and walked out into the warm sunlight. Chief Balasco was a good man. She wasn't so sure about Agent Henderson. He had bugged her. She didn't like the way he had looked at her. It felt like total freedom to walk out of the station away from his stares. He was a colossal jerk, and he was in charge. Poor Matt.

"Dear, I think we should make this normal time for Katie." Sadie grabbed Jessie's arm to slow her pace. "I know shopping doesn't sound like you're doing anything for Adriana, but your mind will keep working. Maybe you'll hear something as we go through the day. After last night, I want to keep Katie's mind off it. Besides, I want you both to have a little fun on this trip despite everything."

"I know you're right. It's hard for me not to get wrapped up in a case once I get going on it." Jessie turned to talk to Sadie. "Besides, Matt will be here soon, and we can talk. He helps me see things more clearly." Jessie walked arm in arm with Sadie to the car.

Katie had remained in the car and at some point had put the top down. "You took long enough. It's hot in the sun," she called out as they approached.

"Now, Katie, I'm old enough to set the record straight. It took all of fifteen minutes, and I tried to get you to come in. I didn't want you to get too warm, remember?" Sadie chided her. "Jessie, you drive. I'm never good when I don't know an area very well."

Jessie followed Sadie's directions and turned down Palm Canyon Drive, a street lined with palm trees and flowers. It was the heart of Palm Spring's downtown area with all its shops and restaurants. "Where do you want to go, Grams?"

"I was told we had to visit this place." Sadie handed a piece of paper to Katie with instructions on it. "It's the El Paseo shopping district, the Rodeo Drive of the desert."

"Wow, it has over three hundred shops, boutiques, and art galleries. El Paseo has just about everything you could want, including jewelry. You know how I love jewelry." Katie's eyes filled with excitement reading the brochure.

It was a floral-filled, well-maintained mile of

beautiful shops and restaurants. Excited to explore the shops, Katie was squealing with delight. Jessie smiled at her, getting into her enthusiasm. Katie was bound to find several things that she loved. Shopping here could do some major damage to Jessie's budget, but she was willing to risk it. She'd probably never be back to the area again. Jessie pulled into the first parking space she came across. "Do you feel like walking a little, Grams?"

"Of course," she replied gaily. "Let's hit a few of these bad boys and shop our cares away." She smiled at them.

****

Jessie settled her bags around her as she sat down on the bench with her grandmother and Katie. The three were exhausted and ready to stop for the day. "I think we did enough damage for the whole week today." Jessie giggled, looking at all the bags.

"Sadie, what are you on, speed? I could hardly keep up with you. Whoever said people slow down when they get older obviously never met you." Katie slipped off one of her shoes and rubbed her foot.

"What do you say we get something to drink as we head back to the car? I think I could use a little nap before this evening. I'm saying that for your benefit, Katie dear, so you can take one too." Sadie smiled at her.

Katie smiled. "I hope when I'm half your age I can be as young as you are."

"I hope you can, too." Sadie patted Katie's hand and laughed.

"I'm sincere. None of us slept much last night and you, sweet lady, just keep going. You're not like any grandmother I've shopped with."

"There are plenty of us out here. Getting older doesn't always mean life is over. As long as you have your health, you can keep on moving." She handed them their iced teas.

When they got to the car, Jessie unlocked it so they could get in. "Thanks, Grams, this was a good day."

****

"Damn, Matt, how'd you put up with the insolence of that guy? I wanted to punch him." Jeremy followed Matt into the room.

"He's in control of the case and that's just how it is. Most guys are cool to work with but now and then you get a guy who loves power and likes to pull rank on you," he said wearily. "I'm going to have to tolerate it to work the case."

"I have a feeling he's going to enjoy pushing your buttons."

Matt took his gun off and placed his badge on the table. He stretched out on the bed. "He'll push, and I'll find a way to work around him. I'll feed him enough to make him happy. We do what we have to do I guess."

"I think I'll check on a few of the other areas you requested. When are we leaving?" Jeremy grabbed his laptop and turned it on.

"I told them we would be out of the room by five." Matt held up the remote. "Will it bother you?"

"No." Jeremy's fingers flew over the computer keys.

"I'll tell Sadie we'll be there a little after five." Matt turned on ESPN, but he couldn't concentrate on it. Matt muted the sound. "There is something that connects all these characters together. I wish I knew what the hell it was."

"Matt, you're not going to believe this." Jeremy jumped up with his laptop. "Look who spent time with Mallory in prison."

"We'll I'll be damned, that changes everything. This case just got real interesting."

Chapter 14

Jessie walked into her room and froze. Propped against the pillow on her bed she found a creepy little doll with a pin stuck through its heart. An envelope was in front of it with her name written in big, bold, black letters across the front. Breathing rapidly she grabbed the doll and threw it forcefully against the wall. It dropped into the trashcan, the perfect place for the ugly little thing. Jessie turned the envelope over in her hands. She hesitated a moment and then tore it open.

"Jessie, Jessie. I'm so disappointed in you. You're not smart. I thought you'd have it all figured it out by now. Adriana was my way to get to you. I'm changing the game. I wonder how Matt will do when he's not just looking for one, but maybe two. We'll see. I'm the Game Changer. Look over your shoulder; I'm often right behind you. Too bad you never see me, though— you've looked right at me. Now don't panic yet, it's not quite the right time. By the way, I bring warm regards from some old friends. See you soon!"

Jessie took deep breaths trying to calm herself. She pulled her dress off the hanger and sat on the edge of the bed. Matt would help her figure it out.

She slipped into her new blue sheath, ran a brush through her hair, and added a pair of sapphire blue heels. Silver hoops and a necklace that her mom had given her completed her look. She could hear male voices. Matt was here. She sighed. She put the note in her purse to give to him after dinner, opened the door, and there he stood. His eyes appraised her, revealing his approval. She had to hold herself back from running to him and throwing herself into his arms. Boy, oh boy, did he look good.

She walked over and stood beside him. "I'm glad you're here."

"I'm happy you're glad. I didn't want to interfere with your girl time vacation." He smiled down at her. "How are you holding up?"

"I'm doing okay, just a little angry." She clenched her lips tight.

"He'd better give up now. I know you well enough to know you'll hunt him down, stay on his trail, and bug the hell out of him until he screams uncle." He grinned at her.

She gave him a tentative smile. "Are you saying I'm a nuisance?"

"Nope, I'm saying you're a damn good reporter and a great partner." He leaned close to her and spoke quietly so only she could hear. "Beautiful dress by the way. It makes it almost impossible to keep my hands off you, and I'm in the same room with your grandmother. I bet you did that on purpose."

"I didn't, but I'll file it away for future reference on how to best torture you if I need to." She laughed at his expression and went to stand behind Sadie's chair.

"Coward." He mouthed the word and winked at her when she looked his way.

****

After dinner and a walk through the downtown area, Matt finally found himself alone with her in the courtyard. Sadie at his request had maneuvered Jeremy and Katie inside to look at something. He stood, stretching out his hand to pull her out of the chair. He pulled her in close to him with one quick move and kissed her. She was a perfect fit. He took a step back so he could see her face, his arms still holding her loosely. He would never tire of looking at her. He could hear the intake of her breath. His heart raced at the sound. With the tip of his finger, Matt traced where his lips had just been. "That, Jess, is for looking so gorgeous tonight." He released her but held her hand. "I guess we'd better get down to business. I'm not sure how much time we have until the others rejoin us." He stroked her face, kissed her cheek, and let her sit down.

"I have something for you." She opened her purse, pulled out the envelope, and pushed it toward him.

"Another note?" His brows rose. "When did you get this one?" He watched her carefully, his hand fisted.

"When we came home today, it was sitting on my bed with a doll." Her hand clutched her purse tight.

Matt saw no fear when he searched her face. "Where's the doll?"

"It fell into the trash when I threw it against the wall. It seemed like the perfect place for it."

"Jess, you know better than to do that. Go get it," he snapped, his hand clenched at his side. "It's evidence."

"I know." She looked away. "It was my reaction to knowing that he was in my room again. How's he getting in our suite? I don't feel safe at all." She sounded defensive.

"Do the others know?" He grabbed her hand as she stood up.

"I haven't told them yet. We were trying to spare Katie."

"They need to know." He stood still, holding her hand. "Let's go tell them together. I don't think you should be alone here anymore. This guy is obviously close. He's found a way to come and go freely in your room. He has to have a room key. There is no evidence of a forced entry on any of the doors or windows."

"How did he know which is my room? Unless, of course, he can see me." A look of disgust crossed her face.

"Don't go there. He could know by having looked at the clothes in the closet. But I'll have your room checked just to make sure." He pulled her close as she shivered. "Will that make you feel better, sweetheart?"

"Yes, but to tell you the truth, I'm mad. I want to get him. If I'm afraid, I can't imagine what Adriana has been up against."

"That's my girl. Like I said before, he'd better just surrender." He placed his hand on the small of her back and guided her toward the door.

Matt held the doll that Jessie gave him, turning it over to look at it before placing it in a bag along with the note. They joined the others in the living room. "I think we need to talk." Matt made eye contact with each of them. "The suspect has been in your suite again to leave this doll and a note on Jessie's bed. I'm concerned about how he's getting in."

"Are you kidding me?" Katie jumped up. "Do something."

"It's not that simple Katie," Jessie reminded her. "They at least have to have an idea who they're dealing with."

"He must have passcode access. What do you want to do about it?" He looked at Sadie. "Jeremy and I can stay here with you, which would mean you would have to double-up. To be close to the doors, I'll sleep on the couch. Where everyone else goes, I'll leave up to you. Or you could move, but I think he would find a way to follow." Matt started to pace.

"By all means stay here." Katie grabbed Jeremy's hand, which he quickly freed, Matt noticed.

"What do you think, Sadie?" He wanted her support and choice. "I hate to interfere with your vacation but I admit I'm concerned. This new note leaves little doubt he's going to try something soon."

"Of course, you must stay here. My granddaughter's safety is all I care about." Sadie gave him a worried look. "Do you think we should stay here or just go home?"

"Honestly, I believe this guy will follow you back home. We have to be careful. I'm hoping he will overplay his hand, and we'll trap him." Matt squatted down to be eye to eye with Sadie. "Jessie understands the procedures of working a case. She's good at what she does. She'll be smart, and I'll do everything I can to keep her safe."

"Okay then, let's move Jessie into Katie's room. How's that sound?" Sadie frowned. "We'll throw him a little curve."

"Now you're thinking." Matt smiled at her.

Sadie quirked an eyebrow at him. "Where do you think my granddaughter got her talent from?"

"No doubt in my mind, from you, of course."

Sadie stood up. "You tell us what to do and we'll do it."

"For now, Jeremy can stay here while I go to the police station. Jeremy, you might want to get your luggage from the car. I'm not sure how long it'll take. They'll need to put this into evidence." Matt pulled out his keys.

"We can move Jessie's belongings into Katie's room, and I'll call for clean sheets. Jessie dear, you go with Matt so the two of you can talk about the other night, and we'll get things ready here." Sadie stood up, grabbed the phone, and called the desk to request more sheets and towels.

"You know you're a lot like her, don't you?" He closed the door behind them.

"One could only hope." She smiled at him as he grabbed her hand.

Chapter 15

A while later they walked out of the police station together. "Who do you think are the old friends he's talking about?" She slid into the passenger seat of his rental car.

"Jeremy and I are working on a theory right now. Mind you, we're building the evidence trail." He clicked his seat belt. "We think the guy's name may be William Mallory. He's had several aliases so you might not know him by that name. He was the big man who got into an altercation with Professor Irwin when you were interviewing the professor about the stalking case at NYU. He also got into your face and threatened you. The story hit the TV news and cost him his job. He was not a happy camper."

"I think I remember the interview, but not the man." She frowned trying to recall the incident.

"At the time, he was going as Brett Peters. I don't know if he's our suspect, but he fits the profile. It's also possible that one or both of the men at the bank are accomplices or inadvertently helped him."

"Do you mean Randy Wallis and Jordon Daniels?"

He nodded. "Did you know the professor dropped off the radar after that interview? No one has heard from him or seen him since. His wife also mysteriously vanished the year before."

"I hadn't heard that." She shook her head.

"Did you know Joel Cummings, the owner of Java Joe's, is Jason Cummings' brother?"

"How could I have not put that together?" She scrunched her face.

"Here's the kicker; William Mallory served his time with Jason Cummings in the same prison where T. J. Booker is being held." He pulled over and parked. "I don't know if they knew each other for sure yet, but this note tells me I'm a part of the game. The last two cases were high profile, and I would think we both probably made some powerful enemies."

"Wow, I didn't see that coming." She pushed her hair behind her ear. "So what's our plan?"

"For now, the plan is to find Adriana and keep you safe while trying to flush out our perp. I think an article for the paper about Adriana being tracked to somewhere in the Palm Springs area might stir a little controversy." He laced his fingers through hers. "We'll start with that."

She smiled at him. "I'm glad you're here."

"I tried to stay away, but too much is happening now to let you go it alone."

She gave him a sheepish look. "You're busy enough keeping order in Blue Cove without having to follow me other places. I can't expect you to come running every time I find myself in a little bit of a bind."

"We're a team, and you're my partner. I got involved when the note came through your mailbox and we found the equipment in your attic. You got that!" He gave her a stern look. "Being partners means we watch each other's back, and we work together. There is no way I would let my best girl and partner face a stalker alone."

Jessie frowned. "I don't know why it's so hard to ask for your help."

"That's easy enough to answer. You're too darn stubborn." He watched her shake her head. "Yes, you are but that's one of the many reasons I'm hooked."

"I don't want you to have to come to my rescue. I should be able to handle this. I did in New York." She turned her face away from him and looked out the window. She tried to pull her hand away, too.

"Oh, no, you don't." He grinned. "You're not getting away with that. I'm not rescuing you. I'm your partner, here to help. Who saved whom the last time? I imagine Booker wasn't very happy that a woman reporter took him down with one shot. The other prisoners must tease him every day. The once notorious hit man was taken out by a mere woman reporter." He could see her fighting a smile. "Besides, if anyone gets to whine about someone coming to their rescue, let's see. When I lay on the ground with a gunshot wound, you were the one running to get the bad guy. I'm embarrassed just talking about it." He heard her giggle and started the car. "You save me, I save you. We're partners. It's what we do." He slipped his hand out of hers, and when she turned to look at him, Matt gently pulled her face close to his. He kissed her. "One more time, sweetheart, we're partners. It's what we do."

"Do all partners kiss? I've never seen you and Dylan kiss, or Kip and Gary." She grinned at him.

"Hell, they're not as pretty as you." He kissed her again and then pulled onto the road.

****

Jessie woke with a start. The room was very dark.

Something seemed off when she sat up. Slipping out from under the sheet, she fumbled to the chair. All the while, she could hear Katie's even breathing. What had awakened her? She leaned back closing her eyes. She heard the faint cry again. *Help me, please someone help me.* It sounded too real to be in her mind. She pulled on her robe and opened the bedroom door. She took a few steps and Matt sat up.

"Where are you going?" He grabbed his pants off the chair and pulled them on.

"I'm sure I heard a woman's cry for help." She paused, trying to feel her way in the dark room.

"Are you sure it's not in your head?"

"Of course, I'm sure. I know the difference. Listen, there it is again." She walked toward the door, and he grabbed her.

"I can hear her, too. Let me get my gun, this could be a trap. We're going together."

Once outside, Jessie found her first. She wasn't far from the suite, lying on the ground, struggling to sit up. "It's okay. We're not going to hurt you." She could see the fear in her eyes. "I'm Jessie," she said. "Let us help you."

"Jessie?" The woman's eyes got wider with a mix of fear and relief. Jessie knelt beside her while Matt called for an ambulance. The next call was the police.

"What happened? Is there someone we can call for you?" Even in the dark, Jessie could see how battered she was. Bruises shadowed her dark eyes and scratches marred her arms and legs.

"My husband is probably worried about me." She told Matt the phone number to call.

"What's your name?" Matt dialed the number.

"Maria Gonzales, sir." She winced when she moved her arm.

"Maria, be real still just in case your arm is broken. It isn't hanging right. I have an ambulance on the way." Matt walked a short distance away to talk to her husband.

"Can you tell me who did this to you?" Jessie let Maria lean against her for support.

"I was leaving work and a strange man came up to me and asked for directions. I told him. When I started to walk away, he grabbed me and told me to be quiet, or he would kill me. He shoved me into the trunk of his car. I don't know where we went, but when the car stopped, he pulled me out of the trunk and starting beating me. He kicked me, and I fell to the ground. He hurt me so bad. I prayed to the saints." Tears ran down her face. "I didn't do anything to him, why would he hurt me like this?"

"I don't know, Maria. Some people are just cruel. How did you get here?" Jessie watched Matt walked toward them.

"He threw me on the ground, right there." She pointed. "He told me to come to this place and tell you something from him. I couldn't make it to the door. I was afraid he would come back and see that I didn't make it and kill me."

"Oh, Maria, I'm so sorry this has happened to you." Jessie gently stroked her face, pulling a strand of dark raven hair that had slipped across her blood-crusted lips back behind her ear. She could hear the wail of the siren approaching until the ambulance turned into the resort. Then the night became eerily quiet.

"The man told me to say to you that your worst nightmare has arrived, and he wanted you to see what you deserved and will get." Maria grimaced. "Go somewhere safe, he's crazy. I could see it in his eyes."

"I'll be safe. You work at getting better for your family." Jessie saw the paramedics getting the stretcher and bags out of the ambulance. She moved out of their way and let them get to work. She turned away when they put the IV in Maria's good arm and felt sick when they put the splint on her bad one to keep it immobile. Jessie wiped the tears running down her face. Maria was in pain, and Jessie knew she would never forget the fear she'd seen in her eyes. Would the mirror show the same fear in her eyes?

"Your husband will meet you at the hospital, Mrs. Gonzales." Matt bent down to tell her. Her patted her hand and said something Jessie couldn't hear. He stood up and walked toward her with a grim look on his face.

"He's watching. I can feel it. He wants to see if we're scared." Jessie started to pace.

"Are we?" He watched her walk back and forth but then stopped her by pulling her into his side.

"No, but I'm angry." She frowned at him. "In fact, I'm going to tell him." Her eyes followed the slight rustling as the wind blew through the palm trees and brush of the thickly landscaped area. He was somewhere close by, gloating. She could feel him. "I know you're hiding out there watching. I'm counting on you being able to hear me. Anyone who beats an unarmed innocent woman is a coward, and that's what you are. You're coward, afraid to show your face. Well, I'm not scared, but you'd better be." She looked at Matt. "I have no idea where he's at, but I know he can hear me even if it is only in his head. Let's get this guy."

"Calm down, sweetheart, we'll get him, but we've got to use our heads. I know you're upset by what you saw." He stopped, turned her toward him, and rubbed her shoulders. "We're going to get him."

"You sound confident." She saw the certainty in his expression.

"I am. It's only a matter of time." He stood in front of her and lifted her chin. "You need to be careful. He's crazy enough and calling him a coward might not be a good idea. Neither is giving him the invitation to come after you."

"I know." She looked up into the starry sky. "I wear my emotions on my sleeve, and I hate what he did to her. How do you remain so calm? I want to hit something."

"I'm not calm, but I won't let him know that." He stood with his arms folded and his feet apart. "Maria put up a hell of a fight. The hospital will gather the evidence under her nails, on her skin and clothing. We'll know his identity quick if he's in the system."

"So we wait." Her voice was barely audible. She rested her head on his shoulder.

He frowned. "We wait."

Jessie went back inside while Matt talked to the police. By some miracle, Katie and her grandmother had slept through it all. Grams sometimes wore earplugs and she'd been tired, so she must have stuck them in tonight. Jeremy had slept through it too, she guessed. She sat down in the chair to wait for Matt. Rubbing her temples, she closed her eyes.

She could see a small figure, her head hanging

down, bound to a chair. Suddenly the woman lifted her head as if she sensed Jessie was observing her. A piece of tape covered her mouth. Jessie's heart raced, it was Adriana. Jessie watched her look around the room as if seeing it for the first time. It was a mess. Dishes piled high in the sink and counters. Everywhere she looked, junk littered the floor. Thoughts were flooding Adriana's mind so fast Jessie could hardly keep up.

Not sleepy. I need to get free before he gets back. Please help me. She started working at the knots. She got one hand free and patted her stomach. I hope you're okay, little one. She kept working until she loosened the rope just enough to wiggle her other hand free. She winced when she yanked the tape off her mouth. The rope securing her feet was next. Her fingers wouldn't work. The knot was too tight. She strained to hear any sounds that said he had returned. Please don't let him back come yet. She kept working at it, cries of frustration punctuating her failure, but she didn't give up. Suddenly with one more tug, she was free. She stood up and stretched her cramped body. How long had she sat there? How many days? Why couldn't she remember? She was wet and smelly. No time to be embarrassed. She rummaged through stuff, tossing junk aside. I know it's around here. She almost gave up and then she found it stuffed in a bag on the table. She held up the flashlight with a cry of victory. She grabbed some bottles of water and a box of crackers and shoved them into a plastic bag. She opened the door and peered into the darkness. Breathe. You can do this. She would rather take her chances against the desert than with him. Adriana found the road the car had come on and she followed it off to the side in case she saw the

*lights of his car and needed to hide. I need help. I wish
someone could hear me.*

"I can hear you. Keep sending me your thoughts
and I will find you." Jessie felt suspended—wanting to
get up but was unable to. She watched Adriana race
into the darkness. She ran with her until she no longer
could see her. Jessie's breathing returned to normal, and
her eyes opened. She jumped up when the door shut,
and she ran to Matt. "We have to find her Matt; we
have to find her." She dissolved into tears.

"What happened, Jess? You're shaking."

"I saw Adriana, and she's free. She's out there
somewhere in the darkness, and we've got to find her
before he does."

He pulled her onto his lap while she told him what
she had seen. "I called Frank earlier today, and he's
arriving tomorrow. Agent Henderson and Chief Balasco
agreed to it. I have one of her shirts that Evan gave me,
so we'll start as soon as the dog is ready."

****

Crouched behind the large landscape rocks and the
lush shrubbery, he had watched it all unfold. He didn't
like her calling him a coward. He wasn't, and he would
prove it to her, soon. He could make her happy. All he
needed was a little time. He stood up when the final
police car left, and the cop went back inside. Sweat
dripped down his neck. His hands were scratched and
bleeding from pulling the leaves from thorny bushes.
He got riled just thinking of that cop touching his
Jessie. She belonged to him. He might scare her, but he
would never hurt her. She was his queen. He had to do
away with the cop, though. He was getting extra money
for killing him. His eyes darted back and forth making

sure no one saw him. He didn't like the cop touching her. His body twitched, and his skin crawled. That feeling was coming over him. He could taste it. He had to get away, or he wouldn't be able to stop himself. He started up his car and drove away. Mile after mile he drove through the darkness, the voices in his head getting louder till all he wanted to do was scream.

A wave of nausea engulfed him, his palms were sweaty and his face clammy. Jessie hadn't meant to embarrass him. He would forgive her; once she understood how it was going to be. It was rising again, clutching at him, threatening to take over him. Wait, wait, calm yourself. It's not time. He pulled off the highway onto a dirt road and stopped the car. "Shut up," he yelled banging his head on the steering wheel. Finally quiet, his head aching and foggy, he slumped sideways on the seat. The quiet darkness settled around him.

He was in his world, and he was at rest.

Chapter 16

The sunlight streamed in through the small opening in the curtains and fell across Jessie's face. Morning! Please not yet. She closed her eyes again and groaned. It was still shining when she peeked again. It was more of a poke than a shine, mocking her with its brightness. She rubbed her eyes and moved her head out of the direct line of the sun. The next line of defense was to pull the sheet over her face. It didn't help, she was awake now, or partly awake might be a more accurate description. The clock showed eight-thirty. All the events of the night before came rushing back into her mind. She threw off the covers and sat on the edge of the bed, pushing the hair out of her face. No amount of rubbing seemed to clear the fog in her brain, though. "Maria," she murmured, shaking her head, trying to erase the image of the woman lying there. Boy, would she would like to get her hands on the man who did it, and put him in a room alone with Matt, Balasco, and Maria's husband.

She stood and shuffled to the restroom. It was a slow start, but maybe a shower would clear the cobwebs. The water worked its magic, and just so she wouldn't be tempted to crawl back into bed, Jessie gave her hair a cold rinse. With a startled yelp, she was wide-awake.

Thirty-five minutes later, she emerged from the

room to Katie's high-pitched chatter.

"There you are lazy bones. The guys left a while ago. I was sure you were going to sleep the day away."

"It was a long night." Jessie scowled. "One you completely slept through, by the way."

"I wore a pair of Sadie's earplugs just in case you decided to take up late night singing again. I wanted to sleep." Katie took a breath. "They worked wonders, let me tell you. I'm feeling great this morning."

"How nice for you," Jessie mumbled, pouring coffee into her mug.

"What happened last night, Jessie? Matt flew out of here this morning saying he had a call in regards to last night." Sadie handed Jessie the cream.

"An injured woman was dropped out front of our room. I heard her crying for help. She had a message for me from the guy who's been sending the notes." Jessie retold the events of the night.

"Will she be all right?" Sadie looked at Jessie, concern written on her face.

"It was bad. She looked awful. Matt thought she might have a broken arm from the way it was hanging. The paramedics wanted her ribs x-rayed to check for fractures too. The guy kicked her several times." Jessie shivered. She knew all too well what broken ribs felt like.

"Oh dear, the poor woman." Sadie grabbed a tissue to wipe her eyes. "Can we do anything?"

"I'm going to check on her today. I thought I would take a bouquet of flowers to the hospital. Do you want to come along?" Jessie sipped her coffee.

"Of course, I do. How about you, Katie?" Sadie glanced at her.

"Naturally. I guess I'm going to have to get used to all these strange things that happen to you, aren't I?" Katie gave Jessie an odd expression. "Just a thought, maybe I should start working the cases with you, but then again maybe not. I think you need someone somewhat normal in your life. I guess that'll have to be me."

"I'm not sure I would go as far as to call you normal." Jessie winked at Sadie and grinned at Katie. "But, I'm glad you live close by, and I can slip over to the Inn whenever I need to laugh. Besides, I've always liked you just the way you are."

Katie rolled her eyes. "I'm normal! Even you can't spoil my good mood today. I like me the way I am, too."

"I think both of you girls are perfect the way you are. As soon as we visit the hospital I think you two should do a little relaxing by the pool." Sadie smiled at them. "Maybe it will do you both some good and help to remove the dark circles from under your eyes." She patted Jessie's hand.

****

They were in the hot tub when Matt and Jeremy got back to the resort. "Good afternoon, ladies." Jeremy smiled and nodded at them as he sat down in one of the lounge chairs. "What have you two been up to?"

"We went to visit Maria at the hospital and to take her some flowers." Katie smiled back.

Jeremy turned to Matt. "I'm telling you, Matt; I'm ready to scream at that guy. I don't know how you put up with his hostile remarks."

"Whatever you do, don't give in to that urge or you'll end up in jail." Matt sat down in the chair across from Jeremy, pulling his shades down from his head and over his eyes.

"Give me some credit, I said I'm ready to, but I won't do it." Jeremy winked at Jessie. "Still I wouldn't mind taking my best shot and punching him. He was pushing you every way that he could. It made me mad."

"Are you talking about Agent Henderson?" Jessie grabbed her towel and wrapped it around herself as she stood. Climbing out of the hot tub, she walked to the chair where her swimwear sarong hung and slipped it on.

"That would be the one." Jeremy grinned at her. "He's got it in for Matt and is making life around the station miserable. That's putting it nicely."

"Don't be nice on our account. We're big girls." Jessie smiled back at him. "I wasn't impressed him with either. He was a little too full of himself." She thought about it a minute. "He could be a nice guy, though. I'm a firm believer that there's some good to be found in most everyone if you take the time to look."

"Always the optimist, Jess," Matt snapped. Jessie frowned at his snap, and he looked away from her.

"I gave *you* a second look, didn't I? We didn't size each other up well in the beginning, either." She flung the beach towel over her arm.

"Touché." His brow rose slightly. "How's Maria this morning?"

"Maria's in pain but doing a little better." She slipped her feet into her sandals. "She was happy to see us. I feel sorry he dragged her into this mess." She frowned at him again. "Is there a reason you're touchy?"

"Henderson." Jeremy chuckled.

Jessie walked over to Jeremy and tousled his hair. "How was your morning?" She smiled at him.

"His morning was all right," Matt snapped again. "Get dressed. We're meeting with Frank in twenty minutes."

She glared at him. "What! I didn't know we had plans, or that Frank was even here. You could have called." She marched into the house, followed by Katie.

Jeremy stood up. "Do you mind if I stay here and do that research we were speaking about earlier? I want to check something out while it's still fresh in my mind." His forehead wrinkled. "I've been thinking of that last note that both of you are the targets. It may be for different reasons, but I would guess that revenge may be at the heart of it."

"I don't mind." Matt sighed. "I need to keep you on my good side. I may be in a bit of trouble. She'll be taking imaginary points off for my behavior."

"Yes, I thought you were acting too male." Jeremy chuckled. "She might be mad now, but she'll remember how Agent Henderson is badgering you. I'll remind her of it, and she'll be her usual sweet self to you in no time."

"Thanks for having my back, not that it's going to help this time." Matt stood and pulled his keys out of his pocket.

"We guys need to stick together." Jeremy grinned. "Women are hard to figure out."

"We're not easy ourselves." He sighed. "But it's pretty straightforward in this case. She didn't deserve how I treated her. I was a jerk. No, excuse for it. She took it about the same way I did with Henderson." He frowned, ruefully. "Only she had no trouble letting me see just how she felt about it. I think I'm about to get an earful." He winced as the door slammed and looked up to find her headed his way. Oh yeah, she looked like she was ready to do battle.

Jeremy patted him on the back. "Hang in there, buddy, the make-up is worth the war."

"That depends on how long it lasts." Matt watched Jeremy walk away and smiled.

Jeremy had stopped her before she got to Matt. "Jessie, when you get back I want to run a couple of things by you. Don't forget." He raked his hand through his hair.

"Sure, okay." She managed a smile that didn't erase the anger in her eyes. "Oh, and I put my article about Adriana on the table in your room. Read it and see what you think. Sadie edited it, but I'd still like you to double-check it." She reached up and straightened the curls he had messed up.

He leaned close to her and spoke softly. "Take it easy on him." Jeremy winked at her. "Henderson put him through the ringer."

She looked skeptical. "He's a big boy.

She walked over and stood in front of Matt. "I'm ready, as you can plainly see, so let's get going."

"Look, Jess…"

She put up her hand to cut him off, turned on her heel, and walked toward the car. "I don't want to talk about it right now."

"That mad, huh?" He ran to catch up with her and opened the car door. He walked around to the other side. "Jeez, am I going to get the silent treatment now?"

"What do you think?" She turned her face away and looked out the window.

"Damn, I don't know what you expect of me." He leaned sideways, trying to catch a glimpse of her expression. "I'm only a man. I've got some guy riding my case, and I'm staying in a small space with a woman who's driving me nuts."

"What's that supposed to mean?"

Okay, no thaw yet. "Nothing, it's not your fault." He straightened. "Forget that I said anything." He started the car but didn't back out of the parking space. "Look, Jess, I'm sorry. I'm a grouch. I don't have a good excuse. I didn't sleep last night. Henderson was being a nuisance this morning. Then to see you half-dressed, getting out of the hot tub, it was too much for this man, I'm at my limits. Since I'm being honest, I didn't like the way you were looking at Jeremy either." He glared at his hands on the steering wheel, forcing them to relax. "I took the path of least resistance and got angry."

"I don't know whether to take that as a compliment, an insult, or both. I'm sorry you didn't like my swimming suit, but I was in the hot tub before you got back." She kept her face to the window. "You didn't call to say you were coming. You just invaded my space."

"I never said that I didn't like the suit. I liked it all right, and what was in it. But, let's not go there." He blew out an explosive breath. He wasn't getting anywhere here. "Right now we both have to do whatever we can to keep our head in this. Honestly, I'm concerned. We have a guy who has real problems, and who is after you. He's unpredictable. The more I find out about him, the worse it is. I have no clue as to what he's capable of, or even what he could be thinking."

"Have you found out something?" She turned finally, her expression worried.

"From the DNA collected from Maria's nails, it is our guy, William Mallory. He was in prison for assault. He beat some guy bad, damn near killed him. He has a long rap sheet starting in his teens. Jeremy's trying to find out more now." He frowned. "We do know he was under the care of a Dr. Hearst for psychotic behavior. As long as he took his meds he was somewhat under control, but more often than not, he didn't take them. That's when the trouble escalated." Matt started to back out of the parking space but stopped halfway.

"So why are you so upset and snapping at me?" She scowled at him. "Is it Henderson?"

He shook his head. "Henderson's a pain, but he's good at what he does. He'll irritate the hell out of me, but he'll get the job done. There's another cog in the wheel, though. Henderson's sources tell him they spotted a known hit man in the area."

"Why don't they arrest him?"

"His sources are snitches, not agents. They have no clue where the man is, and I have to admit that I'm a little concerned about that. You do remember that you shot a hit man. Now there's a hit man in the same area where you are." He adjusted the mirror. "Word is there might be a contract out on you. It may be nothing, but I'm not willing to risk it.

She took a deep breath. "Here's the deal." She turned to face him. "We'll put this aside for now. I want to find Adriana, and personally, I want to survive. But when this is all finished, we are going to have a talk about your constant need to lecture me." Her stubborn chin lifted, and his jaw clenched. "For now, we have a truce."

"Fair enough." He nodded. "But you also need to understand it's my job to give orders when I'm on a case. That's what I do. The niceties don't apply. As much as I would love for this to be a vacation right now, it's not, sweetheart. We're in the middle off a case that I'm working hard to wrap my head around. If making you mad keeps you safe, if pulling rank keeps you safe, then that's what I'm going to do." He tapped the steering wheel.

"I understand orders when it comes to the job, but I won't let you snap at me because you're having a bad day."

"Look, Jess, I can't promise you I'll never lecture you or tell you what to do. I'm a man. I don't even realize, half the time, I'm doing it." He frowned. "And, I'm not like your dad, so don't compare us." He knew once the words left his mouth that he'd blown it.

"I've never compared you to my dad." Her eyes narrowed. "I only got mad when you sided with him. You don't know enough about our relationship to make a call on it either way."

"You may be right about that." He sighed. "But you can't run every time a guy frustrates you—you'd be running for the rest of your life."

"Who's running? So far I've taken everything you've thrown at me."

He softened his voice and turned to look at her. "I know, Jess, I can be a real bear to deal with when I'm on a case. You'll never find anyone who loves you more than I do." He finished backing out of the parking space. From the corner of his eye, he could see her glancing his way with a perplexed look on her face.

"Let's just leave it as it is—we're both tired and angry right now. Maybe this isn't the best time to talk about it. I've already said more than I wanted to. This time, I wasn't pulling rank on you, sweetheart. I was a jerk." He could see the corner of her mouth turn up.

"My description, exactly. A simple call to let me know Frank was here could have avoided all this. I can't read your mind. You have to tell me if you want me to be ready to go somewhere with you." She frowned at him.

"I can live with that." He changed lanes.

"Stress from the job doesn't give you license to jump on me over tight quarters, or my swimming attire. You're the one who suggested you stay there." She turned her face away from him but then turned back around. "And just so you know, I love my dad. The argument I've had with him over the years is not over telling me from time to time what to do—he had the right to do that as my parent. But, he didn't have the right to control my life. There's a vast difference. Enough said." She turned her head from him and looked at the window once more.

He watched her for a few minutes. The silence in the car was deafening. He reached across the space between them and touched her arm. "Truce, Jess, I'm sorry."

She flinched. "Sure, why not."

He noticed she still hadn't looked his way. He had made a mess of this day. *Was* he trying to control her? He needed to figure out how to set this right. He put on the turn signal and turned into the motel where Frank was staying. As soon as he parked the car, she was out and had closed the door.

"Jessie." Frank hugged her when he opened the door. "You've got yourself in the thick of it again I hear."

"It found me and then followed me on vacation." She smiled at him.

"Some vacation, huh?"

"Is Radar in the room?" She pushed past him when he nodded. "Hi, big fella." She petted the dog.

"How are we going to do this?" Frank followed Matt into the room.

"I don't know where to begin. We know she is in the area somewhere but have no clue exactly where."

"I know that Adriana was in the trunk of the guy's car. There must be times when that car has been near the resort because he's gotten into our suite a few times." Jessie looked at the two men.

"Let's start with that. Even if we don't get him, we might be able to find her by following her scent from the resort and the direction the car traveled."

"He can do that?" Matt looked over at Radar.

Frank nodded. "In one of my cases, Radar followed the scent from a coat found in a neighborhood in another area, tracing the same route the perp took. It was over nine miles away. They discovered the body eventually, not far from where we finally stopped the track. Radar re-traced the direction they had traveled."

"That's fascinating."

"I think it is." Frank handed Matt some papers from his briefcase. "This is a list of the cases I've worked and the agencies which you can contact in case the FBI wants my credentials. There is also a list of the convictions made, based on Radar's tracks."

"Impressive. What a way to win over any

doubters."

"It should."

"How about we start at the resort tomorrow?" Matt bent down to pat the dog. "I'll need to take you over to meet the agent in charge, and the Chief of Police to clear it with them; which should be a mere formality. They know you're coming." He waved the papers. "After they get a look at these, they shouldn't have any doubts. Let's say I pick you up at seven-thirty tomorrow so we can start working him no later than nine o'clock. We'll pick you up here later for dinner. I'll call you with the time."

"Sounds good to me." Frank shook Matt's hand. "If she's out there, we'll do our best to find her."

"Oh, she's out there all right." Jessie finally spoke up. "I've seen her." She hugged Frank on her way out the door. "Be sure to tell your wife hi from me."

Chapter 17

It had been a strange day for Jessie. Dinner was okay because everyone was there. Her conversation with Matt was strained and almost non-existent. She decided to sleep in Sadie's room. She needed to be near her grandmother. Her earlier fight with Matt and his concerns were weighing heavy on her mind. A hit man? She didn't even want to go there. Then there was William Mallory, unstable and out to get her. She had read some of her old news archives and had seen his picture. Once she saw him, she remembered the incident. He was scary. She must have buried it deep, trying to forget it.

She could hear Sadie's nice steady breathing. Sound asleep. The earplugs tucked in her ears kept the sounds of the night out, including Jessie's restlessness. What a trouper she was, always so dependable, caring, and selfless. Jessie didn't like to think about the fact that because of her, both Sadie and Katie could be in danger. She would have to do everything she could to keep them safe. Matt would help her. She frowned. She hadn't treated him well, either.

Grams and Gramps had had their share of rough times in the beginning, too. Overall, theirs was an incredible life together. No more pouting. Grams wouldn't let her get away with it, not even for a moment. She wouldn't care if she stood her ground and stood up to Matt, but she wouldn't like the fact that she'd given him the silent treatment. *So what are you going to do about it, Jessie?* She got out of bed, pulled on her robe, and went out into the living room. He wasn't there. She finally found him sitting in a chair in the courtyard.

"Why are you awake?" He watched her walk toward him.

"I wanted to talk to you." She bit her bottom lip, moved a chair closer to him, and sat. He looked tired.

"Before you say anything, let me." He reached over and grabbed her hand. "I've been thinking, and I'm sorry for jumping on you earlier. You had no way to know I was coming back to get you. I was a pain."

"I'm sorry, too. I was pouting and giving you the silent treatment." She bit her lip again. "But, I'm not sorry for calling you out on how you treated me." She smiled at him.

"I need to learn a few things about being in a relationship, I guess." He grinned at her. "The truth is, I've never known a more beautiful woman inside and out. You're kindhearted, Jess, and I hope you'll always stay that way. This business has a way of making one jaded."

"I need to learn a few things, myself." She tried to free her hand as she stood up. She found herself on his lap instead.

"Let me just hold you a minute." He gently pushed her head down on his shoulder. "I don't like it when you're mad at me." His hand stroked up and down her back. "You're my girl, and I'm happiest when I'm with you. I don't like it when we aren't talking." He paused as she lifted her head to watch his face. "I love how you're kind to everybody." He looked into her eyes. "How come you're so sweet?'

"I don't know if I'm that sweet. I got mad enough at you." She chuckled. "From my earliest memories, Sadie drummed into me that life was a gift, and I should be grateful for it. She taught me that love is stronger than hate, so strong that it can stop the hate. I guess I believed it. At least, now and then I try to live it. I'm learning it's not all so black and white, though. Life is tough and even when you try to be nice people might not be nice back. " She traced his brows with her finger. "You look worried. What is it?"

"We're in an awful fix, and we are going to have work together to get through this safely. Jeremy found transferred funds in Mallory's account—in a rather large tidy sum. We also discovered that Mallory has a connection to a couple of the perps from our past. He developed it while in prison. How that influences this situation, I don't know. It adds one more piece to the puzzle."

"How do you think Adriana fits into all of this? Why was she kidnapped?"

"I don't know, but Mallory is a talker. I'm sure he'll let us know. It's a surprise to me that we haven't heard from him since you saw her escape. I think he doesn't know yet that she's gone. So where has he been?" Matt frowned in concentration.

"Good question."

"Dr. Hearst said he could disappear for days when he was in a manic state. I can't imagine what's going to happen when he does find her gone. I think he'll come after you. He'll probably make a mistake in the process because he won't be in control. His anger will get in the way. So you and I, we're going to stick together like glue." He grinned at her. "A nice little twist, don't you think."

"I don't mind. We've done it before." She gazed into his eyes. "But, won't that make us an easy target for a hit man, if there is one?"

"I've thought about that, and we'll have to take our chances but keep our eyes open." He caressed her cheek, then lifted her chin, and kissed her lips. "You need to get some rest. We have another long day ahead of us tomorrow." They walked inside together. As soon as he closed and locked the door, he backed her up against it. With his hands on each side of her head, he kissed her passionately, robbing her of most of her senses. She felt him shudder as he pulled away. Her heart raced, and she wanted him to kiss her again.

His finger stroked her cheek, tracing her lips. "You fascinate me and scare me at the same time."

"How do I scare you?" She exhaled slowly, her eyes meeting his.

"I can't get enough of you and I can't imagine my life without you in it, Jess." He grinned at her as she made a face and gave her a playful push. "Goodnight, sweetheart."

She grinned as she strutted past him her hips swaying saucily. In one quick move, he swung her around. Grabbing the front of her robe, he pulled in close and kissed her one more time. She sighed, and he smiled.

****

Jessie lay awake, tossing and turning. His question kept interrupting her memories of his incredible kiss. *Why hadn't Mallory responded to Adriana's escape?* It was all a mystery to her. Unless, of course, she hadn't seen it at all. Maybe she had wanted Adriana to get free so badly that her mind made it up. It sure had seemed real enough. She relaxed, stretching out on her side, closing her eyes, her arm cradling her head. It was heavenly just to relax for a moment. She was tired.

Jessie's pulse quickened. It was faint, but she could see it just the same. Suddenly the picture in her mind was clear. *It was dark, and Adriana was making her way across a broad open expanse.* Jessie could see the fear in her eyes. *She was looking at something in the distance.* Jessie tried to make it out. *What are you looking at, Adriana? Help me out, please.*

"If I can just get there and take shelter, maybe I can rest. I'm tired. How are you little one? Nighttime is the only time I can travel. I don't want him to see us." Adriana patted her stomach. *"I hope there are no snakes out."* She shivered. *"I hate snakes. I know your daddy won't give up looking for us. We can't give up either. Just a little ways more and then we can rest."* Jessie saw the landscape ahead—maybe rocks of some kind. As fast as the scene had appeared, the vision was gone.

Jessie sat on the edge of the bed and then lay back down. One more time she sat up, sighing. Why fight it? She threw off the covers and headed for the chair in the corner. Why had they abducted Adriana? She sat down, turned on her laptop, and combed over the articles on mental illness, one by one. She found herself feeling a bit sad for Mallory and others who suffered from mental illness. Mallory had his problems to be sure, but so did the doctors treating him. Treatment was often a case of trial and error. His doctor struggled to find the best combination of drugs for him. To be fair, there were some success cases. People who stayed on their meds and whose doctors monitored them closely did the best over time.

So where was he now? He apparently had left Adriana alone long enough for her to wake up and to be able to escape. If what this report said was true, he could be sleeping off an extreme excitable or manic event. How was she to know? If he weren't on his meds, his behavior could be unpredictable. Jessie knew what he was capable of when he was angry. They needed to find Mallory before he hurt someone else, including himself. No wonder Adriana was afraid. Had he beaten her too? She followed her train of thought and continued to search for something. Her excitement began to build. She crept to the door carefully, opening it on a whim. She could hear Matt's even breathing and started to close the door again.

"Are you coming or going?" He sat up and pulled on his T-shirt.

"I was checking to see if you were awake."

"I wasn't, but I am now. Why aren't you asleep?"

"I saw Adriana again." She leaned against the doorframe. "I couldn't sleep so I got up, searched through some old files, and I found something. I should have waited until morning, but I got too excited."

Light filtered into the room as Jeremy opened his door. "Is this a private party or is anyone invited?"

"You may as well come join in. Jessie saw Adriana again and has some new information she was about to tell me."

"Now isn't that a coincidence. I have some information, too." Jeremy walked into the room.

Jessie realized she hadn't slipped on her robe and darted back into the room to put it on. She brought her laptop out with her, placed it on the coffee table, and sat down on the couch between Jeremy and Matt. She pulled up the page she had been on so they could see it on the screen. Matt nodded at her.

"I was watching this unedited video of my interview with Professor Irwin. Do you see Mallory standing there?" Jessie pointed him out. Both men nodded their acknowledgment. "This is after everything was over. Brian, my cameraman, continued to roll the camera." She froze a frame and enlarged it. "You can't see this when the video is running. It was happening too fast. The professor slipped Mallory an envelope. Money maybe? Was the interview staged or the professor being blackmailed? Their argument could have been for show." She stopped the video and went back a few frames letting it play at regular speed. "See, it only looks like they're shaking hands."

"What I found makes a little more sense now." Jeremy looked at her. "Mallory must have had something to hold over Irwin. The college was hush-hush about the stalker. The case remained unsolved according to them. I couldn't find out any information. They terminated Irwin's tenure, which I find strange. It doesn't happen very often. His records were sealed, and they wouldn't say why. A few weeks before his tenure termination, Irwin resigned. This is even stranger. Adriana never filed any charges against anyone. The good prof dropped off the radar after that. The other thing I learned is Irwin spent a good deal of time in Haiti and overseas during his vacations and sabbaticals. I found that interesting. Could Irwin or someone from the bank be the stalker? No one is talking."

Jessie's eyes lit up. "I wonder if that's what she meant when she said that death had found her again. It seems I can remember an article that I read at the time that suggested some unusual things had happened to her and her roommates." Jessie stifled a yawn. "Her stalker must be somewhere in Rocky Pointe."

"Or here," Matt added to the conversation. "If she's here, he would want to be nearby. Nice work both of you. It looks like two or three different cases have somehow found a common link. It gives us a lot more questions to think about and answers to find. Is Irwin still paying Mallory, or is someone else doing it, and why? How does our past case fit into this?" Matt looked at them both. "Let's keep a lid on this for now. We need to think it through before we tell Henderson our theory." Matt yawned. "What did you see this time?"

"She was walking across a vast open expanse. She headed for what appeared to be a safe place to shelter herself and the baby. It looked like maybe a small rock or sand formation of some kind."

"It will be like finding a needle in a haystack. The desert area is vast. I'll ask Balasco if he knows of any rock formations in the area."

"I'm wondering, with Mallory's troubled life, if he could come up with all of this on his own. I could see blackmail, but who else is involved and how do you both fit into it?" Jeremy looked at them both.

"While you're figuring this all out, remember there's a body of at least one other woman somewhere. I'll leave you boys to your collaborations. I'm finally tired. Good night, you two." Jessie caught Matt's wink at her and smiled back at him. She went to her room, yawning all the way.

****

The next morning, Matt and Frank cleared the hurdles with Henderson and Balasco and headed back to the resort. Henderson was following behind with Tony. They wanted to see the dog work. This time Matt had called Jessie and had given her the heads up.

"How do you want to go about this, Frank? You're the handler, and I want you calling the shots. Don't let the others force you into anything that's not right for you and your dog."

"Yeah, I think I got the situation." Frank gave him a wise look. "But I'm pretty particular when it comes to my dog and I know what's best. Believe me, I won't let him push me into anything. I've worked with a few law enforcement agencies over time, and I found a way to work with all of them—which hasn't always been easy." He chuckled, his eyes crinkled at the corners.

"You've got to know there's a lot of male ego in law enforcement." Matt joked with him, smiling.

"There's no doubt about that." Frank grinned back at Matt. "I think we should start the track at Jessie's place. You said he had been there. Radar may pick up one of their scents. It's worth a try. We might at least get the direction he drove when he left the area."

"Sounds good to me. I'm looking forward to seeing Radar in action again. The last case was eye opening. I admit I'm a bit of a skeptic. I want to see if he does it again."

"Even I can't guarantee that he will, but he still surprises me all the time with how good he is."

Chapter 18

Everything hurt. What the hell had happened to him? He tried sitting up and groaned. How long had he been slumped over like this? He looked at himself in the rearview mirror. Jeez, his face looked like it had been through a meat grinder. Dark, sunken eyes, wild, uncombed hair standing on end, and dried blood plastered on his shirt. Was it his? He looked like he had been on a binge. Had he? He raked his hand through his hair. He didn't recognize himself. If only he could remember. Think. What had he done? Long scratches stretched from his forehead to his chin. Scratches covered his hands. Who had scratched him? He frowned in concentration.

Wave after wave of panic pulsated through his body—first from the not knowing, but then they built even higher as the flashbacks played through his mind. The feel of her flesh bruising as he pounded it without mercy, the snapping sound of her bone, and the pleas for him to stop filled his hazy memory. He covered his ears, but it didn't block out her screams. Who was she? Not Jessie, please, not her. "Make them go away. Please, make them go away," he yelled, hitting the dash with his fist.

The windshield had clouded over. Sweat beaded on his forehead and trickled down his chin. A strange rumbling erupted from his stomach as he fumbled for the door handle. With a groan, he staggered a few feet in the darkness, doubled over, and vomited. Gulping for air, he wiped his mouth with the back of his hand and gagged at the vile smell. He walked a few steps in the darkness and then fell against the hood of the car. In the cool dark cover before dawn, he slid to the ground, and collapsed in a smelly heap. The desert was silent with only the sound of the crickets to keep him company. There was no traffic on the road. No one to see him. His body relaxed and his head came to rest against his folded arms.

"When was the last time you took your meds?" The voice in his head thundered at him.

"I can't remember." He rocked back and forth where he sat.

"They'll be mad at you. You know they will. They'll beat you like when you were a kid."

"Stop talking to me. I don't want to hear you. I'll fix everything, they'll never know." His eyes became flat, his body was rigid.

"He already knows, and he's mad as hell, you idiot," the voice taunted him.

"I hate when you call me names. I don't have to listen to you. Do you hear me? I won't listen to you." He stood up and flailed wildly at the air with his hands. "Get away from me...Get away from me." He knew now what he had to do. He lifted the hood of his car, changed his shirt, cleaning up the best that he could, and sat down to wait. He hadn't seen any cars for a while, but the fewer cars, the better. All he needed was one. Be patient Billy-Boy. He smiled.

The sun was climbing in the sky when someone finally stopped. A man in a business suit stepped out of his car. "Looks like you could use some help. What seems to be the problem?"

"The dang thing overheated."

"You're lucky I came along. I don't usually take this route back to town," the man said.

"You wouldn't happen to be carrying some water on you, would you?" He saw the man nod.

"I always carry some, just in case. Cars overheat all the time out here." The man smiled at him.

"I should have prepared better, but I'm new to the area." Mallory shook hands with the man.

The man nodded at him and walked to the back of the car to open the trunk where he kept several bottles. Mallory came up behind the man and hit him, taking him by surprise. He groaned and staggered. Eyeing the lug wrench in the man's trunk Mallory grabbed it and hit him again on the back of the head. The man went limp and fell to the ground. A pool of blood puddled on the sand. Mallory tried not to look. He closed the trunk, got in the car, and left.

It was a beautiful car. Mallory looked around at the interior. One day, he would own something like this and wear one of those fancy suits. Jessie would be sitting right next to him. He had hated to hurt the man. Adriana had been alone too long, and he had to get back to her.

He needed the car. It was the only way. *He had to hurt the man, he had to*, he repeated over and over as the tears fell from his eyes.

Chapter 19

"He's on to something," Frank called back to Matt, as Radar started toward the road in front of the resort. "I'll let him go far enough to make sure of his direction and then we might have to go by car for a few miles. At which point, I'll let him back out and see what he does."

"Okay, Frank, you're in charge." Matt followed behind with Henderson, Balasco, and Jessie.

Frank stopped. "You guys might want to follow behind me in your cars with lights. It might keep it a little safer for the dog as he follows the scent."

"We can do that." Matt nodded.

"I'll walk with Frank." Jessie stood beside him.

"Let's move it out." Henderson started for his car.

"Radar, let's get to work." Frank gave the command and the dog moved forward, head up, sniffing the air for a bit until his nose went down to the ground. He started trotting at a steady pace along the road heading out of town.

Jessie fell into step with Frank and the dog. "Adriana came to me in my dreams last night. She's out there, and Mallory hasn't found her yet."

"Did you see anything that might help—a landscape, or mile marker?"

"Not much." She shook her head. "I only saw her. She was alive but afraid. It was her second night out in the elements. She's pregnant; we can't forget that. All I could see was a small rock formation. I remember thinking it seemed out of place in a desert location. Radar appears to be working it." She pointed at the dog.

"He's doing an excellent job." Frank smiled at her. "He's tugging on my arm. He seems to be in a bit of a hurry." Radar came back to them. "What's up, fella? Do you want me to move a little bit faster?" Radar took the length of the line and pulled harder. A couple of miles out of town, Frank stopped, and Matt pulled up beside him. "Let's put him in the car, go about five miles, let him out, and see what he does."

"Sounds good." Frank, Radar, and Jessie got in the backseat.

At five miles, Frank let Radar out, and after he had scented, he continued in the same direction. "He's still working it." Frank broke into a brisk walk as the dog pulled on the line. The track went on for another three miles. Radar paused suddenly. Up went his nose, and he started pulling harder. "Radio Matt and tell him he's on to something, but I don't know what side of the road we're looking at."

Jessie nodded and made the call. "Look, Frank, over there." She grabbed his arm, "Is that a car on the side of the road? Right there?" Jessie pointed at sunlight bouncing off something, maybe metal, a ways up the road.

"It could be, let's see if he takes us there." The closer they got, the harder the dog pulled. Jessie broke into a run when she saw the car and something lying on the ground. "Matt, there's a car. Oh goodness, hurry! There's a man on the ground. We may need help."

Matt sped up and pulled off the road by the car.

Henderson followed him closely. Matt jumped out of his car and squatted beside Jessie and the man, feeling for a pulse. "We have a pulse, faint, but it's there." He nodded at Balasco, who was already calling for an ambulance. Matt noticed the pool of blood behind the man's head. "Jess, get the bottle of water out of my car. See if you can find something clean to pour it on and make a cold cloth for his head. It's warm out here."

Jessie went to the car and found both. She poured the water over the bandanna she found in the car. She ran back to the abandoned car and handed him the wet cloth and the water. "Will he make it?" She squatted beside them, her eyes on Matt's face.

"I don't know, but if we hadn't gotten here when we did, he surely would have died."

She watched Radar. He kept pacing back and forth, sniffing at the trunk before he finally sat down. "Did you find something, fella?" Frank patted the dog's head. "Good boy, Radar, good boy." He gave him a treat and water.

Henderson looked inside through the car's wide open door. "Wow, what a mess." There's blood on the steering wheel and junk everywhere. Whoever left this, wasn't very smart. He left his keys in the car. Tony, get a crime unit up here to go over the scene. I'll call it in to the Agency to put a rush on the evidence you send them." He pulled on a pair of rubber gloves.

"Henderson, if you've got the keys, could you open the trunk?" Balasco called out to him. "The dog has hit on it. I want to make sure there's no one in there."

Henderson moved to the back of the car and opened the trunk. "We might want to have this towed to the Agency when your guys are done and let our team go over it too. At least one of our victims has obviously been in the trunk of this car. This car is like the one Maria described to us."

"There isn't a body, but we have a woman's shoe which could belong to either one of our victims."

Jessie watched Matt, Balasco, and Henderson at work. Her eyes kept returning to the quiet man lying on the ground willing him with her every thought to live. He was too pale and had lost some blood. The wailing sirens were closing in fast. She sat down beside him, fanning the air around him with Matt's clipboard, trying to keep the flies away from his face. He made a sound, startling her, and she jumped. "Matt he's groaning. Do you think he's coming around?"

Matt squatted down beside him as the man tried to move. "Sir, lie real still. You don't want to make your injuries worse. We're not going to harm you. The ambulance is on its way."

"He, he hit me…" His faint voice trailed off. "Big man…said he needed help, stole my car." He groaned again.

"Don't try to talk, sir."

"Please don't leave me." He grabbed at Matt's hand. "My wife, my kids, the number is in the wallet."

"I'll take care of it for you, sir." Matt pulled the man's wallet from his pocket. He wrote the number on his notepad, along with Rodney Owens' name and address, taken from his license. The ambulance pulled up beside Mallory's car. Matt watched them remove the stretcher. "They're here to help you." Matt stood up and noticed the man trying to reach for his hand. "I'm not leaving, but I'm getting out of their way so they can work at getting you home to your wife and kids."

Jessie was impressed once again. Matt went the extra mile to reassure the man. She watched as the paramedics worked on him. They brought a backboard to keep him immobile, which they slipped carefully underneath him. They lifted him and the board onto the stretcher. They checked and reported his vitals to the doctor. A drip line inserted into his vein began the flow of a drug cocktail that a physician from the trauma unit prescribed to stabilize him enough to transport.

Matt walked beside the stretcher to the ambulance. "I'll be at the hospital to see you in a while." The man blinked at him. "We're going to get the man who did this to you." The man blinked again, and tears slipped out of his eyes. Matt grabbed his hand. "You work hard at getting better and we'll work hard at taking care of this." Matt placed the man's wallet near his hands. He watched them lift the stretcher into the ambulance and close the door. It took off the way it had come.

Jessie watched a weary-looking Matt walk over to Frank and Radar.

"It's a darn shame when someone stops to help what he thinks is a stranded motorist to be attacked and left for dead." Frank refilled the water bowl in front of Radar.

"What do you think we should do? They'll be here to process this before long." Matt patted Radar's head. "Jessie saw Adriana last night. I think we need to keep looking."

"I know. She told me. I would like to let Radar take another sniff of one of her items and see if he does anything. He's had a little time to rest, and he drank plenty of water."

"Let's do it," Matt talked to Balasco and

180

Henderson about continuing the search.

Henderson scowled at them. "You both go with the dog. I'm going to stay here and make sure they don't bungle this crime scene up. You radio me the minute you find something if you do. But, I doubt you will." The agent walked away. "Watch where you step," he snapped at one of the officers getting out of the car that had just arrived. "This is a crime scene and don't forget it."

Tony winked at Matt. "I'll be happy for a little space from that one, but I feel sorrier than you know what for my poor crime unit."

****

"Let's go find her." Matt walked over to Jessie.

"I hope we can before Mallory does." She gathered her hair, pulling it into a ponytail.

"We're ready." Frank attached the line to Radar. He took out one of the shirts Adriana's husband had given them and placed it near Radar's nose. "Find the girl, fella, let's bring her home."

Radar's routine began. His nose went up in the air, and he started sniffing. His tail began to wag, and he took off, moving at a good pace. Jessie continued to walk with Frank, and Matt followed with Tony in the car, lights flashing to warn any traffic.

About thirty minutes into the new track, Radar crossed the two-lane road and headed along a dirt road that wound through a vast open expanse of cactus and sand. Jessie talked with Matt and kept him apprised so that Matt could turn down the same road.

"Is he still working it?" Jessie watched the dog pause and sniff the air.

"He sure seems to be." Frank started walking when

the dog pulled harder on the line. They moved farther off the main road. Radar was getting more excited and pulling harder on the line. Another thirty minutes passed, and then Jessie saw what appeared to be a small formation of rocks in the distance. "Frank, look over to the left. Do you see those rocks in the distance? It might be what I saw last night."

"I see them. We'll find out soon enough if she was ever there. He's pulling hard. I'm going to be sore tonight."

"He's veering to the left." Jessie's voice sounded excited. "Hold him up. Matt's going to have to walk this and so is Tony. The car can't go out there."

The car pulled up beside them, and Matt rolled down the window. "What's up?"

"You're going to have to walk this next part. He's headed out through the sand toward the rocks or whatever that is over there." Frank pointed in the direction. "Jessie saw them in her head last night. I should probably give him some water and take it from there." Frank poured water into the bowl and placed it in front of Radar. He took a few laps but then trotted to the end of the line and began pulling. "He wants to go. I think he's on to something. We need to keep moving."

"Nothing is as close as it appears." Jessie wiped the sweat running down her cheek with her hand.

"You ought to be grateful this is winter and not summer, little lady. We'd all be a puddle by now. No one can survive long out here in the summer heat," Tony mentioned as tried to keep pace with them. "How does he do it? That dog is pulling something fierce. His arms must feel like they're going to fall off at the end of a track. I guess it's all worth it if that dog finds something." He slowed down and started to fall behind as the dog picked up speed.

"Watch, and you'll be amazed how good he is. I know I was the first time." Matt lagged behind with Balasco.

"We're getting closer and he's getting harder to hold back." Frank tried to slow him down.

"Let him have his lead, we'll follow behind and catch up soon enough."

They were surprised when they found Adriana ten minutes later curled up out of the sun in a crevice in the rocks. The dog's excited howl awakened her from a deep sleep.

Jessie could see the fear on her face. "Don't be afraid, Adriana, I'm Jessie. Frank is my friend, and so is his dog Radar. We've been looking for you." When Matt and Chief Balasco caught up to them, she introduced them. "We'll get you to safety."

"Do you think you can walk a little ways?" Frank asked her.

She nodded at him. "How did you find me?"

"This good old boy right here did the work." Jessie patted the dog's head "With a little help from one of your shirts that your husband gave the police." They gave her water and started the trek back to the car. "I'm so glad that we've found you."

Tears filled Adriana's eyes. "I only traveled at night for fear he would find me."

When they reached the car and she was safely inside, Matt handed Adriana his phone. "Would you like to call your husband and let him know you are alive and safe now?"

"Yes, please." She touched the phone's numbers

and began to cry when her husband answered. "Evan, it's me. Honey, I'm safe. They found me. I'm safe. I don't know where I am. Here you can talk to the policeman." She cried and laughed as she handed the phone over.

"Evan, this is Matt. We met in the bookstore in Blue Cove."

"I remember you." He sounded as if he was crying. "How did you find her?"

"It's a long story and I'll let her tell you all about it later. We are several miles outside of Palm Springs. We need to take her to the hospital and have her checked out. I'll make sure she calls again the minute she gets settled."

"Is she okay?"

"A checkup is routine for any victim. She appears to be fine, but we want to have her checked out thoroughly and ask her some questions. You understand?"

"Yes." He drew a gasping breath. "I'll book a flight there right now. How can I ever thank you?"

"Hey, it's our job. See you when you get here. Evan, the phone is on the speaker. Do you want to say anything else to your wife?"

"I love you, sweetheart." His voice broke again. "I'll be there as soon as I can get there."

"Okay, I love you too, Evan."

Matt smiled at Jessie. "I'll let you make the next call. You can tell Agent Henderson that Radar found her, and we are en route to the Palm Springs Hospital." Matt handed her the phone.

"Agent Henderson speaking."

"This is Jessie. Matt is driving. Radar found

Adriana and we are taking her to the Palm Springs hospital now."

Matt grinned when he heard the colorful language coming over the line. "Henderson, you missed a thing of beauty. We'll fill you in as soon as we see you back at the station. Balasco and I will put it all in our report." Matt hit the lights and siren as they passed the crime scene on their way into town.

Chapter 20

He had looked everywhere. He swiped at the sweat dripping down his face. He was in big trouble, and no amount of thinking was going to get him out of this one. She was gone. How'd she get free? He knew he had tucked her in nice and tight. She'd hardly awakened the whole trip. Not even when he'd tied her to the chair. His heart was pounding as he ripped through the trailer, overturning furniture as he went. He kicked a pile of clothes, scattering them. Back outside, he looked in the lean-to, and the small outbuildings a second time, throwing things around. She was gone. Damn, *damn*. He hit the side of the trailer with his fist, staring out over the desert landscape, miles and miles of nothing but sand. He swatted at a fly buzzing around his head.

How long has she been gone? He cleared the clutter from the couch, throwing it onto the floor, and sat down. Jeez, this place stunk. He rested his head in his big hands. The medicine bottle stared at him from the table. When had he taken the last one? He rubbed his temple. He couldn't remember. One, two, or ten days, what difference did it make? Grabbing the bottle, he counted the number of pills inside, but he still didn't remember. He hated them. Each one of these little pills sucked his life away, making him woozy and sleepy. He didn't need them, but everyone said he did. He unscrewed the lid and popped one in his mouth, swigging an open bottle of water from the table in front of him. It was warm and tasted awful.

She was probably dead somewhere out there in the damn desert. He had just killed someone to get back to her, and she wasn't even here. What a mess. His boss would have his hide.

What would he tell him? Think, stupid, think. His phone rang, and he knew who it was without looking. He let it ring a few times and then answered.

"Mallory, what have you been doing? I've been trying to reach you for hours."

"I was in town, doing what you told me to do. And then, my phone's battery died, and I was just able to plug it in." Quick thinking, he smiled.

"Have you been taking your meds? You know how you get if you don't stay on them."

"I just took one right before you called." He had a silver tongue, yes, he did.

"How's my girl? Is she there waiting for me? She'd better be fine, or you're in trouble. I don't want her hurt."

"She's okay, all safe and sound, right here, just like you wanted." He was holding his own; the lies were rolling out like water. He grinned. Maybe these pills did work.

"Now you see, Bill, you don't mind if I call you Bill, do you?"

"Not at all." He sat up taller on the couch. He was ready for the next question. He didn't like the way the boss had just called him Bill.

"I'm having a little problem with what you just told me."

"Oh, yeah? Why is that?" Here it comes. His hand

fisted.

"You see, I just heard the news the cops and some reporter found Adriana in the desert. You know the same reporter that you wanted to have for yourself?"

"You must have heard wrong." A lightning bolt of fear ripped through him. "She's here all right. Maybe it's a trap to get you or keep you from your work." He covered his ears as the cursing began. "I don't know how she got away." The words, bubbled out, treacherous tongue, betraying him. "I had her tied and gave her the pills just like you told me to. I don't know how she got away."

"The guys aren't happy about the publicity. They weren't supposed to know. It was our secret. Remember? You know what that means, don't you?"

"You want the money back." He scratched his head and wiped the sweat running down his cheek onto his sleeve.

"Screw the money. I'm going to kill the reporter. She's what you wanted, right? Well now, she's going to die because of you. That's how it goes when you mess things up. And boy, did you mess it up. You know how it works. I don't like messy situations or unanswered questions."

"I would've had them both in my hands if your stupid magic tricks would've worked."

"They're not tricks. I can refresh your memory if you need me to. I'm in town working on our little project, and now I'm going to have to stop working and check on you. You'd better be there, or you'll be the next one dead after the cop and the girl."

"Don't threaten me. I was smart enough to blackmail you, wasn't I?" His voice rose. "If you ask me, you should be taking the pills, not me. You're sick and twisted. The worst thing I ever did was to get to know you. I know where the bodies are buried, don't forget."

"You won't talk. You're too afraid of what I can do to you. You can complain all you want, but you have money sitting in your bank account because of me. If you want to keep it, don't go anywhere. Stay where you are. You hear me?"

"I heard you." He ended the call.

He looked around the trailer, his mind racing. Billy boy, it's time to think. You can't let them kill her. She's yours. What are you going to do about it?

He stretched out on the couch, folding his hands behind his head. From the first time he'd seen her, with her hair blowing in the wind, with those killer legs, and interviewing that stupid Irwin, he'd fallen hard for her. She wouldn't give a guy like him the time of day. But, he had a plan to make her love him. All he needed was the time to convince her. What was he going to do? He was resourceful and they were about to find out what he was capable of doing.

Chapter 21

Jessie stopped to check in with the young officer sitting outside Adriana's room. "You're fine." He motioned her on. She smiled when she saw Adriana sitting up in bed.

"How are you feeling?" Jessie hid the large gift bag she was carrying behind her back.

"I'm much better now that I've had a shower and got out of those filthy clothes." Adriana blushed. "I must have smelled something awful."

Jessie waved it off. "It couldn't be helped. Here are a few items for you." Jessie handed her the bag and sat in a chair by the bed. "We did a little shopping. Knowing that you had to be in those same clothes throughout this whole ordeal, I wanted you to have something new."

"Thank you. May I open it now?" Adriana smiled as Jessie nodded. She pulled out lacy undergarments, a nightgown, a pair of navy blue pants, and a blue floral twinset. A bottle of her favorite perfume was next, followed by a pair of black ballet flats. "How did you know my size?" She sprayed perfume on the back of her hand. "This perfume is my favorite perfume. Who told you?" She grabbed the shoes and clutched them to her chest. Her eyes sparkled, and her smile showed off the tiny dimple in her chin.

Jessie smiled at her. "Evan helped us. He must

have gotten sick of our calls, but I wanted you to have something to wear before he got here with your clothes." She reached into her purse and handed Adriana a gift-wrapped box. "This is from my friend, Katie."

Adriana opened it and smiled down at the silver necklace with a small turquoise stone and a matching pair of earrings. "Oh, these are lovely." She dabbed at the tears filling her eyes. "I can't tell you what this means to me."

"We loved shopping for you." Jessie searched for her phone in her purse. "Do you mind if I take a picture of you, for Katie and my grandmother?"

"It's all right. You've all been so kind to me." She smiled for the picture.

Jessie snapped a couple of pictures and sat back down. "It must have been scary for you." She crossed her legs. "I can't imagine all the emotions you must have experienced during the whole ordeal. Worry about the baby, wondering if you'd ever see Evan again, I don't think I could have done it."

"I didn't have a choice; I just tried to survive." Adriana pulled the blanket over her legs.

"Did he ever hurt you?" Jessie was afraid to hear her answer.

"A little." Adriana shrugged.

"The first picture I had of you in my mind was in the trunk of his car. He stood looking you over, but you didn't seem to be moving. Did you ride in the trunk?"

"The trunk is where he kept me the whole trip, but to his credit he left water in case I woke up. The upper part of the back seat had been removed so the cool air could get to me." Adriana frowned. "I was aware of what was going on, but I didn't want him to know it. It was strange. At times, he was so nice, and other times he was frightening. I never knew who would show up. As much as I was afraid of him, someone else scared me more. I thought maybe he had something to do with my abduction, I never saw him, but still I know he was there."

"Who?" Jessie watched her.

"Just someone from my past." A strange expression came over Adriana's face.

"Do you mean the stalker you had in college? Did you know who he was?"

"How did you know about the stalker?" Adriana looked surprised.

"I had interviewed one of the professors when it was going on. Another girl went missing around the same time. I searched the records and saw no one was ever arrested."

"He never showed himself, but I always knew when he was there."

"You never saw him?" Jessie saw her shake her head.

"No! Thank God! He's the scariest person I've ever had to deal with in my life. I've never seen him, but I know when he's around." Adriana pulled her covers up to her neck. "He's behind this somehow. I know it. I can't prove it, but all the same, weird things were happening."

Jessie saw the fear on Adriana's face. "Is that what you meant when you told Jayla death had found you again."

"Yes," her voice grew softer. "He is death in a person."

"I hope you don't mind me asking. Can you remember much of what happened to you?" He must be the dark shadow that Jessie kept seeing in her mind, not Mallory.

"The man was always trying to force pills down me." Adriana's expression changed. "There was something off about him, too. He talked to himself all the time. Other times he would lash out, hitting anything in sight, including himself." Adriana shivered. "I pretended to sleep most of the time. I didn't want him to give me too many drugs. They could hurt my baby." Adriana's hands went protectively to her stomach. "All I want to know now is that this ordeal hasn't hurt our baby. The doctor is supposed to be in later to tell me the results of all the tests." She folded the new clothes and placed them neatly beside her.

"Do you want me to put those back in the bag for you, and get them out of the way for now?" Jessie picked up the clothes when Adriana nodded and placed them neatly in the bag, setting it on the telephone stand. "If you like, I'll wait with you until the doctor comes."

"Thank you. I don't want to be alone until I know how everything is." Adriana stared off into the distance.

"I wouldn't want to be either." Jessie fluffed her pillow. "I don't want you to answer anything if it makes you uncomfortable. Tell me to back off if you don't wish to talk about it."

Adriana looked thoughtful. "I need to speak about it. I don't even know how many days he stole from my life. I felt so powerless, and I never want to feel like that again."

"Believe me I know what it feels like to be powerless," Jessie told Adriana about her own time in the trunk of the car and the potent drug they had used on her. "You always wonder what you could have done differently. I still second-guess myself. I have a therapist who has helped a lot, and I've trained to use a gun. I'll never go down again without a fight if I can help it."

"I don't know what more I could have done to fight against him. He was such a big man and his fists." She shivered and hugged herself. "I saw the damage they could do when he hit things."

"If you heard about Maria Gonzales and Rodney Owens, then you know what he's capable of doing. Not challenging him was the smart thing. You're alive because of it."

"Agent Henderson told me about them both earlier. I would like to visit Maria before I leave." Adriana wiped the tears that were running down her cheeks. "I can't remember much about the day he took me. My car stalled. I managed to get off the road. A car came up behind me. I saw the man in my mirror, but there is nothing after he opened the car door."

"Do you know where you were held?" Jessie listened, taking mental notes as she spoke.

"The place was a dump. He tied me to a chair and left me there the entire time. I couldn't even use the restroom. You can imagine the smell." She shook her head. "I don't think I'll ever forget it."

"I'm glad he never hit you." Jessie touched Adriana's hand. "After Maria, I have to admit that I was afraid for you. Especially, if he had found you before we did."

"I feared that more than anything. I believe he would've killed me." Adriana shuddered. "You never know your strength until you face a crisis and have a desire to survive."

"I'm amazed you're doing as well as you are." Jessie patted her hand.

"I'm so relieved that you guys found me. I could still be wandering around out there. How can I ever thank you for everything?" Adriana's eyes lit up as she sniffed her hand where she had sprayed the perfume. "I smell nice again. Not to have the dignity of using the restroom has to be one of the worst things in the world. I think I'll be more grateful for the little things from now on." She tucked the blanket around her legs.

"It was our pleasure to do whatever we could." Jessie dabbed at a tear running down her cheek. "I sent the story of your abduction to my boss and he was going to run it. I asked him to hold it. I want to add to it the story of your escape and rescue. Would you like to read it, too?"

"I would love to. I hope they catch my stalker this time. Every day I'll be grateful if they do. Mallory was scary, but the other man is evil."

"Write your email address on this and I'll send it to you." Jessie handed Adriana a piece of paper and a pen.

They spent the next hour talking, and Jessie was pleased to hear the good news when the doctor gave Adriana a clean bill of health for both her and the baby. Jessie stayed long enough to see Adriana in her new outfit. She watched Evan walk into the room and head straight for his wife. He embraced her passionately, kissing her cheeks, her eyes, and lips.

"My love." He touched her stomach and Adriana beamed. He shuddered and then began kissing her again. Jessie walked out of the room not wanting to disturb the touching scene. She smiled. They were a cute couple.

"Keep an eye on them, you hear." She smiled at the officer sitting in the chair outside her door.

"You've got it." He smiled back at her.

Jessie got into her car. She locked the doors and let the tears flow. This story could have ended so badly, but it hadn't, which made her cry all the harder. Her phone rang, and she searched for it in her purse.

"Hey, sweetheart, where are you? Are you okay? What the hell, you sound like you're crying."

"I'm just leaving the hospital. My waterworks turned on, but I'm okay." She looked in the mirror to see how much damage she'd done to her eye makeup.

"Are you alone?"

"Yes, why?"

"You shouldn't be. No lecture, but you shouldn't be anywhere by yourself right now. I'm near the hospital, and I'm going to have Jeremy drop me there. I don't want you alone. Remember the glue, the new twist, and all."

"I'm sorry I forgot. I wanted to check in on Maria, Adriana, and Rodney."

"I'll be right there."

Jessie quickly ran a brush through her hair and put on some blush. The longer she waited, the more nervous she got, searching out all the places someone could hide. What had seemed like a long time in truth had been only about ten minutes when she looked at her watch again.

Finally, he was there. She watched him get out of the car. Her stomach fluttered. He did look good. The blue shirt set off his killer eyes, and those jeans were a perfect fit. She fanned herself and blushed. He was her eye candy today, and she was happy to have her fill until he opened the car door.

"Jess, I don't want to have to go over the rules again, but you can't go anywhere alone with that guy still out there. Before you bite my head off, don't shake your head. I can see the fire in your eyes. Until we catch this guy, you always travel with someone. Got it?" He pushed his sunglasses firmly onto his nose.

"Yeah, sure, whatever." She handed him the keys and jumped out of the car. He met her halfway around the car. "I wasn't leaving." She looked at him warily. "I was just letting you drive."

He walked beside her until she got in the car and then closed the door. "I wouldn't put it past you to take off." His face showed no emotion, and she couldn't tell if he was teasing or not.

"Have I ever deliberately...never mind, you don't need to answer." She wanted to smack the grin off his face, but she couldn't keep a straight face long enough.

"Let's start over. Hi, sweetheart." He leaned over and gave her kiss. "Did you miss me? Ah, come on honey." He smiled at her. "You know you did."

"That's debatable." She turned away to hide her smile.

"It's your lucky night. You and I are going out to dinner. Tomorrow is the street fair. Frank is tired tonight and is going to order room service. Jeremy has taken pity on me, and he's taking Katie and Sadie out. It's just you and me, kid. I have to go to the station, but I'll be around to get you right at five." He pulled into the parking space in front of their suite. "I'll give you the info to write a good story and you can just be with me, which is more than enough." He held up the keys. "Do you mind if I drive it?"

"Go ahead. I'll be waiting for you." She was still smiling as she walked in the door. What had him so happy? He wanted a date, and she wanted to give him one to remember. She promised.

****

He missed her the minute he pulled out of the resort. Another three hours and she'd be his for the evening. He needed to be with her, to look at her, and to hear her voice. She was his calm in the storm. His excuse was they needed to talk about this case. Frank seemed to think, given the opportunity, Radar might be able to track which direction Mallory had gone with the stolen car. He didn't doubt that dog's ability for a minute. Tomorrow they would try it. He had come up with a great idea to get her away from Palm Springs for a few hours. Balasco and a couple of the officers helped him put it all together. Not even Henderson could dampen his mood.

Matt walked into Balasco's office grinning. "Hey, Tony, how's it going?"

"Not bad. I just checked with the hospital, and they upgraded Rodney's status to stable." Balasco stood and shook Matt's hand. "Thanks for the way you handled that with his wife. You did a damn fine job."

"No problem. I felt sorry for the man. He didn't deserve what happened to him. Hell, he just stopped to help the guy." Matt frowned.

"And we wonder why no one wants to help anymore. I think we have our answer." Tony took a swallow of his coffee. "Now, if I could get Agent Henderson to try a little diplomacy, life around here might be pretty damn good." He sat down again and motioned Matt to do the same.

"Have you heard about any more sightings of the hit man?" Matt tapped restlessly on the arm of the chair.

Balasco shook his head no. "We know this one calls himself the Hunter. He likes to toy with his victims for a while before he kills them. They become his prey, the hunted. Henderson seems to think he's observing for now. He's not your problem, at least not yet. He likes to inform his victims first so he can give them a chance to run. It's all about the thrill of the hunt for him. Here's a copy of the file that we have on some of his past victims, and what we've learned so far.. You may need it in the future. He's hard to pin down. We haven't gotten his real identity yet, but the FBI is working on it."

"He sounds like a sick bastard." Matt stretched out his legs. "Thanks, Tony, I'll read this over."

Tony nodded. "What did you learn in the interview with Adriana earlier?"

"She couldn't give us much information about the location although it sounded like it the place was a real dump. She ran for it. She tried to stay clear of the road where he might have spotted her." Matt pulled out his notepad.

"She was one lucky lady." Balasco took a sip of his coffee.

"I realized talking to her, just how lucky we were to have found her. The dog made all the difference in the time that it took. "I don't think we would've found her in time without him. This story would have had a different ending." Matt sat forward in his chair.

"I'm willing to write Frank and his dog a glowing report." Tony made a note to write one.

"I'm not sure she's safe yet. That's why I'm here, the stalker's obsession with her. She did tell us he came into the bank in Rocky Pointe. She never saw him, but he left her several messages. Notes like the ones someone left Jessie. He holds something over Mallory. I wouldn't put it past him to use it against Mallory, forcing him to attempt to get her back. What do you think should be our next step to protect her?"

"We have to convince Henderson that we should put Adriana and her husband in a safe house for a few days until we're through questioning her. Then she can return home until his trial." Tony glanced out in the hall. "Henderson was pretty pissed off that he wasn't there when we found her. That would have looked good on his record. He'll be ready to pounce on you if I don't miss my guess."

"Not to worry." Matt lifted an eyebrow. "I can live with him not liking me. There's no love loss on my side either."

"What do you think we should do about Adriana?" Tony picked up his pencil and notepad.

"I agree we should put them somewhere safe. I think we should keep the hospital room as if she's still there and hope our guy will bite."

"I don't know if Henderson will go for it." Tony tapped his pencil idly on the notepad. "But it doesn't sound like a bad idea."

"Maybe Tom Maxwell could help convince him. Look, someone wants Adriana. My gut is telling me that this guy promised Mallory he could have Jessie if he handed Adriana over to him. I think Jessie may be the prize for Mallory, and he needs to have Adriana to claim her. So I'm ruling him out in my mind as trying to harm Jessie, but he still might try to kidnap her."

"What about all the notes and stuff?"

"Scare tactics. One of our suspects has a connection to voodoo. One of the things we found out during the interview was that Adriana and her roommate had some bizarre experiences in college. It had started happening again at Rocky Pointe a few months ago."

"Do you think Jessie is in the clear?" Tony frowned.

Matt shook his head. "No, not by any stretch of the imagination. There is someone behind all this who wants both of us gone, and I'm not sure yet who." Matt pulled out his phone and scrolled through the messages. "I'm waiting for word now. Dylan is working some angles for me back in Blue Cove."

"Interesting logic. I need to think about this for a while. I'm willing to stick my neck out with Henderson if you can give me something to go on."

"I should have something for you before I leave here today. The thing is, in the last couple of cases we worked, Jessie's writing and research is what exposed them. She brought it all out in the open where we could pursue it. Either one of the cases, and both of them were big, could have made us a lot of enemies." Matt leaned forward in the chair.

"I remember hearing about both of the cases. You're right about making some enemies. You broke up some big money schemes. People don't like having the money spigot turned off." Balasco sipped his coffee again. "Yuck, it's cold." He grimaced.

"Adriana said they were going to release her today. Henderson won't be back until this evening, so you should call him. We need to slip the Fosters into a safe house and convince the hospital to leave the room unoccupied." Matt's phone alerted him to an incoming message. He read the text.

"Henderson will do what's best for her. He wants this case to end well. That's all the better for him. He's an all right guy. A little on the controlling side, but he does a hell of a job."

"I agree with you. That's why I've put up with all his crap. Let me warm up your coffee." He took Tony's cup and filled it up with the hot brew. Balasco was talking animatedly to Henderson. As Matt walked back into the office, Tony hung up the phone. He handed the hot coffee to him.

"He okayed it. He hardly put up a fuss about leaving guards on the empty hospital room. Of course, it helped that I made it my suggestion and not yours." Tony grinned.

"Whatever it takes to get it done. I'll try to get that information for you before I leave tonight, but you can always reach me by phone. Thanks for your help with my other plan." Matt smiled thinking about the evening he had planned.

"I enjoyed helping you. It's all about the romance, the ladies like it." Tony grinned at him. "Henderson wasn't happy that you weren't going to be here tonight." He chuckled. "I think he's a little taken with your Jessie."

"Hell, who isn't? He gave a lopsided grin.

"Well, it's hopeless for Henderson. I've seen the way she looks at him. Jessie's not impressed."

"She has a mind of her own; that's for sure."

"I've noticed. I'd say she's a nice problem to have."

Matt grinned. "Yes, she is."

Chapter 22

Jessie was excited to see Matt. He had called to say he was on his way and would be on time. He was mysterious, evading all her questions about their evening. Her curiosity had kicked in. She loved a good mystery and found herself fully engaged in trying to figure it out why he was evasive.

Jessie could hear Katie's happy voice in the other room. She was excited about Katie going out with Jeremy, even if Sadie was going along with them. Jessie thought they looked great together. If only Katie could settle down and not scare Jeremy off. When she got nervous, Katie chattered in hyper-drive. Jessie grinned. It would make her so happy if Jeremy and Katie got together. They both meant so much to her. She'd promised Jeremy to stay out of it, but maybe she could give a little nudge here and there to help them along the way. Why not? Katie had done it to her often enough. Jessie knew she didn't have the finesse that Katie did, but she'd like to keep trying her hand at it. Katie was like a bull in a China shop. She did not attempt to hide what she was doing at all. She jumped right in. Jessie looked in the mirror one more time. It would have to do.

Jessie walked out into the living room. "Where are you guys headed?"

"Jeremy didn't say, he just said we were going."

Katie stood up and turned in a circle. "How do you like it?"

"It looks great on you. A new dress?" She smiled. The jade color made Katie's green eyes pop, and the fit showed her figure to perfection. Maybe there was hope for her plan yet. "I think it's perfect for you. When did you get it?"

"I found it earlier when I bought the necklace for Adriana. When you were busy shopping for her clothes." Katie smoothed her dress as she sat back down. "How is she, by the way?"

"Physically, she's been given a clean bill of health, but emotionally it will take a while."

Sadie patted the couch beside her. "Sit down, dear. You look lovely in that dress. I have just the thing to go with it. Wait right here. I'll be back." Sadie went into her room and came out carrying a strand of pearls. "The perfect accessory for the little black dress, I always say." She latched them around Jessie's neck.

"Thanks, Grams." She kissed Sadie's cheek.

"Enjoy yourself tonight. Try to forget about everything for a few minutes if you can."

"If only..." Jessie sighed.

Matt walked in with his suit coat slung over his shoulder. "All this beauty in one room and you're all waiting for the guys. Something is wrong with this picture."

"In my day, it was the other way around. It was always the lady who made the grand entrance and the man had to wait until she was ready." Sadie grinned. "Making them wait was the fun of it. Waiting for your entrance was the build-up; the look on their faces was the payoff. It was all very romantic." Sadie blushed.

Well, I'll be…" Matt chuckled. "I would have never taken you to be a romantic girl, Sadie."

"There're a lot of sides to this old girl, Matt. I guess you're going have to get to know me a little better."

"I think I would like that." He winked at her and kissed her cheek. Do you mind if I take my gorgeous date now and leave you girls to wait? Where is Jeremy, by the way?" Matt looked around the room.

"He's getting ready." Katie giggled. "It's too sad when the guy takes longer than the girl."

"Now, Katie, you know that he only got back a few minutes ago and ran in to change his clothes." Sadie smiled at him. "You two run along and have fun."

****

Once in the car, he turned to her. "You're a knockout as usual. I don't know what I ever did right that fate dropped you into my hands, but I'm sure happy for whatever it was."

"You have such a way with words; a regular smooth talker." She smiled slightly. "You don't look half bad yourself." Jessie slowly exhaled. "Where are we headed?"

"We'll now, ma'am, that's a surprise. I have a few surprises for you tonight. Sit back and enjoy yourself." He winked. "I can be a bit of romantic if I try."

"Is this a new side of you that I haven't seen yet? I mean you have to admit it's a little different than the tough guy cop who likes to lecture me." She grinned at him.

"Time will tell." He drove to the Palm Springs airport.

"What are we doing here?"

"You'll see." He stepped out of the car and walked around to open her door. "I didn't want you to leave the West Coast having never seen the Pacific. I hope you don't mind a short flight to San Diego for dinner."

Jessie's jaw dropped as she shook her head. "When did you have the time to plan all this."

"I have my ways. I wanted to get you away from Palm Springs so you could relax for a few hours without worrying."

"Did Sadie know about this?" She glanced sideways at him.

He grinned. "She sure did. I had to tell her just in case you needed a little convincing." He placed his hand in the small of her back, escorting her to the waiting small jet.

Jessie sat in a seat by the window. She looked at Matt as he sat beside her. "I'm speechless, thank you." She glanced at him again, a bemused look on her face.

"Buckle up, sweetheart, and you're welcome. I chartered the flight with a little help from Tony."

From takeoff to the landing, it took all of forty minutes. Another surprise for the night was the limousine that waited their arrival. It was a luxury plus, and the driver negotiated the area with flair. Matt put his arm around her shoulder and pulled her close. "One of the perks of letting someone else drive." He grinned and bent his head to steal a kiss. A quick turn sent her sliding into him. "We used to call those turns opportunity curves."

"Why is that?" Jessie asked him.

"You did live a sheltered life." He grinned at her. "You're closer to me now and I didn't have to do anything. I can take the opportunity to kiss you." He glanced at her. "I forget you didn't have a brother to torture you or educate you. Boys pretty much think about girls all the time. It's what we do. I think about you all the time."

She blushed. "I thought you wanted to talk about the case." She took a deep breath, gazing into his eyes.

"I'll get to that soon enough. For now, I want to enjoy you and pamper you. Most of our relationship has been about saving one another. Let's just enjoy being together."

Their first stop was a restaurant nestled at the water's edge. They sat at a table by the window with a beautiful view of the San Diego Bay and the downtown skyline. The waiter poured dark, lush Merlot into their glasses, leaving them to enjoy their meal. It was the perfect setting. Jessie enjoyed a salad of field greens, tossed in a ginger orange vinaigrette, topped with mandarin oranges and candied pecans. Matt had the house specialty, Lobster Bisque followed by Prime Rib.

Matt leaned back in his chair resting one arm on the back of her chair. "I've wanted to ask you for a while what it was like to grow up as an only child. Our house was wild with my brothers and me. My mother was a saint to put up with it. We pushed her to the limits almost every day. What one of us didn't think up, the other one did. We had a lot of crazy good times. We fought often and nearly ate my folks out of the house and home—especially in the middle school and high school years when we were playing sports."

"Ours was a quiet house, as you can imagine." She smiled when he nodded. "I used to read a lot. I would have had an older sister, but she died when she was a baby."

"I'm sorry." Matt touched her hand.

"I never knew her of course, and after me, my mom couldn't have any more. I think that's why my dad was so over-protective." She glanced at his handsome, unreadable face. "No, need to feel sorry for me. I had Katie. We were always together. She made me laugh, and we got into trouble together on many occasions. Her house was like yours, filled with laughter, pranks, and constant teasing. Katie's older brother, Liam, tormented her." Jessie giggled. "And I tormented him. I had such a crush on him when he was in high school. He thought I was a pest, and he was right."

"When was the last time you saw him?"

"I think it was when I was in high school. He went away to college. He never came home much after that. I think he's a couple of years older than you."

"I bet he'd kick himself if saw you now," he said under his breath.

"He's supposed to come to visit Katie in the next few weeks. It should be fun to see him again."

"Is he married?"

"No, but I'm sure there's someone special. He always had a gorgeous girl on his arm. Katie is thrilled that Liam is coming. The Donovans lived up to their rowdy Irish heritage. I loved to be at their house growing up." She smiled. "Between them and Sadie, I had a grand childhood."

"You turned out amazing—that's all I know."

"Thank you; I have my good and bad moments, like everyone."

After the meal had been finished and the check paid, Matt held her coat so she could slip it on. "Would you like a tour of the city, Cinderella, before you have to return to reality?"

"Mm…that would be nice." She smiled and leaned briefly against him.

"Your carriage awaits you." He motioned to the entry, where the chauffeur was waiting with the limo door open for them.

Their tour began downtown in the waterfront district of the Embarcadero, winding its way through Point Loma Peninsula. Then the driver took them on a short drive through Old Town San Diego where the city had begun in 1769. The shops, restaurants, and museums all embraced and preserved its rich history. They veered along the coast to La Jolla to the north with its pine-forested oceanfront bluffs. The last stop of the night was Seaport Village. He told her he wanted her at least to see it. Most of the shops closed early, but it was still worth seeing. It looked like she imagined a seaside town would look.

"This has been lovely." She smiled at him. "I think I would love to come back for a real vacation. Maybe see San Francisco, the Wine Country, and of course, the Redwoods."

"My parents brought us out here years ago. Naturally, we did the whole Disneyland and Sea World thing. But, I remember being in awe of the giant redwoods."

"Thank you. I've had a great time."

"The evening isn't over yet. I have one more place I want to take you." They drove to a scenic overlook at Mount Soledad Park where they could view San Diego sprawled out in all directions. They walked hand in hand for a few moments, taking in the lights of the city and the smell of the sea air.

Jessie stopped and faced him. "I've always loved the ocean; that's one of the reasons I moved to Blue Cove. I find a sense of peace, hearing the waves crashing on the shore."

"That's how I feel when I'm with you." He gazed into her eyes. He pulled a small wrapped box at of his coat. "I've always loved the ocean too. I think I'd always have to live near it." His hand holding the box moved toward hers.

Her eyes questioned him as she took the box from his hand when he nodded. "Should I?"

"You can open it."

She carefully started the process. Nestled under the cushioned front was a silver necklace with a starfish pendant. In the center of the starfish was a small diamond. Her eyes lit up. "This is lovely, and an excellent reminder of our special time." She reached up pulling his head down and kissed him. "Thank you," she whispered against his lips.

"I take it you approve." He wrapped his arms around her, holding her tight.

"The necklace is beautiful and the whole evening has been fantastic. I guess I can add a romantic to the list of your qualities." She sighed. "You're full of surprises."

He looked at his watch. "As much as I hate to have this evening end, it's time we get back to the airport."

Chapter 23

The sound on his phone alerted him to a text as they strolled back to the limo. Once inside the car he read it. "It's from Dylan. He wants me to call ASAP. Do you mind if I do it now?"

"Go ahead." She listened to what was a one-sided conversation for the next ten minutes. Dylan was doing most of the talking as Matt scowled.

He cradled the phone between his shoulder and ear, all the while looking at her. "Let me mull this over, Dylan, and I'll call you back tonight. I'll run some of it by Jess while I'm at it. Yeah, she's right here. Dylan says 'Hi,' sweetheart."

"Hi, Dylan."

"Did you hear her? Okay, we'll talk later." He put the phone back in his shirt pocket.

"What's up? You have that look about you." She had watched his face tense as he talked.

"What look is that?" He looked at her quizzically.

"You know—the look that you get when you're ready to get back to business." She scooted close to him and rested her head on his shoulder.

"Dylan found out who wired your store. He also had some interesting talks with Jordon Daniels and Randy Wallis. Where do you want to start?"

"I want to know about the hit man, do I need to be worried or not?"

"Eventually, I think you might, but then again, maybe not." He shrugged.

She lifted her head off his shoulder and frowned at him. "What's that supposed to mean?"

"We haven't seen his calling card yet telling us he's engaged. But, from everything I've read about him, it could be something we have to worry about in the future. He might even be in the area to stalk someone else. Balasco thinks he's only observing right now, and I tend to believe that too. First, there's someone else involved, and he works alone. Nobody can have the credit for his kill but him. I'll let you read some of his files. He calls himself the Hunter." Matt frowned as he said it.

"Isn't that just peachy."

"Let's take him out of the equation for now. We still have to deal with a stalker, Mallory, Daniels—which may not be his real name, and Wallis. I think that's the tip of the iceberg."

"I haven't had any dealings with Mallory since the interview. The stalker is only interested in Adriana, so what does he have to do with us?

"It's a little more complex than that, and we are only beginning to see the pieces coming together." He frowned. "I may be wrong, but I believe Irwin may be the stalker and he was going to give you as a reward to Mallory for kidnapping Adriana. You were Mallory's queen, his perfect bride that he spoke about." He smiled at her. "I tend to agree with him there."

"But he messed it up. What does that mean for me?" She watched his face. He had a stony stare that didn't bode well.

"It's probably not good. Let me be blunt, someone

is going to try to kill you. That's the easy part to figure out, but this is where it gets a little confusing—we have no idea who." He pulled her tight when she shivered.

"Killing me is the easy part! I swear I'm getting tired of being everyone's punching bag. I don't even know those people at the bank. So why am I in the center of it all again?"

"Only one way and that's through our past cases. We haven't found the direct connection, though. We've found some old enemies all around the edges. Mallory spent time with a few of them in the same prison. Joel is the brother to Jason Cummings. The guy who put the equipment into your store was a cousin to Ed Jones our ex-city councilman who's now serving time, and someone not yet identified at the bank is another relative or friend."

"Is that what it means to keep it all in the family?" She tried to smile. "Are you sure Irwin is the stalker."

"No, nothing is firm yet. If it makes you feel any better, Dylan thinks I'm a target too."

"I would rather that neither of us were the targets if I had my druthers. Sometimes I wonder if you would be better off had I not came into your life." She wrapped her arms around herself. "You never had crazy cases like this before."

"Don't even speak of it." He put his arm around her and pulled her against him. "My life was just a job until you came in and added the spark to it. I haven't laughed and enjoyed myself like this in a few years. Those cases were there all along, but we didn't know it. We'll find a way through this together." He hugged her tighter.

Jess fingered her necklace and snuggled closer to

Matt. "I love this by the way, it's perfect."

He brushed his lips across her temple. "Just like you, sweetheart."

Content to let him hold her she rested her head on his shoulder until the limo stopped at the airport, and they had to board their jet for the return flight back to Palm Springs. Once back in Palm Springs, Matt opened the car door for her. He smiled at her. "I guess we should have left the case out of it tonight and just had an evening to ourselves." He started the car and backed out of the parking space.

"It was a lovely evening, great food, a beautiful city, and a nice gift." She smiled at him. "The best part was doing it all with you."

"You know what..." He stopped the car and got out. He opened her door and pulled her gently out. "You always give me that look when I start to drive and have my hands full. Now you're in them, and I'm going to give you my reply." His lips descended on hers, simply and divinely ravishing her mouth. She exhaled slowly, and he smiled. He started to walk away, and she pulled him back around and kissed him again.

"Now that's what I call the perfect ending to a perfect date." Matt caressed her cheek.

****

The rose bush poked his side. He was getting tired of crouching there. They had told him to wait, but he didn't care. The boss had pissed him off, and he had taken matters into his own hands. He had tried to get Adriana back, but she wasn't in the room. The police officer didn't know what had hit him. He felt bad, he didn't like hurting people.

He watched a car pull in and park. It wasn't her. He

needed to see her tonight, but it wasn't wise for him to hang around too long, but he couldn't go back to the trailer either. The boss would be watching for him. The smile on his face broadened. He had changed the game. Call him dumb, huh? He'd show his so-called friend. A different car, a new place, and he would have Jessie without his boss' help. Who was stupid now?

Mallory's whole body began to hum like a tuning fork. She was near. He could feel it. Tension filled him from head to toe, all he wanted was a glimpse of her. Another car pulled in, and he knew she was inside. The cop got out and opened her door. He needed to remember that. She laughed at what he said to her. He put his arm around her, and Mallory's hands fisted. She took his breath away. What was it that he saw? There in her eyes. It was in the look that passed between them when she gazed at the man. It ripped at his heart. Grief filled him. She would never belong to him. He could take her, but she wouldn't belong to him. Her heart belonged to the cop. The darkness of the night shielded him from view. He stumbled to his car. When inside, he drove out of town and stopped at the first turnoff he saw. He might not be able to have her, but neither would anyone else!

Chapter 24

Jessie changed into her nightgown and slipped into bed, listening to Katie's snoring. Yes. Jessie smiled. She was snoring. Jessie could hear Matt moving around out in the living area. He was talking on the phone, probably to Dylan again. It had been a night to remember. She would never have guessed that Matt was such a romantic. Everything had been perfect. The flight, the dinner, and the kissing, it was all magical. He was her prince. She sighed, a smile curving her lips.

In the middle of the night, Jessie awakened to fear licking at her senses. The darkness settled over her like a heavy weight. She sat up in bed, her heart beating frantically. He was near. Breathing became work. She could feel him trying to get inside her thoughts and take them captive; strong, pulling her into his web; choking the life out of her. She fought, singing the song in her mind. When she grew weary, and her eyes closed, the shadows began to dance, and the voices mockingly sang *you will die, you will die.* Jessie got up and sat on the floor. *I will not let you in. I will live, I will live,* she repeatedly whispered until his power was broken and the night gave way to the gray light of dawn. Strange. She should still feel fear, but it wasn't there. Why?

If Irwin was the stalker, then he was in Palm Springs and near enough for her to know it. Matt needed to know. She opened the door.

Matt jumped up. "What is it?"

"It happened again—that strange ritual or curse." She walked over to where Matt was sitting, pulling on his shirt. "I know the stalker is near. It felt different this time."

"How was it different?"

"The last time it was more about fear, but this time was about threatening my life. He's going to try to kill me." She sat down beside him.

"Are you sure?" He pulled her close to him.

"Yes, I know it, but I'm not afraid. I don't know why. It's going to be okay. I know I'll survive this, too."

"I guess we need a plan." He smiled at her.

"I may as well get dressed." She stood up. "I'm wide awake and I need to make a phone call." She walked into the room and sat on the floor not wanting to wake Katie. It was later in the East. Jessie was sure Reba would be up as soon as she touched the numbers on her phone.

"Jessie, finally. I've been waiting for you to call. I was worried. Your vacation is not a vacation at all, is it, dear?"

"No. I need to ask you some questions." She explained to Reba all about what was happening to her. "Your words about me being the gatekeeper came back to me both times and helped through each attack."

"It sounds like someone has gotten involved with the dark occult and is trying to get at you with fear and threats. It's hard, I know, but what you're doing is right. It must be infuriating to him, to find someone stronger than he is."

"Could he be manipulating people this way?"

"Yes, of course. You mean Mallory, I suppose?" Her sigh came through the phone.

"Not just Mallory, there are others. But, mostly Mallory because he is the most vulnerable. It makes me livid to think of someone doing this to another person." Jessie stood and began to pace. "Can you tell me why I believe it's all going to be okay? Am I too casual about the seriousness of the situation?"

"You are at peace, Jessie, because you have handled everything he has thrown at you and beat him at his own game. You're going to be okay. The others involved are in for a bumpy ride. I do have one warning; there is more to this than what you see on the surface. What comes to an end in the next few days will rise again in the future."

"That doesn't sound too inviting."

"All you need to remember is, at this moment, it will be okay. As you know, Jessie dear, that's the only assurance that any of us has."

"I know you're right. There are many unknown variables. I think I should be more worried than I am."

"Worry doesn't do anything. It takes away your ability to respond quickly and accurately. You have no need for it. Keep doing what you're doing."

"I will and thanks."

"You're welcome, dear girl. You'll be back here before you know it, your store will open, and another chapter in your life will begin. What a great novel your life would make, Jessie girl. You're living an adventure."

"You always make sense out of it all, Reba. Why is that?" She pushed her hair out of her face.

"I have faith in something greater than me, even if

I'm a little strange in my approach. I love you, and can't wait to see you at your store's grand opening. Call me, and let me know how it all turns out. I'll be waiting, dear."

"I will. See you soon." Jessie ended the call, feeling better after hearing Reba's take on it. She stepped into her favorite jeans and pulled a comfy tee over her head. She pulled her curls into a ponytail, hoping to calm them a little. Gliding lip-gloss onto her lips, she pinched her cheeks and was ready to plan. Boy, she hoped there was coffee.

****

He couldn't take his eyes off her when she walked in the room. "Did you make your call?" He took his glasses out of his pocket and put them on. "How is it you can look so good in the morning after the night you had?"

"I hope there's coffee." She followed him into the small kitchen area.

He had ordered room service while she was talking on the phone. He filled her cup, and she grabbed a muffin. "So what's the verdict?"

"It's going to be okay, don't ask me how I know, I just know it will all work out." Jessie sat down in the chair across from him.

"Mallory is unstable at best, but in my gut I don't think he'll hurt you." Matt grabbed his pen and scribbled a note on a napkin.

"Probably not intentionally, but he's vulnerable. Someone could manipulate him to try to hurt me. I'm not sure if he's strong enough to fight it."

"Oh hell, that means he can't be ruled out." Matt took a swig of his coffee. His expression was grim. "I

220

forgot to tell you last night that Frank is coming by today, and we're going to take Radar out to where we found Mallory's car. Frank seems to think it's possible for the dog to pick up Mallory's direction from there. Do you want to come along?"

"You bet I do. Radar can do it. He's done it before. What time are we leaving?" Jessie took a bite of her muffin.

"He'll be here at nine. Who knows what we'll run into if we find the place; you know how the safety protocol works." His jaw clenched. "Are you sure you remember your training?"

She rolled her eyes. "Yep, I'll do it by the book with the gun, badge, and everything." She licked her lip to get the muffin crumb she could feel.

He was staring at her as he handed her a napkin. "Is there anything else I need to know?"

"Not that I can think of at the moment. Thanks." She wiped her mouth and stood up.

"Sure." He poured himself another cup of coffee.

She walked around to where he was sitting and leaned forward to kiss his cheek. "Thanks for a great evening. I liked learning a little more about you. Knowing your brothers, I can imagine how your family was. You are something, Matt Parker, so full of surprises." She ruffled his hair. I'll be ready in a few." She walked out of the room.

He watched her until she disappeared into the bedroom. Matt was glad she wasn't worried because he was doing enough for both of them. When he had talked to Dylan last night, he'd found out a few more details. They were getting close to figuring out how their past was catching up with them. Soon they would find out how it tied into the whole mess with Irwin and Mallory. Irwin was involved, no doubt about it. Dylan felt they were getting closer to identifying them. Maxwell was tracking down what he could for him on the Hunter. A hired gun didn't come cheap.

Tony had told him this morning about an attack on the police officer on duty outside of Adriana's empty room last night. It verified what he had thought would happen. One of them had taken the bait, but he had slipped through their fingers. Probably Mallory. He was still roaming around out there. Jessie was right; manipulating Mallory was always a possibility. At least the officer was going to be okay.

"Good morning, Matt." Sadie walked into the room. "You look like you're carrying the weight of the world on your shoulders this morning."

"Morning, Sadie." He glanced up at her. "I'm okay."

"Nope, that's a worried look." She sat down across from him. "No sense in denying it, I know a worried look when I see it."

"Well, maybe just a little." He smiled at her.

"Your job doesn't give you much rest does it? I admire your dedication, but everybody needs a little break. You know what I think?"

"No, what?" He watched her sit down.

"My granddaughter is good for you. At least she makes you think of something else once in a while."

"You've got that right." He picked up the coffee carafe. "Would you like some?" He poured her a cup when she nodded.

"Was Jessie surprised last night?"

"She was. It was a great evening." He smiled at the

memory of her kiss then took an enormous bite of the muffin he had grabbed.

"That's not enough for you to eat. You should have a full meal." Sadie scolded him.

"I'm okay. Did you know that your granddaughter had a visit again last night?"

Sadie frowned. "Good or bad?"

"It was like the night you described to me when you asked me to come out here."

"Oh my, the dear girl. How is she?"

"Remarkably well. To tell you the truth I don't know how she deals with it."

"Ever since she was little, Jessie has taken on tough challenges. She's quiet and sweet, so most folks don't see her tenacity. As the old saying goes, 'still waters run deep.' It's certainly true in her case. Whatever she set her mind to do, growing up, she somehow found a way to do it. Even to stand up to the pressure of her father. The downside to that is she can be stubborn. Watch out when she starts to lift that chin of hers." Sadie laughed. "You're in for a major battle. Still I couldn't be prouder of my granddaughter. Watching her grow into a strong woman has been a source of joy for me."

"She's something, all right." Matt smiled down at her. "She moved to Blue Cove, and straight into my heart."

"I'm glad you've come to appreciate her because you're just the sort of man she needs. You bring out the best in her. Plus you can handle her stubbornness."

"I don't know about that." He grinned and then became serious. "I wish I could do more to protect her and keep all this from happening."

"You would be taking away her chance to breathe, grow, and to soar in life." She sipped her coffee. "It's not like she needs you to solve her problems, but rather to be there to catch her if she falls. Let her fly. You can do your best to protect her and still let her fly."

"Sadie, you're something, you know? How'd you get to be so smart?"

"I've lived a long time." Her eyes twinkled.

"A lot of people live long, and they're never smart."

"They don't live; they survive. There's a difference, and my husband was my greatest supporter."

"I suppose you're right. There are a lot of people just barely holding on out there."

"You're not a survivor, Matt. You grab hold of life and go after it. In that way, you're both a lot alike. You're a brooder; you think about something, you go at it from every angle. She's a planner and does the same thing. You both vie for control; you do it through vocal strength and leadership. She does it quietly but does it nonetheless. I have to admit I've had fun watching the two of you." She grinned at him. "It is endless hours of entertainment for me. I trust you with her heart and with her life, because she does."

"Thanks, Sadie." And he meant it.

"What's on your agenda today?"

"Another dog track. We're looking for the place where Mallory held Adriana."

"Don't forget the street fair tonight. Tell that man with the dog to come to dinner with us tonight. I'll pay for it. What's his name again?"

"Frank Wagner and you can invite him yourself—

he should be here any minute. I want him to meet you."
He smiled and touched Sadie's hand. "Your granddaughter has told him a lot about you. He'll want to meet you, I know." Matt stood up. "I need to get ready, but I'll bring him to meet you when he gets here."

Matt went out to wait for Frank's arrival. Hell, he wished there was no street fair or anything that put Jessie out there. Henderson wanted her to be the bait. They had argued over it, of course, and Henderson had pulled rank. The agent wanted to be the one to talk to her about it, and would this morning. So far, he'd kept his mouth shut. He was on record that it was a bad idea. She'd do it, of course. Matt knew that much. He ran his hand through his hair. At least it would go by the book, and she'd have to wear a vest. Not that it made him worry any less.

Chapter 25

They reached the turnoff where they had found Mallory's car by nine forty-five. Frank got the dog out and was ready to get started.

"If he picks a direction, we can follow for a while and then put him back in the car. We can drive until we see a road where Mallory might have been able to drive his car. By the process of elimination, we might just get lucky."

"Okay, Frank, you're calling the shots." Matt handed Jessie the radio. "Let me know when you all are ready to get back in the car."

"Sure enough." Frank bent down by Radar. "Radar, it's time to get to work. Find the man Radar, let's find him." He held Mallory's shirt for the dog to smell.

"I'm glad we found the shirt in Mallory's car."

"It makes it easier for Radar, that's for sure."

Jessie watched the dog begin his track. "Thank you for taking the time to meet Sadie. I've told her so much about you and your dogs." She kept pace with Frank step for step.

"You're just like her you know." He smiled at Jessie. "She's spunky and game. There's still a twinkle in her eye that makes me wonder if she still doesn't cause a little mischief now and then."

"You can bank on it. She loves to give my dad a run for his money."

"I think Matt, too. She's checking him over pretty thoroughly. He's holding his own so far in this match, but then again, so is she." Frank chuckled.

"Did you know Agent Henderson wants to use me to lure the stalker out into the open?"

"I know. Matt told me." Frank frowned. "And he's not happy about it."

"Matt worries too much about me, and he's not thinking like a cop. We have an excellent chance to get our guy. What none of them understands is that it's all about the mind games with him. I don't have to lure him. He knows I'll be there tonight." She noticed Frank's worried expression. "I'll be wearing a vest, which is good." Jessie touched his arm to reassure him. "If he shoots at me it could be easy for him to hide in the crowd. We might need Radar to walk along with us so he could find him. Remember how you told me he could pick a man up even in a crowd." She adjusted her sunglasses and used her hand to shield them so she could see Frank's face.

"I remember, and he can."

"You have to come along tonight. You can keep him on a leash and walk with us." Her eyes pleaded with him.

"I already told Matt I would be there. If they're going to put you out there, then I'm going to make sure we get the guy if he's in the area."

"Thanks, Frank. I knew I could count on you." She kissed his cheek.

"Radio Matt, and let's ride or this could be a long day."

They rode in the car until they reached the first dirt road and got out, but Radar didn't hit on it. They did that for the next twenty miles. Nothing other than the highway. They came up empty-handed. Twenty-five miles out of town, they came upon another dirt road. "Frank, let's try this last one. If nothing else, it's a good place to turn around." Matt looked back at him in the mirror.

"Sounds good. He's capable of doing it, but this is a big challenge and a lot of ground to cover. At least we know Mallory stayed on this road for some distance." Frank took Radar out. He knelt beside him letting him smell the shirt once more and gave the command. Radar took off down the dirt road. Jessie and Frank followed him as he moved down the road for a couple of miles. Suddenly, Radar veered to the right onto another smaller road. At the end of the small dirt turnoff, it stood, a gleaming silver piece of metal, with the sunlight reflecting off its roof. Out in the middle of nowhere, right where no one would have thought to look, was the trailer that had been Adriana's prison. Jessie had seen it the night that Adriana had escaped. The dog was pulling hard. Matt and Balasco's cars sped past them as soon as Jessie radioed Matt that this was it.

Jessie watched as they secured the perimeter with guns drawn. Henderson waved to them to stop where they were. Henderson was at the front entrance of the trailer, and Matt and Tony were at the back. They disappeared inside on Henderson's command. Before long, they came outside again. Jessie heard Balasco make a call for the crime team.

She walked over to Matt. "Nobody there?"

"Nope, but that is Rodney's car, the one that Mallory hijacked." Matt pointed. "The plates are a match. Frank, what is Radar doing?" Matt noticed the dog digging and pawing at the ground.

"You might need to get someone digging over here. I think we might have some decomp or blood evidence the way he's acting." Frank pointed to the spot, and two officers started digging. As soon as they were digging, Jessie saw Radar go to another spot and do the same thing.

"What about in there? Can I look around?" She pointed at the trailer, glancing at Matt.

"Believe me; you don't want to go in there. The smell alone will kill you." He held his nose. "I've never seen anything like in all my years of police work."

Balasco walked out of one of the outbuildings. "It's better out here than in there. I don't know how that poor girl stood it."

"As she told me, she had no choice." Jessie shook her head.

"Well, Frank, he did it again." Tony walked over to them. "There's a body buried in each spot he hit on. Forensics will work on identifying them. You can add another successful case to your file. This dog is good. I read your file the other night. I'm impressed. We should use these animals sooner rather than later in cases. I was impressed with how many cold cases he helped to solve."

"Thanks, sir." Frank looked shyly proud. "He still amazes me."

"We might've found this place eventually, but it would have taken a lot longer. I'm not sure we'd have found the bodies without probable cause to look, though."

Henderson walked over and shook his hand. "He did a damn fine job. When Matt told me his abilities, I thought he was exaggerating a little. Your dog took care of business, which is no small thing. You can count me in to write you a glowing report about your work here."

"I would appreciate that." Frank patted Radar's head.

"I hear you're going to be there tonight?"

"Jessie asked me to, and so did Matt." Frank glanced at Jessie standing beside him.

"I'm glad. We may need you." Henderson smiled thinly.

"You've got it, and I'm happy to do it for her." Frank looked pleased. He nodded at Matt.

Balasco walked over to where Matt leaned against the car petting Radar's head. "You know, Matt, I feel a little sorry for my crime unit. I wouldn't want to have to go through that mess."

"I was just thinking the same thing. It will be a miserable task. With the sun beating down on it, I imagine it must have felt like being in a tin can."

"If that's how you live when you have the kind of money Mallory has in his account, what's the use of having any?" Balasco wiped the sweat from his forehead. "This sun gets warm when you're standing out in it with no shade."

"You could always go in and turn on the AC." Matt smiled at him.

"I think I'll pass that up. I would rather be hot."

The minute the crime unit arrived, Henderson started barking orders. Jessie couldn't believe the way he talked to Matt. Henderson told Matt to get on his way—to take Balasco back to town, and he would make sure the crime unit didn't mess up.

Once they were in the car, Henderson strode

toward them, motioning Matt to roll down his window.

"Jessie, make sure you're ready tonight." He pinned her with his gaze.

"I will be."

"We'll do our part to keep you safe if don't you do anything stupid."

Stupid? Jessie could see the angry look on Matt's face in the mirror. "I'll do my part," she snapped back.

"Matt, be sure to get her in a vest, and I suppose you'll need one, too." He turned his stony gaze on Frank. "We're doing this by the book. Do you have something for your dog?" He waited for Frank's terse nod. "Okay, you won't know where our guys are, but we'll keep you covered the entire time. Let's hope he tries something tonight."

"I hope he doesn't try anything tonight for Jessie's sake and her grandmother's," Balasco said to him.

"You can leave." Henderson straightened and shoved away from the car.

"Sorry, Jessie, I don't think that guy has an ounce of diplomacy in him." Balasco frowned at Henderson's back as he walked away.

"Don't worry, Tony. I understand the waiting part of any case is the hard part."

"He could use some work in the area of people skills. He's shown poor judgment in that area since I've been here. I wonder if he missed that class when they were teaching it at the Academy," Frank muttered.

Tony and Frank got into a conversation about the dog, and Jessie's attention wandered. She kept looking at Matt in the mirror. He still had a grim set to his lips. She couldn't tell what he was thinking, but she wouldn't want to be on the receiving end of that look.

"Hey, Tony, I've put up with some dumb crap to work with that guy. I'm warning you, don't leave me alone in a room with him for long, or he might be picking himself up off the floor. There's no reason a seasoned officer or agent should talk to his peers the way he just did. When this case is over, I'm going to file a formal complaint." Matt's lips tightened.

"I can't say that I blame you, I might have to do the same." Tony winked at Jessie.

"I wouldn't mind adding my two cents worth," Frank chimed in.

Well, I'm glad that's settled." His tense face visibly relaxed. "Jess, you don't have to do this tonight if you don't want to. I want to make that clear. You aren't a cop; you're a civilian."

"I'll do it." There was no way she'd look at his expression in the mirror. She kept her eyes on the arid landscape sliding past the car. Jessie knew it would take him a little while to adjust to the idea. He was only looking out for her. She wouldn't put it past him to trip Henderson tonight on the sly, he was that mad.

The ride back to town was quiet and gave her time to think.

Chapter 26

Where was his boss? Mallory knew he was in town. So far, he had avoided running into him. It was a good thing this old car ran or he would have been at the trailer when his boss got there. The cops were looking for the stolen one. Still he could feel the weasel breathing down his neck. He took a swig of water. His eyes darted to the parking lot entrance as a car drove in. He frowned and ducked low. He strained to hear any sound, his hand on his gun under the seat. The car pulled into a parking spot a few spaces down from him. Doors opened and shut with a slam.

"Be careful! Don't shut your brother's fingers in the door," a woman yelled. He sneaked a quick look. It was a woman with two young boys.

"Mom, he hit me." The smaller of the boys pulled on his mother's shirt and started screaming.

"Toby, leave your brother alone." She sounded exasperated. The hitting and screaming continued.

"If you two don't stop it now, I'm going to lock you both in the car," she yelled at them.

Mallory covered his ears. Damn kids, they were all too noisy. He pushed the gun back under his seat as the mother grabbed one by the shirt collar and thumped the other on the back of the head.

He groaned and crouched out of sight. Once again, it was his mother's hand reaching out to grab him. She slapped the back of his head, as she pushed him toward the dark, dank closet. His body twitched with the memory of the sound of the turning lock and the slide of the bolt from the outside. How long would it be this time? He never knew. Some days he would get food, and sometimes they forgot him altogether. The darkness surrounded him; the loneliness was his companion, and the smells turned his stomach. His breathing became rapid, his face flushed, and anger coursed through him, bringing with it awful memories. Hell, he hated this feeling. He never knew what would set it off, but his mother's screaming was always there, at the edge of his mind. Her belittling words were there, even though she was long dead. He would never be free of her. Never! His hand clenched.

It took many years, and several foster homes, but he finally was able to take care of business. He smiled slowly and ran his tongue across his lip. Oh, he had hurt them. They had treated him like some damn animal, not their son. In the end, they had begged and pleaded. He had simply done to them what they had done to him. An eye for an eye! He had given them the same, all right. He smiled. The last thing they saw was his angry face as he locked them away. The last thing he saw was the fear on *her* face.

Tonight he would follow Jessie because Irwin would. Only the Game Changer could determine her fate. He had to get to her first and hide her.

Chapter 27

Matt dropped Jessie off at the resort. She had called Sadie earlier to let her know she was on her way back. It was warm enough that a dip in the pool sounded like the perfect way to spend the afternoon. All she needed was her suit, and she'd join them.

"Hey, Jessie, can I talk to you?" Jeremy called out to her as she walked in the door.

"Sure, what's up?" She poked her head into his room.

"The article you did on Adriana was great and is ready to send off. It's this one on Mallory that's got me thinking." He looked over his glasses at her. "If this is true, it explains a lot. How did you get all this information?"

"It's true all right. I found a lot of it in the transcripts from his trial. Some came from the public record including the unsealed records from his childhood. I also talked to Dr. Hearst, who gave me some of the hypotheticals I used." She leaned back against the doorframe.

"It almost makes me feel sorry for the guy. The whole angle of the abused becoming the abuser takes on new meaning."

"I know, to me too." She folded her arms and frowned. "His parents should be put in prison for life for what they did to their son. The strange thing is no one has seen them for years. Mallory said they had died in a car accident, but there's no record of it. It is as if they disappeared from the planet. Dr. Hearst believes it's possible that Mallory killed them."

"It got me thinking." Jeremy rubbed his eyes. "How many other kids have been so horribly abused by their parents? It's hard to stand idly by while this could be happening to other children. I could become an activist against child abuse. This made me sick." Jeremy looked thoughtful. "I had great parents. I can't imagine what a kid must go through when the people they depend on for survival and love are the ones who hurt them."

"I hear you." She leaned against the doorframe.

"You need to publish this at some point. It's a good place to begin." He pushed his glasses up on his nose. "It makes you wonder how many criminals were abused as kids."

"It has a way of changing how you feel about them, doesn't it? I know that Mallory has done a lot wrong. Nothing can change that." She shook her head. "I can't imagine you can have a proper sense of what justice is when year after year, you went through torture."

Jeremy nodded. "Did you ever find out who turned his parents in?"

"It was his grandparents. They noticed at his birthday how thin he had become and the bruises under his clothes. They wanted to take him but decided not to because their daughter would find a way to have access to him. They never wanted her to be able to get near him again." Her face softened. "The sad thing is that Mallory never knew his grandparents had tried to help him. It would have been nice for him to have known that someone loved him."

"That's sad. Look what it did to him." Jeremy walked toward her. "Not to change the subject, but are you okay about tonight?"

"Yeah." She relaxed her stance. "I'm a little nervous, of course. I hope they catch him so that he can't hurt anyone else. Maybe he'll get the help that he so desperately needs." She gave Jeremy a dubious look.

"I'm beginning to think, like Matt, the professor has something to do with this. A large sum of money was deposited in Irwin's account. You both need to be careful and on the lookout for him tonight. I already told Matt, but I wanted you to be aware." He touched her shoulder. "We'll all be looking out after you, but be careful out there."

"Thanks, Jeremy. I'll try. But for now I'm going to chill out at the pool with Katie and Grams." She walked away and then turned back. "You can join us if you like."

"You know, that sounds good." He grinned. "I'll meet you at the pool."

While Katie and Jeremy played a game of volleyball in the pool, Jessie lounged back in the chair next to Sadie, her sunglasses shielding her eyes and an umbrella shading both of them. "Where's Matt?" Sadie stretched luxuriously.

"Probably still at the station filling out reports." Jessie took a sip of the iced tea the waiter had just brought her. "The man is virtually buried under a mound of paperwork. I think Agent Henderson is doing it on purpose. I heard how he goaded Matt, and I don't know how Matt has put up with it. Matt did all this so he could be here to work on this case with me." Jessie looked over at Sadie. "He's a gem, you know?"

"I know. Your Matt is a hard worker. It seems his job takes up most of his life." Sadie fanned herself. "Oh, that little breeze feels nice."

"It does indeed. Speaking of the hard-working man, here he comes now."

Matt came through the gate and walked toward them. He bent down to kiss Sadie's cheek and winked at Jessie. "How are my two favorite girls?" He sat down beside Jessie, grabbed her hand, and laced his fingers through hers.

"Were you ears burning?" Sadie winked at him. "We were just talking about you."

"Is that right?" He grinned at her. "Do I need to be worried?" He looked at Jessie as he asked it.

She shook her head. "We were talking about how hard you work, weren't we, Grams?"

"Among other things." Sadie stood. "I think I'm going to take a dip and cool off."

"What did she mean? What other things?" Matt's eyebrows rose.

"Nothing. She's baiting you. That's my grandmother being a stinker. Did you notice how she put that little idea out there and then left me to deal with it? She's good." Jessie chuckled.

"I'm on edge. I don't want you to do this tonight. I've spent the last hour arguing with Henderson over it." His eyes hardened. "I've about had it with that guy."

"You don't have to put up with him too much longer. We head back on Sunday morning."

"I wish it was that simple. Until this case is solved, I'll be traveling back and forth for a while. You'll have to come back out yourself for trials if we catch them here, unless we can have them extradited."

"I forgot all about that part of it." She sighed. "I hope it's not until after my store's grand opening."

"The law gives them the right to a speedy trial, but it won't be that fast." He smiled at her. "As long as we can get you home without anything going wrong, it should be okay for a while."

"That's nice to know."

"Look, Jess, I want to talk to you about tonight." His smile vanished.

"I figured you might. You have that look about you."

"What look is that?" He glanced over at her.

"You know the look that says it's time to get down to business, just when I'm trying to chill out." She gave him a crooked smile.

"You mean the look that means I want to talk about keeping you alive?" he said bluntly.

"Yeah, that's the look. The one that usually has some lecture attached to it." She turned her head so he wouldn't see her smile.

"What's this really about, Jess?" He sat up with a frown, and then saw her smile. "I think there's a lot more of Sadie in you than meets the eye." He gave her a lopsided grin.

She laughed as she saw his smile. "Sorry, but you need a break from your job even if it's only for a moment. Consider me here to help you out." She sipped her tea. "I know we need to talk, and that you're worried, which is sweet by the way. I'll listen to all your instructions, and I'll do what you tell me to do. But every now and then, you need to lighten up, if only for a moment."

"You're something." He stroked the palm of her hand with his thumb.

"I know. I'm good for you." She felt the familiar flutter in her stomach. "So what do you want to tell me?" She exhaled slowly, a whoosh of air, trying to steady her pulse, and pulled her hand from his.

He grabbed it right back, and a tug of war ensued. She let him win. "I have the vest you're wearing tonight in the car. It should be cool enough when the sun sets for a light jacket if you have one. The vest won't be so obvious that way."

"Okay, I can do that."

"Frank will be walking with us, and so will Radar. I was talking to Tony. The fair attracts large crowds. It could be a nightmare trying to keep track of what is going on around us. There is a risk, and I want you to be aware of that. You can say no, and I can keep you home if you want. No plan is foolproof."

"I know," she said quietly. "But, if not now, when? At least I'm aware now in this situation. What happens if I go home and let down my guard? They'll probably follow, won't they? What then? Maybe it will be when you're out of town." She lifted her sunglasses and gazed into his eyes. "I would rather it be here, with you by my side. The odds are a little more in my favor. Who knows, maybe they won't even come out to play with all those people around."

"Oh, they'll be there all right." Matt ran his hand through his hair.

"You sound pretty sure."

"I am. Here's the plan." He adjusted his sunglasses. "At some point Jeremy is going to take Katie and Sadie off to look at something. Frank will move away just a little leaving us to walk alone."

"Thank you for thinking of Katie and Sadie. I don't want them caught in the crossfire."

"We'll do everything possible to keep them safe. I will tell them why it's important that they go with Jeremy. I think they should know about what we believe might happen so they can choose to stay here if they want."

"I agree that they have to be given a choice."

"Mallory will be there. I'm not sure what he'll do. You keep a watch out for him and Irwin in case he shows up. You've seen them both before."

"I can do that. Will you be wearing a vest, too?" She drew a slow breath.

"Yes." He tightened his hold on her hand.

"I'm good with that." She released the breath she had been holding.

"As soon as we've finished here, I'll talk to Katie and Sadie."

"I appreciate you telling her. Sadie likes you. She'll weigh everything you say. If she decides to go, it will be because she wants to. I thought you should know."

He let his free hand follow the line from her cheek to her jaw. "Do you have any idea what you mean to me?"

"I think I'm beginning to." She caught her breath.

"I want you to know it. I love having you in my life, and I'll do everything I can to keep you there."

****

Her nerves were starting to kick in. She'd looked at the clock several times in the past ten minutes. *Get a hold of yourself.* She took a pair of slacks out of the closet and pulled them on. She buttoned her shirt in all wrong places and had to start again. *This will simply not do, Jessica Lynn.* She slid her feet into a pair of shoes but had to change them when she realized that they were from two different pairs. It was all because of the item she had to put on next. The vest. She held it up to look at it. Matt wanted her to wear it. He had wanted her to wear the vest during their first case, too. He was right then. It had saved her life. So why did she dread putting on the vest?

Maybe because it made it all real. Anything could happen. Matt had made it clear—you can do everything right, and still it's a risk. There is always the unknown factor, the one variable you didn't plan for that can happen.

"Jess, are you about ready? I want to make sure the vest fits you right." Matt knocked on the door.

"Give me a second." She ran the brush through her hair and put on her lip-gloss. "Okay, you can come in now."

"Are you all right?" He looked at her.

She nodded. "Just thinking," she answered softly.

"About what?" He reached for her hand.

"This." She held up the vest. "And the last time I wore it."

"I thought maybe it was something like that. Why don't you stand up and let's make sure it fits right."

She shook her head no. "I know when I put this on it will be real, and I don't want it to be."

"Do you want to back out?" He raked his hand through his hair.

She shot him an irritated scowl. "No, I just don't

want it to be real, that's all."

"Jess, that doesn't make sense. It *is* real, and you can do it, or not. You're not logical."

"Who says I have to be logical." She stood with her hands on her slim hips. "I wish the whole thing that makes this necessary didn't exist, that's all."

He stood and wrapped his arms around her. "You're just having a case of nerves."

"Of course, I am. The last time, this vest may have saved my life, but the bullet still bloody well hurt."

She looked at him in time to see the corners of his mouth twitch. "I suppose you think that's funny."

"Nope, not me, but I think that's the strongest language I've ever heard you use. I bloody well think it probably did hurt." His chuckle morphed into laughter.

With his laughter, her tension eased. She picked up the vest and put it on. "Am I good to go?"

"You're good to go." He smiled at her.

Chapter 28

"I sent Jeremy on with Katie and Sadie. We'll meet up. We need to go pick up Frank and Radar." He had noticed her expression as she looked around the room. "Plus I wanted Jeremy to have a car to get them out of there if something comes down."

"It makes perfect sense to me." She put on her lightweight jacket over the vest and buttoned a few buttons. "Do I look like I can bench press a Buick?"

"You're something…most girls would be totally freaked out now…I'm not sure how to answer your question?" He winked. "Other than to say you'll be safer."

"It's this darn vanity of mine. I don't want to look like I've gained weight." She tossed her head. "I would rather look like I lifted weights a little too long. You look like you've been working out. I just appear, you know, lumpy."

Matt chuckled. "Sometimes I'm a blockhead. Sweetheart, even with a vest under your jacket, no one will think you're fat. I sure as hell don't."

"Since you're the one that will have to walk with me, I can live with that." She walked in front of him and out the door to the car.

****

Matt swung by to get Frank and Radar. Once on the main street, he pulled into a parking space just as

244

someone was pulling out, near the café where they had arranged to meet Jeremy and the others for dinner. He had a feeling it was going to get crowded—the streets were already beginning to fill up with people. While they waited for their order, Matt watched the interaction between Jessie, her grandmother, and Katie. They were fun to watch. Jessie was a little more relaxed. He smiled. Sadie was telling a story about her and Jessie was laughing. Her eyes were lit up. Damn, she was pretty. He draped his arm possessively over the back of her chair.

"Do you think they'll show up tonight with all these people around?" Frank asked.

Matt noticed Radar curled up at Frank's feet. "No doubt in my mind. I think they'll be here. Whether they're stupid enough to try anything, I don't know. I've found no matter how smart they are, a perp will risk it all by doing something dumb. Our stalker doesn't think straight when it comes to Adriana. She's his weakness, and Jessie is Mallory's Achilles' heel. I'm counting on them taking a risk and messing up, so we can catch them." Matt's fingers played with Jessie's hair, where it hung over his arm.

"We had better prepare for any possibility. I was hoping it would be an enjoyable evening for her. She looks relaxed right now. It's hard to believe she has had to face what she has. Between the dreams, and people after her, she's stronger than I ever gave her credit for." Frank leaned in a little closer to Matt. "Is she handling it okay?"

"For the most part, I think earlier the reality hit her when she put on the vest. The last time she wore one she was shot, and it was a rather painful experience."

Matt chuckled. "She told me, it bloody well hurt."

Frank smiled. "I think that's akin to cursing for Jessie."

"I think you're right. I admit I laughed." He grinned at Frank. "Seriously, though, we need to keep our eyes open out there tonight. Who knows where it could come from, or if it will even come at all?"

"I'm hoping it won't come at all." Frank gave Radar a treat from his pocket.

Her hair felt like silk running through his fingers. She looked at him. "I'm sorry. Did I pull it?'

"No, what are you doing?" She changed her position slightly.

"I like touching it."

"That's sweet, but don't get sentimental on me right now. I'm this close to falling apart." She snapped her fingers.

"You don't look it. What can I do, sweetheart?" He looked into her troubled eyes and swore under his breath.

"Make sure you keep them safe." She looked at Sadie and Katie.

He understood. She was more worried about them than herself. "You're something."

"You keep saying that," she teased. "I would like to know what this *something* is that you're talking about."

"All I know is it makes me want to be a better man."

"If you must know, I kind of like you just the way you are." She leaned in closer to him. "No need for you to change. You're my big, strong, hunky cop." She bit her lip.

"Jess, play fair, I don't want to shock your grandmother." Matt heard Frank laughing in the background.

She jabbed her finger into Matt's chest. "Feeling a little bothered, are we?"

He grabbed her hand and put it in his lap, pinning it there. "If you're not careful, I'll tell you what I'm feeling." He grinned as she blushed. "You're playing with fire. I don't embarrass easily. I wouldn't try me, if I were you."

"I'll behave." She turned her back to him and answered Sadie's question.

"Chicken." He liked this playful side to her. Matt looked at Frank, who was still chuckling. "I think she's nervous."

Frank grinned. "I've never seen her this way. Thanks, I've enjoyed watching the sparks flying between the two of you. I would say she's more than halfway to being in love with you."

"I wouldn't mind." He turned on his earpiece. Henderson wanted to follow their progress and bark out his orders most likely. Tony's was the first voice he heard.

Finally, you turned it on. I have men in place along the route.

"We're about ready to get going." He gave the server his card.

Good luck out there. Stay safe.

"Thanks, Tony. Keep your eyes open." He signed the receipt.

Matt leaned over and whispered in Jessie's ear. "It's show time." He looked around the table. "Everyone knows what they're supposed to do."

"We understand. We've prepared for the worse but hoping for the best." Sadie spoke up while the others nodded.

"My sentiments, exactly." Matt smiled at her and stood. "We'll go to the first few booths together. After a while, Jeremy, you take them on to another area." He pointed at Sadie and Katie. "Frank will remain close by in the area, never out of sight. The others are already in place." Matt's jaw tightened. "If everyone is ready, let's go."

The city closed several streets of the downtown area for the fair known to the locals as the Villagefest. Booths filled with artwork, unique food items, and handcrafted items were all along both sides of the streets. The ad said it drew thousands of people and Matt believed it. The streets were full, and more than once someone in the crowd bumped into him. He didn't like it. Matt maneuvered Jessie around an Army private with his petite, redheaded girlfriend on his arm that had stopped suddenly in front of them to look at some rings. He smiled at the besotted look on the private's face. He knew the feeling. Matt halted when Jessie paused to look as silk scarves. They attracted Katie and Jessie both. What was it with women? They could shop anytime. He shook his head. His eyes scanned the crowd looking for anything that seemed out of place. So many things could go wrong. How could they ever see Irwin or Mallory in the sea of faces? "Tony, can you hear me?" Matt turned his head when someone bumped his side.

I hear you, Matt.

He grabbed Jessie, pulling her closer. "Have you seen anything?" A middle-aged couple strolled past him carrying several bags. They eyed his holstered gun warily until he pointed to his badge. They smiled and continued.

No, but there's a lot of people to watch.

"I'm not sure we could pick them out until they're standing right in front of us. I don't like the vibe I'm getting." Matt's eyes tracked the area in front of them as they walked. He jerked when a young boy ran past him, hitting his arm. The boy's ice cream cone fell to the ground with a splat. He watched Jessie give the boy some money to go buy another one.

Henderson's voice came across the line. *We are doing it as planned. Do you hear me?*

"I hear you, all right. You're not the one putting your life on the line. If I feel I need to abort the assignment, we will abort."

I'll back you on that, Tony added.

Matt motioned to Jeremy, who headed off in another direction with Katie and Sadie. Frank paused to look at something and lagged behind them a little but kept them in sight the entire time. Frank had an earpiece so Matt could call to him as needed.

Matt grabbed Jessie's hand. "It's just you and me, kid."

"So I noticed." She stopped to look at some artwork. "I wish I could enjoy looking at this for real. There's some beautiful stuff here. Look." she pointed at a sculptured piece. "That would look great in your house." She took the man's business card. "I think you should buy it. It's only sixty-five thousand dollars." Her eyes widened. "Only…"

"Sounds like a good bargain. I'll take two." He chuckled, pulling her along.

An hour later, Matt looked at a text on his phone. "Jeremy is taking Katie and Sadie home. Your grandmother's getting tired."

"Good, I'm glad. I want them away from here." Jessie glanced at him.

"We'll give it another thirty minutes or so and then call it a night ourselves. The fair is starting to wind down. Vendors are packing."

They strolled on and the crowd began to thin out considerably. Jessie yawned. "I'm getting a little tired." She shut her eyes and rubbed her temples.

He noticed a strange look cross her face. "Is everything okay?"

"Let's turn around and start walking back," she spoke softly to him. "He's close by. I can feel him. I can hear him in my head. There's something else, but I'm not sure what."

"Did you hear that, Frank? We're going to start heading back, so stop and fall in behind us. She feels he's in the area."

Okay, Matt. Frank paused to look at the wooden carvings on the table until Matt and Jessie passed his position.

"Tony, did you copy that."

I heard. We're watching.

Matt steered her back the way they had come. He felt the tension radiating from her.

"He's getting closer, but I have no idea where to look." She picked up her pace.

"Are you copying this, Henderson? She can feel him closing in. You guys keep your damn eyes open."

I hear you, Matt, Tony responded. *Henderson is the closest to your location, but he's not responding.*

I'll keep trying to reach him.

"Thanks, everyone, look alive out there." Matt took her arm and picked up the pace.

"Matt, one of my guys found Henderson. He's out cold. I'm closing in on the site, but still a little ways out from you."

Matt swore under his breath. "It'll be okay, sweetheart, we're all looking." Matt's eyes scanned back and forth across the crowd.

****

Mallory kept his eyes on Irwin as he skulked along the edges of the crowd following Jessie with his beady eyes. He had seen Irwin hit the dumb mule. Out cold, Henderson never saw it coming. Mallory didn't mind if there was one less of them. No cop was a friend. They'd never been there to protect him. What were they thinking? Irwin wasn't an ordinary person. All of them were too far away to get to her in time. Irwin could outmaneuver them any day. Mallory moved quicker to keep pace with Irwin. The game was on.

Irwin was bearing down on Jessie, weaving through the crowd toward her. Suddenly he stopped. Mallory planted himself across from Irwin on the other side of the street, a few steps away from Jessie, but near enough to grab her if he needed to. Jessie knew Irwin was coming. Mallory could see it her eyes.

Standing behind a tall man where the cop couldn't see him, Irwin opened his jacket slightly. The game was on. No more time to think! Mallory was about to change the game on them all.

Chapter 29

Jessie turned to look at Matt. "They won't get here in time. It's too late for them to help." Her voice sounded resigned.

In a blink of an eye, a huge form rushed past Matt, shoving him aside like a rag doll, sending him crashing to the ground. The man jumped in front of Jessie at the precise moment the gun fired. The bullet's impact propelled him backward taking Jessie with him to the ground with a sickening thud. The smell of sulfur and blood filled the air, mingled with the sound of the chaos that ensued. People screamed, scattering in all directions. Matt rose up on his elbow so he could see her. She lay quiet and motionless on the ground. His breath caught in his chest. Time played out for him in slow motion. Mallory lay splayed on top of her, his face contorted with pain.

"Jessie," He shouted her name, scrambled to his feet, and lunged toward her. Frank had already squatted beside her.

"Matt, she's okay." His broad face was bright with relief. "She got the wind knocked out of her. Help me get her out from under him."

Matt felt for a pulse on Mallory and found a weak one. They got Jessie out from under him, and she sat up to catch her breath. "Tony, can you hear me?" he snapped into the wire. "Did you see what happened?

We're you able to get the guy?"

Not yet, we're sealing up the perimeter, but in the confusion, I don't know if we were fast enough.

"Get an ambulance here."

It's on its way.

"Tony, don't let Irwin slip away."

"We're trying, Matt. If he's here, we'll get him."

"I'll get Radar out there looking." Frank brought Radar over and put the line on the dog. "It was the damnedest thing I ever saw." He shook his head. "The guy flew out of the crowd, jumped in front of her, and took the bullet himself. He saved her life." He drew a ragged breath. "I thought you should know. I saw the whole thing."

"Thanks, Frank." Matt could see Jessie out of the corner of his eye, rubbing the back of her head. She moved over to Mallory and knelt beside him, lifting his head into her lap.

He got busy on the radio, listening to the reports coming in, but he never took his eyes off her pale face. He could see her talking to Mallory. Matt could tell from the wound, he probably wasn't going to make it, even if the ambulance got here fast. He decided that moment to give Jessie her space.

****

"Thank you, William, for saving my life." She saw his eyes flutter open. "Why, why did you do it?" She pressed a towel Frank handed her over the wound in his chest, trying to apply pressure.

He grimaced. "I couldn't let him kill you..." He struggled to breathe. "You were my..." His voice trailed off, and his breathing became labored.

"Shh, don't talk, save your energy. Help is on the

way. That was a kind thing to do." She swallowed and went on, raising her voice slightly, to be sure he heard her. "Did you know your grandparents were the ones who saved you? Who got the state to take you away from your mother? They loved you."

His eyes fluttered, opened. "I never knew."

"They never wanted your mother to find you again, or they would have raised you themselves. They tried to find you before they died." She gulped trying to hold back the tears.

"Sorry..." Blood trickled from the corner of his mouth.

She laid her hand on his. "Thank you, how can I ever thank you?" She sat holding him that way for what seemed an eternity. He opened his eyes one more time and looked into hers. His breath gurgled in his throat; he shuddered a few times, and he was gone. Her tears dripped onto his lifeless cheeks. She didn't move, not even when the paramedics got there.

"Ma'am, you can let go of him, we'll take care of him for you." The young man looked at her. He knelt down a little closer so she could see him. "You can let go of him." He gently removed her hand from Mallory's hand. We'll take good care of him, I promise."

Matt squatted down behind her. He placed his hands on her shoulders. "Come on, sweetheart, we need to let them do their job." He stood up and helped her up, too. Her jacket was splattered with Mallory's blood, and she was dazed. He picked her up in his arms and they motioned him toward the ambulance.

"Let's have you checked out." The woman paramedic on the team told Matt to set her down. "Your friend will be close by. He won't leave you." Jessie held tight to Matt's hand.

"Could you check the back of her head? She's been rubbing it. I think she landed pretty hard on the asphalt." Matt watched the woman treat her.

"Here, honey, you can wipe your hands with this." She talked quietly to her for a few moments, then turned her attention back to Matt. "She's had quite a shock. They're waiting for the arrival of the coroner before moving the body. You can go take care of things you need to out there. I'll work with her. I'm going to see how she responds, and you can probably take her home pretty soon." She faced Jessie. "Jessie, do you hurt anywhere?"

Jessie focused on the woman. "My head hurts and my ankle, a little." She pointed at her right foot.

"Let's have a look, shall we?" She lifted her pant leg when Jessie nodded at her. When she poked around her ankle, Jessie winced. "It seems a little swollen. You probably twisted it when you went down."

"He saved my life." Jessie rubbed the back of her head.

"Did he now?" She patted Jessie's hand. "That was a brave thing for him to do."

"How can you repay someone who died to save you?" Jessie touched the medic's arm. "I didn't know what to say to him."

"I don't imagine there's much you can say besides thank you. Did you tell him that?"

"Yes." Jessie raised her arm so the paramedic could check her pulse. "Thank you doesn't seem quite enough when someone dies in your place."

"Do you think he heard you?" She put on the blood

pressure cuff.

"Yes, I think he did." She nodded. "He opened his eyes and looked at me."

"Then you did all you can do." She smiled at Jessie. "Your pressure is good, considering what you just went through.

"Thank you." Jessie smiled slightly.

"For what, honey." The medic looked at her.

"For letting me talk." She folded her hands in her lap. "I need to speak about it."

"I'm good at listening." The woman felt the knot on her head "I'm going to wrap your ankle. Someone will need to monitor her for a while to make sure she doesn't have a concussion."

"What should we be looking for?

"A persistent headache, lack of coordination, memory loss or pupil dilation are a few of the signs you'll need to watch for. I'll give you a sheet to take with you. If at any time tonight, she becomes nauseous or has blurred vision, get her into the ER. Don't leave her alone if possible."

"She won't be alone."

"Jessie, I'm going to let your friend take you home so you can shower and change your clothes. How's that sound?" She reported to the doctor on duty over the radio.

"I would like to go home." Jessie watched her wrap her ankle.

"The doctor has prescribed something for you to take tonight. It will help your system to recover, and rest. I'll give them to your friend to keep for you."

"Okay, thank you."

The medic handed Matt the pills that the doctor had

prescribed for Jessie. "See that she takes this when she's all cleaned up at home. Tonight for sure and tomorrow night if she needs it."

"I will." He helped Jessie out of the ambulance. "Let's get you back to your grandmother, sweetheart. Can you walk on that foot? Better yet, you sit here, and I'm going to get the car."

As soon as Matt took off, Jessie limped her way over to watch them working on the crime scene. She saw Frank standing there and heard him tell the officer what he had seen. She watched them as they photographed the body. It was hard not to look at Mallory and the gaping wound in his chest. He hadn't had much of a life. It was sad what people were capable of doing to each other. She would always remember this strange man. Not for the bad he had done, but for this one moment. It had erased the rest from her mind.

"Jessie, why don't you sit down?" Frank pointed to a bench on the sidewalk.

She shook her head. "He saved my life."

"I know. I saw him," He told her what he had seen.

Jessie smiled. "I don't think Matt appreciated being knocked on his backside."

"I think he was more worried about you than anything else. You were pretty still for a few minutes."

"I couldn't catch my breath."

"It's scary having the wind knocked out of you, if you ask me. I've had it happen to me a couple times, and it's not a pleasant feeling."

"I thought I left you sitting over there." Matt walked up to them.

"I needed to see him again." She pointed in Mallory's direction. "I'm okay now."

"Let's get you home and the ladies can help you get cleaned up. Sadie's waiting for you." Matt looked over at Frank. "I can take you back to the motel now, or come back for you."

"They want me to hang around since I saw it all, and they're still looking for Irwin."

"I'll take her to the resort and then be back myself." He took her hand.

"Okay, see you in a while." Frank patted Radar's head when the dog nudged Jessie's hand.

Mallory's body was covered when they walked by it. "Frank told me you got knocked to the ground."

"I did. He apparently saw what Irwin was going to do. None of us could see him. I owe him, and so do you."

She nodded. "It's strange isn't it? A person can make many wrong choices and in one moment do such a selfless act. I'm not sure I'll ever understand people."

"He probably changed the game at the last minute. I think he meant to kidnap you until he saw what Irwin was going to do. At that moment, he decided."

"I guess we'll never know for sure." She gave him a sideways glance. "I want to believe my version more than yours. I want to believe he chose to do something good."

"You believe it, sweetheart. I've seen too much over the years. Anything is possible, I guess. You may convert me yet." He grinned at her and opened the car door.

Chapter 30

Matt left Jessie in capable hands. He headed back to the crime scene, parked the car, and got out.

"How's Henderson?" Matt walked up to Tony. "Has he come around yet?"

"He's sitting in the ambulance with a pretty big headache." Tony pointed to where the agent was.

"I can imagine. Did he see anything?" Matt crossed his arms.

"Nothing. He doesn't even remember being hit." Tony scratched his head. "It makes you wonder, doesn't it?"

"All night I watched for the professor, and only Jessie knew when he got near because she could feel him. How do you deal with something like that?" Matt's hands clenched, and his jaw tightened.

"I've never seen anything like this before."

"It's been the same in every case but with a little different twist to it." Matt shook his head. "Our first case together it was a ghost. I would have never believed it, but when they were fighting to save Jessie's life, I saw it for a moment." He shook his head. "Now this case, with its dreams and voodoo." Matt frowned and shook his head again. "I'm afraid we are going to need Jessie to find Irwin. My gut tells me he'll be here because of her. She has thwarted his plans more than once. He can't like her very much." He looked at Tony.

"Tell me how I can ask her to put herself out there again after this? She's tough, but I don't know how she's going to process this. How much can I ask of her? I just don't know."

"That's a lot to think about, but if he's angry, he'll keep coming after her. You know how it works, no matter what you do to protect her, he'll keep trying. I wonder if Irwin is even in the area. There's no sign of him. I don't understand how he slipped the noose." Tony let his breath out in a gusty sigh. "He must have slipped away in the confusion when it first happened. He might think he's invincible." Tony scowled. "I have to tell you; I was surprised by what Mallory did. I thought he might try to grab her."

"I think he intended to and changed his plan at the last moment, but that's just my guess. He wanted her."

"I never thought I would see a day when a guy could toss you on your backside." Tony shook his head. "You're not exactly a little guy. He sure was moving. None of us could have saved her, and at point blank range she would have suffered some damage even with the vest on."

"Oh, I'm grateful, believe me, whatever his reason."

"This has been a frustrating night. Even with all the planning we did, we have one person dead and no idea where Irwin is." Tony leaned against the lamppost and folded his arms across his chest. "I'm thinking Jessie is the only way we have to get to him, just like you said. Maybe with her and the dog we'll catch him. Between the two of them I think the odds are in our favor."

"Do you have anything you want me to do here tonight?" Tony asked as they watched a scowling

Henderson get down out of the ambulance.

"I guess we should check with Henderson."

"I think I'll stay here and talk to Frank." Matt grinned at Tony as he walked away. He went over to stand beside Frank. "What are you thinking, Frank?"

"I can't figure out why Radar couldn't find him. I'm stunned." Frank shook his head. "Experience tells me he's in the area somewhere. He's probably watching us right now. If that's true, and he is, then Radar should have found him with no trouble. I guess this evening didn't go the way he had planned, either."

"True, he wanted to kill her, and was willing to do it in a crowded place filled with witnesses. He had to have seen the heavy police presence, which tells me he's bold and isn't afraid of being caught. His survival was a long shot, and yet he didn't see it that way. Why?" He shook his head, angry. "What are we missing? Something!" Matt frowned, throwing his hands into the air.

"I was thinking about the same things. Didn't you tell me that scary things happened at the sheriff's department that was first handling the case?" Frank stared directly at Matt.

"I did, which means Irwin could be manipulating some of the edges of the case. I also believe I'm missing a logical piece too." He leaned against the front of the building. "In our first case, we had a touch of the supernatural, but I missed the guilty party right in front of me because I was afraid to accept that he was involved. The chief was a nice man, my mentor, and like a father to me. I couldn't wrap my head around his involvement. I know I'm missing something simple." Matt scowled in concentration. "What is it?"

"Good question. I'd like to know how he got away so quickly. Even if he could fade into the crowd in the confusion, Radar should have picked up his scent, but there was nothing. Could he use mind control on a dog? Is that even possible?"

"I suppose anything is possible." Matt shrugged and shook his head.

"Could be there was too much going on for Radar to pick up his scent. He was off his game or distracted." Frank looked confused.

Tony walked up to them. "Henderson said you are free to go. We'll wrap it up here, but there's nothing more for you to do."

"Good, we're out of here then. See you tomorrow." Matt pushed away from the wall.

Tony nodded. "I admit I'm perplexed about a few things that happened tonight." Tony scowled. "It all feels off to me."

"We understand the feeling, man. We're overlooking the obvious, but damned if I know what it is." Matt motioned to Frank. "Let's go."

"Radar, let's go, fella." Frank picked up the leash as the dog stood up.

****

Matt walked into the suite and found Sadie waiting up for him. She looked worried, and he didn't know how to tell her not to be. "How's she doing?"

"I think she's still in shock. She fought us about taking the pill. But finally she took it, and she's sleeping." Sadie fiddled with the pillows on the couch. "What kind of medicine was it, did they tell you?"

"A sedative so that she could rest. What she went through is traumatic. It may not all have registered yet.

When it does, she'll need our help to cope with the guilt of it."

"When you put it that way I see what you mean." Her eyes searched his face. "What happened out there, Matt?"

Matt retold the night's events up to the time where Jessie held Mallory as he died. "I swear, Sadie, she was trying to comfort him. The look on Mallory's face, when he drew his last breaths was one of peace as if he was looking at an angel. Whatever she said gave him great comfort."

"She told us that she thanked him." Sadie's eyes filled with tears. "She told us about all the abuse he had experienced as a child."

"How did she know that?" Matt sat down across from Sadie.

"Jeremy said she found it out when she was doing research on him. You'll have to ask her."

"I will. I guess Mallory was looking at an angel, aye Sadie?" He smiled at her. "She's probably writing an article on him."

"You know me well enough to know that I think she's an angel." She glanced at Matt. "Young man, you look tired. I think what you need is sleep. You're going to get him. Jessie told me earlier today that you were the best and won't stop until you've got it figured out. Rest so you can start with a fresh head tomorrow." She stood up, gave him a kiss on the cheek, and started for her room. "You know I like you, Matt. You're good for her. So don't blame yourself for anything tonight. She's safe. Someone is watching out for her."

"Thanks, Sadie, I appreciate it. I feel like I'm missing something important." He shook his head.

"Good night." He watched her walk toward her room. "By the way, I believe she's an angel too," He said softly.

Matt stretched out on the couch and stacked his hands behind his head. He sat back up and grabbed his phone. "Dylan, I know it's late, but I need you to check on some things for me."

Matt explained what had happened. "I want you to start looking into everyone at the Rocky Pointe Bank. See if you can trace anyone who hung out with or knows Irwin. Now that Mallory's dead, Irwin is our frontrunner."

"We already found out that Irwin came into the bank all the time. He befriended Randy Wallis and Jordon Daniels. I don't believe Jordon Daniels is his real name. I can't find evidence that Randy knew what was going on. He didn't seem to like Irwin much. Jordon is questionable. They both said he was strange, and they were often afraid of him. That came up in several interviews we did. Randy said more than once that Irwin would suddenly be standing at a place where he hadn't been a minute before. He could sneak up on them without a sound."

"Interesting. Maybe Henderson didn't hear him, either. Keep checking for me, Dylan. Think about it, go over the files. Maybe you'll see what I'm not seeing. Something connects all of this somehow. Email anything you find. You need to check with Tom about a warrant to search Mallory's place in Rocky Pointe."

"I'll keep my ears open. I'm sorry about what happened to Jessie. Take care of her. I'll send you any information that I find."

"Sorry to have awakened you. I'll talk to you

later."

Matt shut off his phone. Sleep came quickly, but a few hours later, Jessie's scream awakened him. He jumped up and ran into the room. Katie was shaking Jessie, trying to rouse her.

He knelt beside the bed and gently patted her back. "It's okay, sweetheart." He stroked her face, pushing her hair off it gently. "Jess, it's only a dream. I'm right here; you're safe now." He watched her calm down as he soothed her.

"Why won't she wake up?"

"It's probably the sedative. She's struggling to wake up. I would say she's semi-awake, but can't shake off the effects of the drug."

"What's going on?" Katie's voice caught.

"The reality of what she went through, and what she saw, is starting to catch up with her."

"Will she ever have a normal life again, or is this her new normal?" Katie scowled at him.

"My guess, knowing her the way I do, is that this is her new normal." He still stroked her face gently, but she was sleeping quietly now. If it happens again, you know what to do." He smiled when Katie nodded at him and rolled her eyes.

"You're a bossy fella, aren't you?" Katie glared at him, her lips turning up at the corner.

"So I've been told."

When he left her room, Jeremy was standing in his open doorway. "Is she okay?"

"She's having nightmares, which is to be expected."

"I thought you should read this stuff about Mallory she let me read earlier. It'll help you understand some of her emotions in the next few days." He handed Matt the papers.

He turned on the light, slipped his glasses on, and read. "Wow, that helps me to understand the poor guy. He didn't stand much of a chance, did he? Sometimes the cards are so stacked against an individual that you wonder how they survive as long as they do. It doesn't excuse his behavior in any way." Matt handed the article back to Jeremy. "It's a shame we always see it after the fact."

"I thought you needed to see it so you could help her through this. I have a feeling this will be real hard for her."

"You're right, and thanks."

"I'm working on tracking the bank employees and I'm starting to see some connections. I have a few more things to check out. We can go over it tomorrow." Jeremy glanced at the clock and winced. "I guess I should say later today. Get some rest, man. You look like you could use it." He walked back to his room and closed the door.

Matt heard her call out a couple more times, but she settled down quickly. He left her in Katie's capable hands and went back to sleep. The next time he opened his eyes, she was sitting in the chair across from him, smiling. She looked like the sunshine and the angel he had seen last night.

"Good morning, Jess." He sat up on the couch, still wearing his clothes from last night.

"How could you sleep like that? You look uncomfortable." She shook her head. "You didn't even take off your shoes."

"I've learned when I'm on a case to catch sleep

when I can. Is that coffee that I smell?"

"Yes, and Grams ordered you a big breakfast. She's worried that you're not eating enough. So be sure to eat it."

"No problem, I could use some food, I'm hungry. I'll clean up and be right there," he called back over his shoulder. "Don't go anywhere. I have some questions I want to ask you."

"I'll be here. Someone told me I'm not supposed to go anywhere alone. I'm obeying your command." Her mouth twitched as she said it.

Matt turned around and stared at her. "Wow, now that's a first. I wish I could have got that on tape." The pillow hit his head as he turned around, and he heard her giggle. His aim was perfect. He got her full in the face with the pillow. She fell back onto the couch, laughing. "Sorry, I had brothers. It's reflex now."

Chapter 31

By the time he got to the kitchen, Katie and Sadie had left to do some shopping. Jeremy and Jessie were at the table drinking their coffee and talking.

"Your breakfast is warming in the microwave," Jeremy told him. "Sadie made me promise to tell you to eat it or else you'll have to deal with her." He grinned at Matt. "My job is done."

"This seems like the perfect time for us to talk. We still have a suspect on the loose, so it's not a time to let down our guard." Matt took a bite of his egg.

"I'll get my computer." Jeremy walked out of the kitchen.

"I know we need to talk, but it makes me feel sad." The smile on Jessie's face faded.

"It will make you feel that way for a while, probably. You have to deal with last night, and it won't be easy. I'm sorry." He reached for her hand. "Why don't you start by telling me what you said to Mallory?"

She told him what she remembered. "He said he was sorry, and he looked at me strangely, and that was all."

"Can I tell you what I saw?" He smiled when she nodded at him. "I saw a man who was dying in the lap of a woman he had obsessed over. Whatever you said gave him hope—so much so, that before he died he looked like he had seen an angel. You helped him in his last moments in life."

"Thanks, words failed me last night. How do you thank someone who just gave their life to save you?" She looked away. "No words seemed adequate."

"From my vantage point it looked to me like they were working."

"Do they know where Irwin is?" She sipped her coffee, gazing into his eyes.

"No, he got away. Even Frank was a little shocked by that. I think we'll need to keep a real close eye on you. No more being a target. If Henderson wants to play target, he can do it. He's tall enough and blond. All he needs are the right clothes and some padding."

Jessie laughed. "I doubt that he'll go for it. I think I'm sensing a little vengeance on your part."

"Who me? Not at all." He saw her skeptical look. "Okay, well, maybe a little."

"I don't trust Irwin. He doesn't play fair." Jessie tapped her cheek.

"Sweetheart, no bad guy plays fair." He saw her frown. "I'm game, what do you mean?"

"In most of the cases I've been a part of, here and in New York, there are some predictable patterns. Mallory was a little hard to figure out because of his imbalance. I thought I had it figured out, and then he threw us a huge curve last night. Irwin, on the other hand, is almost too cocky and sure. He was willing to kill me in front of witnesses. What's to stop him from doing almost anything to get back at me? He's a manipulator. He saw the weakness in Mallory and took advantage of it. Can he see a weakness in me to exploit?" She scrunched her face. "The other thing is

Adriana never saw her stalker, but she knew when he was there and she was afraid of him. He's the dark shadowy figure that I've been seeing."

"Damn, Jess, you're right. I knew I was missing something." He looked on his phone at the email from Dylan again. "Do you remember when we interviewed Randy, and he told us to check out the strange man that came into the bank who was always looking at Adriana?"

"I remember, but then Jayla told us he was harmless and shifted the guilt toward Randy."

"That's right. Randy was pointing us in the direction of Irwin. Randy didn't like him and was afraid of him. He thought something was off with the prof. He went into the bank where he was very visible. Adriana saw him but didn't know him as her stalker. She could feel the darkness, but she still couldn't stop him from getting to her if he had wanted to."

"That's why she said what she did to Jayla, about death finding her again."

"Do you remember what you said to me at the time? You wondered if Jayla was such a good friend, how come she didn't show more emotion about Adriana when she went missing."

"Sure I remember."

"You were spot on in your thinking. I think Jayla is involved in this somehow." He glanced again at his phone. "Dylan is trying to make a connection now. You're right about it not following a particular course. I think three different crimes have merged, and they are playing off each other. I have no idea what we're dealing with. It is all muddled together and unclear. First, it was Mallory; you were to be his prize if he got

Adriana for Irwin. Irwin manipulated Randy and Jordon, who set Adriana up, unwittingly or not, for Mallory. I think Irwin knew when he told Mallory he was going to kill you that Mallory would try to protect you or kill you himself. Irwin forced Mallory to react out of his obsession for you. That much we know for sure. Jayla was trying to throw us off Irwin's track. Why? There's something bigger here than Irwin, although he is the one we have to deal with now."

Jeremy walked in, carrying his computer. "I was searching the old Harvest Club site to see if it had been taken down. Low and behold, see what I found." He set the laptop down on the table. "It's a new site that is recruiting civic-minded people wanting to make a difference in the world. It reads suspiciously like the old Harvest Club site. They call themselves The Collector's Club. It's set up the same way with lots of protections. It's hard to maneuver around in it unless you're a club member or me." He grinned at them. "This is just my thought. I'm attempting to trace the origin of the site now. It isn't in Blue Cove. I know that for sure."

"The picture is getting a little clearer." Matt wrote a few names on a piece of paper. "Could you check and see if any of these folks have an offshore account with recently added money in them?"

"I would be happy to." Jeremy picked up the paper Matt pushed toward him.

"I'll call Tom Maxwell as soon as we have a location or a little more evidence. For now, I have to stay clear-headed so I can deal with Irwin. It's not easy to figure out what his next move will be. You're awfully quiet." He looked at Jessie. "What's up?"

271

"Irwin is active. I can feel it."

"What do you mean by active?"

"He's planning his next action. Unlike Mallory, he won't announce it. He wants to keep us guessing and off our game. It's like a chess match—we have to see the big picture and anticipate his next move. For whatever it's worth, he has shifted his attention."

"I don't know if I like the sound of that. What do you mean?" Matt frowned.

"I was someone to keep Mallory under control. Irwin will do whatever he needs to do to walk away from this mess unscathed. He'll use whatever situation presents itself. The thing is a guy like him would be a premium to a group that needed to recruit new members and keep its people in line."

"Jess, you're an angel—" Matt's phone interrupted his thought. Jessie's phone rang next.

"Hi, Grams, is everything all right?" Jessie's voice rose. "Stay calm, we'll be right there. Remain in the car with the doors locked where he can't see you. Did you call the police? We're on our way."

"Jess?" He looked at her.

"Irwin kidnapped Katie and some others at gunpoint." She started running toward the door.

"Wait a second. I'm right behind you." Matt grabbed his gun and badge off the table as he raced after her.

"I'm going with you guys. Don't even think of leaving me behind." Jeremy followed them out.

"Katie is in the middle of a hostage situation. The police are on the scene." Matt grabbed her arm. "Slow down, Jess, remember we're a team. We do this together."

Chapter 32

Matt stayed in contact with Tony en route to the store. "Don't worry, Jess," he glanced at her briefly. "Sadie's fine and she's waiting in a safe place." He saw relief sweep across Jessie's face. "She kept her head and called the police first. Your grandmother is one sharp lady."

"She is at that. I should have known something like this would happen. I said he was going to change his tactics," she said brokenly, "but I had no clue he would take Katie."

"You can't know everything, Jess. Besides, the police are there. They have the store surrounded, and the perimeter is secure." He signaled and changed lanes. "So far they haven't heard any demands from Irwin. There's no word on the hostages either."

"Is that good or bad?" She fiddled with her badge.

"It tells us very little." Matt glanced quickly at her. "If Irwin is anything like other perps in a similar situation, he'll want to control the way it plays out. He'll make demands when he wants to make them. They surrounded the store, so there's no way out for him." Matt frowned. "I wish I knew what he was thinking."

"The thing is he's not like others; he doesn't fit the norms." Jessie closed her eyes. It was silent in the car, but the atmosphere felt charged. Matt waited. "He's not in a panic," she said eventually, her eyes still closed. "I know that much. He's methodical. He has a plan." She looked at Matt. "He's not worried about being caught. Katie was at the wrong place at the wrong time. I don't feel he's even thinking about her or about anyone else that might be in there."

"They'll just be collateral damage if anything happens to them," Jeremy spoke from the back seat. "Can't you go any faster?" He gripped the back of Matt's seat.

"I'm not in a cruiser, so the answer is no. I'm going too fast as it is, and we have no time to be stopped. Hold tight, we're almost there." Matt rounded the corner quickly, slamming on his brakes and skidding to a stop. His door flew open as he leaped out, followed by Jeremy.

"Stay put," he called to Jessie who was running toward Sadie. Matt spotted Tony and headed toward him. "What are we looking at?"

"This is what I know so far." Tony motioned to one of his cops to head around to the back of the store. "Irwin followed the owner into the shop when she opened up this morning. He forced the customers waiting for the store to open to go inside at gunpoint. Sadie was in the car and saw him grab Katie and push her in with the others. Sadie said he didn't seem to recognize Katie. He was acting strangely is how she put it."

"How long did it take you to get here and set up operations?" His eyes narrowed as he scanned the storefront.

"We were here within five minutes and had the store surrounded." Tony ran his hands through his hair.

"We've called to him on the bullhorn. No response, nothing. We have no way of reaching him to talk him down. I've tried calling the store, but he's not picking up."

"So no demands and no communication." Matt frowned. "I don't like the sound of that. Have you had any sight of the hostages?"

"We've seen no movement inside the store since we arrived."

Matt stood with his legs apart; his arms folded across his chest. "It has to be some kind of trap. I wish I knew what was going on in his freaking mind." He frowned in concentration. "Suicide by cop, do you think? I mean, what are we looking at?"

"He was carrying a bag, Sadie said. It could be a sniper situation. But, he doesn't seem to play by the same rules." Tony glanced toward the storefront as he spoke.

Matt noticed Jessie walking toward them. She was wearing that look of hers. "What's on your mind?"

"I think he's planning something unusual; an event that's spectacular in his mind. With his knowledge of the occult, the store's name is a dead giveaway to me; Strange Artifacts." She frowned. "I don't think he's worried about you guys being out here, which makes me wonder."

"You're right. He controls things in a different way." Matt looked at Tony. "Let's not give him time to put his plan into action. We need to get the hostages out of there."

Suddenly a small explosion rattled the glass windows and door. Smoke filled the store. "Let's use it!" Tony waved them into the shop, and they ran in.

Bursting through the door, they spread out, guns drawn.

No fire. No sign of Irwin, just the hostages.

Katie was sitting propped against the counter with the others, coughing now as the smoke settled to the floor. He had bound their hands behind them and tied their feet together. Matt bent beside her, pulling the tape from her mouth and motioning for her to be quiet. They quickly untied the hostages, helped them up, and hustled them away from the store.

"Where is Irwin," he asked Katie as he half-carried her out of the building at a near run.

"He went upstairs, but he's not right in his head." Katie tilted her head and shrugged.

"What do you mean?"

"It was like he never saw us; he just looked right through us. Once he had us tied up, he never came to check on us again." She paused and rubbed her wrists. "He had us tie each other up while he held the gun to us. He was chanting and swaying back and forth. I couldn't understand what he was doing." Katie shivered. "To tell you the truth, he never needed to come back to check, we were all too afraid to move. I can't explain it, but we couldn't have moved if we tried." Katie turned when she spied Jessie and Sadie.

"Don't go anywhere. The police will want to question you." He saw her nod.

More small explosions followed, a few minutes apart, each creating new billows of smoke.

Jessie sat down on a bench across from the store. Matt caught the movement out of the corner of his eye and sat down beside her. "What are you thinking, sweetheart?"

"I thought I would try something. It's the only idea

I have. I'm going to try what I did the two times he came to me. I'm not sure if it will do anything. But in case it does, you guys should be ready to take him down." Her face was pale, but her gaze was steady. "He'll be coming after me."

"Are you sure that's what you want to do?" Matt studied her face.

"We have to do something." Her lips tightened. "He's up to no good."

"I think you could say that about most bad guys." He grinned at her and patted her hand.

"True, but I'm talking about something *big*. And dramatic. We are meant to be here for a reason." She pushed her hair away from her face.

"I'll give Tony the heads up. Wait a few minutes until I signal you before you begin. He may want to get some men in position first." He stood up and then bent to look her in the eyes. "Look, Jess, from the beginning, this whole case was different. This case drew you the moment Evan Foster walked into your store and told you about his dream with you in it. I believe that you'll be the one to finish it with Irwin." He noticed her puzzled expression. "What can I say? I'm starting to believe all kinds of unconventional stuff since I started hanging out with you." He touched her cheek. "Besides, it would be nice if we could get through this day without anyone getting hurt."

"You sound like Reba." She grinned at him. He made a face and then smiled.

****

She sat alone and watched for Matt's signal. He was standing by Tony and a few other officers next to a patrol car. He motioned to her a few minutes later.

Suddenly, she saw Tony's eyes go wide with terror. He stumbled back, grabbed at his neck, and fell to the ground. The shadow power, the one that had nearly killed her. She had to find a way to stop it, to break Irwin's control over it. The words began to tumble through her mind as Tony writhed on the ground and officers raced to his aid. They couldn't help him.

She was the gatekeeper. The battle began. Shadowy figures were dancing all around the store, inside and out. Drumbeats filled the air while the shadow dancers moved in ritualistic unison. Each time she said the words to the song, they stopped and stared at her. She heard Tony gasp for air in the distance. He was still alive. But, the shadows moved around him in a frenzy jabbing at his throat with spears. Irwin had worked them up again, and she fought to calm them down. Time stood still. At one point, she felt herself gaining strength and felt theirs start to diminish. Yes! She grew stronger the more she spoke the words. Finally, they stopped, all facing her, eyes tiny sparks of black light. She drew on every bit of strength that she had. *Go!* She told them. *Go away and never do the bidding of this man or any other ever again*! For an instant, they stared at her, and her heart trembled. *We depart.* The whispers filled her head resembling the sound of the wind. *Thank you for freeing us. We will honor our word to do as you say.* They slunk away into nothingness, no longer moved by Irwin's bidding. They were gone. She saw Tony struggle to sit up rubbing his neck. His officers would not let him move until the paramedics looked at him.

Her eyes slowly closed as she concentrated her thoughts one more time. *Come and get me, Irwin. I'm the one you want,* she taunted. His anger was building. She could feel it. *Come and get me if you're strong enough.* She knew the minute he began to move. He was coming. She opened her eyes just as he came crashing through the door. He picked up speed, shaking his fists in the air, screaming insults. His eyes locked on hers; he rushed toward her, his face contorted in a rage, screaming obscenities at her. Dimly she heard people shouting. Two of the officers tackled him, and he flung them away like toys. He slammed another officer aside, still coming. Matt was running toward her, his gun drawn. She had her gun out; her hand had closed on it without conscious thought. Slowly she lifted it. He was close now, huge, looming over her. Her arm shook as she forced the gun higher and finally, finally squeezed the trigger.

Click!

He was almost on her! Suddenly he fell forward, an officer on his back. She heard herself scream and kicked at his hand as his fingers fastened like a claw around her ankle. It took several police officers to hold him down. Matt had to pry Irwin's fingers away from her ankle. Finally subdued, Irwin was cuffed and shackled.

Jessie watched a large black shadow lift out of Irwin's prone body and fly away. Irwin was powerless. She stood up at the same time Matt and Taylor stood Irwin on his feet. She gasped for breath, trembling. She met his hate-filled glare and, one eyebrow rose slightly. "I hardly know you and I don't understand your hatred."

"You've ruined everything, you and your news articles, your misplaced sense of justice, and your

279

stupid crusades. Look what you've done to me." She jerked her head back slightly as spittle spattered her face. "You'll never know what you've ruined. I didn't want Mallory to die." He twisted to scream the words to her as they hauled him to the waiting cruiser. "I wanted you to die." He started cursing her, struggling at every step.

The screams continued as they forced him into the backseat of the cop car and drove away.

"What the hell did he do? Not one gun would fire." Matt looked at her face. "Will you be okay?" Matt put his arm around her and pulled her to his side.

"I think so. I just don't understand his hatred or his power." She looked up at him, her face pale. "Why me?"

"That's beyond me, Jess. Hatred is a tricky thing to figure out. There's often no good reason for it." He stroked her back. "What did you do to rile him?"

"I'll explain later...go do what you need to get done. I think I need to sit down for a minute. It was a strange experience, which has left me drained. I hope I never go through this again." She pulled out of his arms and her lips tightened.

"I want to know what happened." He frowned at her. "Are you sure you're okay."

She nodded at him. "I'm fine. Go on, you need to check on Tony. He should be okay now. They're gone." She shivered.

"Who are gone, or should I ask?"

"It's a little hard to explain, but they're gone. I'll tell you later."

"Are you sure it's over?" She nodded at him. "I thought he was going to die. He couldn't breathe." Matt glanced in Tony's direction. "None of this makes any sense. You and I, we'll talk later." He walked over to where the paramedics were checking Tony, who was still rubbing his neck. His officers huddled off to the side with concerned faces.

Jessie sat with Sadie for a few minutes and then went in search of Katie. She found her locked in an embrace with Jeremy. He was talking to her, and she heard Katie sigh. Jessie backed away and turned so they couldn't see the big smile on her face. Her two friends, how cool was that? Sweet, at least something good might have come out of this fiasco.

"Sadie, do they still need to question you or can I take you home?

"I'll talk to the officer and see, but I'm ready to leave if they say I can." She went to speak to Matt and one of the officers. Jessie saw him nod.

"Grams, this hasn't been much of a vacation for you." She linked her arm through Sadie's as they started for the car. "I think you should come to Blue Cove for my store's grand opening."

"I'd planned on it, dear." Her eyes crinkled, a smile lit up her face. "This has been the most excitement I've had in years."

"Be careful, Grams, it has a way of growing on you." Jessie smiled at her grandmother. "I moved to Blue Cove for a quiet life and looked what happened to me."

"It's put roses in your cheeks, given you a handsome young man, and more excitement than any girl could ask for." Sadie climbed into the passenger seat of the car and clicked on her seatbelt.

"I want to get away from here and go home." Jessie

fastened her seatbelt too.

"I think we should fly home tomorrow. I'll call the airlines and see if we can change our tickets." Sadie patted Jessie's hand.

"I'd like that, and why don't you come stay with me at the Cove." Jessie pulled the car out of the parking space.

"Should we wait for Katie and Jeremy?"

"I don't think so. The police want to question the hostages, and Jeremy will take care of her." The corner of Jessie's lip twitched.

"Katie likes him a lot." Sadie looked out the window. "Even better, I think he likes her, too. He steals glances at her when he doesn't think anyone is looking. She bewilders him a little. Maybe this little event will awaken him to just how short life is, and he'll stop dillydallying."

"I think you may be right about that. It was the perfect wake-up call for him." She smiled. "I have a feeling we'll be seeing more of Jeremy in Blue Cove. I wouldn't even be surprised if he moved there." Jessie smiled and then chuckled when she saw that they were still hugging as she drove past them.

****

Matt stood with Tony as he questioned each of the hostages. Tony let them leave after they gave one of his officers their personal information.

"Are you okay?" Matt noticed Tony's pale face.

"I checked out okay, but my head still can't grasp what happened to me."

"To tell you the truth, I can't figure any of this out." Matt frowned.

"I don't have a clue either." Tony put his hand to

his forehead and rubbed his temple.

"Whatever is upstairs had his undivided attention." Matt looked at the building. "I hope we can get in there soon to check it out."

"I know. We'll know what he was up to in a while. The store is being swept by our explosive expert to make sure it's clear before the crime team goes in." Tony checked a text on his phone. "The explosions were the results of some simple chemicals compounds used in magic tricks, according to Carl."

"Something meant to impress us, I guess." Matt raised his brows. "I wasn't impressed, were you?"

"Nope. Although, it did give us the time we needed to get the hostages out of the store." Tony frowned. "When did you ever hear of the bad guy creating a diversion so the good guys could free his hostages? I wonder, can he do something like this at the jail." Tony rubbed at his neck. "What are we looking at?"

"I think it's what Jessie said to me earlier. He wasn't even thinking of them. Out of sight was out of mind for him. He was controlling them another way. Katie said they were afraid to move."

"Exactly. I wonder, can he do it again?"

"I don't think so. Jessie said his power was broken." Matt read a text that came in on his phone. "I can't wait to hear what Jessie did to rile Irwin up like that. He had no clue what was going on around him. He only wanted to get to her. I have a theory that Jessie knows more about all of this than any of us."

"Hell, it's not normal. I don't know how to begin to write up the reports. Whatever Jessie did, though, it worked." He put a hand briefly on his holster. "I'm just glad that more bad guys don't know how to pull that gun trick." He shook his head. "I want just one expert to explain what made all our guns misfire, eh? Just one. Crazy." He shook his head again. "I thought I was going to die. I felt hands around my neck like a vice." He rubbed his neck and frowned. "What was it? It took all of us to hold him down and get him cuffed and shackled."

"Jessie was concerned that Irwin was up to something major. And whatever caused the gun thing." He shrugged. "I have more questions than answers right now. Irwin has the answers, but I doubt he'll cooperate. Jessie might be our best bet."

Tony answered his phone on the third ring. "This is Tony. Thanks, we'll be right with you. Matt, we're cleared to go in, but he said watch where you're walking. They haven't removed all the wires yet."

Matt followed Tony in the door. "I imagine Henderson will be upset he wasn't here for this."

"You've got that right." They approached a tall, sandy-haired officer. "Matt, this is Carl."

"Nice to meet you, Carl." Matt shook his hand.

"Tony, you won't believe what this guy had planned. Those first little explosions were your basic magic tricks. If you guys hadn't stopped him, a good portion of the city block would've been leveled and most of our police force gone with it." He led the way up into the attic and pointed out where the wires had been rigged and snipped, so the explosives had no triggers. "Plastic. C-4. Not nice stuff. This one had been rigged to detonate by this handheld device."

"He couldn't have done all the work this morning." He stared at the neat stacks of plastic explosive wired in sequence. "I wonder if this is where he got off to last night. Do you think he hid up here?" Tony leaned against the wall.

"It's possible." Matt shrugged. "We didn't see any sign of forced entry, but that doesn't mean he couldn't have gotten in. He also couldn't have done this alone."

Carl waved at the tangle of wires. "If he worked around the clock for days, he needed someone else to work with him to accomplish all of this. Set on a timer, it's an elaborate set-up. There's more going on. It wasn't just about today, although, I think he had changed his mind and was trying to take this building out today. His schedule might have been pushed up." Carl pointed to the smaller makeshift bomb rigged to go off. "All this," he motioned around the room, "has all the earmarks of something bigger."

"Jessie thought he was planning something big and dramatic. She was obviously right." Matt squatted down to get a better look at one of the dirty-white bricks of plastic explosive. "I wonder how and where he got his hands on all this stuff."

"We have a trace going in on the serial numbers. Stolen. This material is illegal to possess. We are talking weapons grade, and the damage could have been phenomenal." Carl shook his head. "Your perp must have had some training in bomb making. He knew what he was doing. If I don't miss my guess, I'd say he was a military man at some point."

"I guess when Uncle Sam trains these boys, he never knows how some of them will end up using their training." Tony walked around the attic looking at the equipment. "So why take hostages. They weren't necessary to his plan. And why did he go to the front of the store and risk being seen?"

"I was wondering the same thing. I don't have an answer. It doesn't make sense. Even if he had planned for this eventuality, why would he risk it on anything as trivial as a few hostages?" Matt leaned his shoulder against the wall. "Given the right incentive, he might be in the mood to talk when you question him."

"I doubt it. The text I got earlier was that Irwin is causing problems. He's going nuts, and no one can calm him down. They're keeping him cuffed and shackled for the time being." Tony leaned against the wall.

"He didn't think they'd catch him. It sounded like he never intended Mallory to die. It surprised him and threw him off his game plan. Or was this his game plan?"

"Damned if I know." Tony folded his arms across his chest. "I just hope Jessie is right that his power is broken." He touched his throat nervously. "I never...want to feel anything like that again."

"If Jessie's sure they're gone, you're safe," Matt said soberly. "That's why he wanted Jessie eliminated—he must have guessed she might be able to break his power. But what is this all *about*?" Matt squatted down to look at one of the timers. "Why multiple timers when the first one will blow everything." He looked up. "I wonder if any of the other stores have been rigged."

"We'll need to check that out. It's a possibility."

"Is this the result of a political movement or maybe domestic terrorism? There are more people involved than just Mallory and Irwin." Matt looked at Carl as he asked it.

"All are real possibilities." Carl picked up a piece

of the wire and looked at it. "It's been in the works for a while. Someone knows what they're doing."

"I wonder how Irwin plays into this." Tony frowned.

"Who owns that trailer where they found Adriana? That might be a good place to start." Matt stood, holding a scrap of wire in his hand.

"I'll check it out when I get back to the station. I'm not sure if we know yet."

"I bet that when you find the owner, you'll find someone with some military training, or at the very least, access to this kind of munition."

"Carl, check the adjacent stores and see if they've got explosives hidden anywhere. Call me as soon as you know."

"Yes, sir."

"Damn, I moved from New York to get away from this, I guess you can never really get away." Tony stood and dusted off his knees. "I'm going to check in with Henderson. I'll let you know, Matt, when we'll start the interrogation."

"Thanks, Tony. I appreciate you letting me be a part. We've walked into something bigger than a kidnapping." Matt saw Tony frown and nod his head.

"These guys play it cool for years running under the radar and then something stupid takes down their operations. I've seen them do it time and time again." It was Matt's turn to nod.

****

When Matt walked in the door, the first thing he noticed was Katie and Jeremy sitting on the couch side-by-side holding hands. He smiled at them. "What took you so long?" He walked on through to the kitchen where Jessie and Sadie were sitting at the table. "Good afternoon, ladies. You two turned out to be the heroines of the day."

Sadie blushed. "I only made a phone call. My granddaughter, on the other hand, baited him to come and get her. As you clearly saw, that's what he was doing when you guys stopped him." Sadie poured him a glass of iced tea.

Matt frowned. "Let's hear it, Jess." He sat down beside her and took a swig of his tea.

She told him what had happened. He was still frowning. "You're something, you know. I don't suppose you ever thought about what would have happened to you if we hadn't been able to stop him."

"I was never in doubt of you stopping him. You wouldn't let anything happen to me." She smiled sweetly at him.

"I appreciate your faith in me, but as I've told you before, there is always a risk. I've never dealt with shadows and occult power." He made eye contact with her. "If you're not challenging them in newsprint, you're challenging them in mind games. You're something; that's all."

She gave him an arch look. "I would like to understand just what this something is that you keep talking about."

"When I fully understand it myself, I'll explain it to you." He grinned and grabbed her hand. "Sadie, I hope you don't mind, but I can't resist any longer." He leaned over and kissed Jessie. One long, slow, hot kiss. He could see the smile on Sadie's face and the pink tint on Jessie's as he pulled away. "Boy, that was good. I don't mind if I help myself to another." He kissed her again and then winked at Sadie, who was still smiling.

"I don't mind passionate looks, kisses, and love in the air. I remember what it's like, believe me. You can kiss her anytime she says you can." Sadie chuckled. "Don't mind me."

"What do you think about you guys starting home tomorrow instead of on Sunday?" He looked from one to the other. "I know it's a day early, but this hasn't been much of a vacation."

"We've already talked about it and I've changed our tickets. I'm going to go back and stay with Jessie. I'll help her in the store until it opens. I called my son. He wasn't happy about it at first, but I convinced him that it would be good for his daughter." Sadie grinned. "He melts like butter when it comes to what's good for Jessie."

"I'm telling you, it's those blue eyes of hers." He grinned at Jessie when she rolled them at him.

"I'm ready to be home." She placed her hand on top of his on the table. "I want to see my store." She tapped his fingers. "By the way, did they clear all the surveillance equipment out of there?"

"Yes, it's clean as a whistle. They've kept an eye on it to make sure no one put any more in."

"How about you?" Jessie looked at him. "Will you be going home, too?"

"I'm going to stay through the interrogation process. We're close to knowing more about the Collectors Club. I would like to put a stop to it before it gets a foothold again. Tom Maxwell is already on the case. One thing for sure, I'll be at your grand opening." He grinned at her. "I wouldn't want to miss your big day. I'll give you plenty of information for a few articles."

"What's in it for you?" She sipped her tea and smiled at him.

His pulse quickened. "Let's see, I'm hoping for a little laughter in my life, an endless supply of kisses, and several dates with the girl of my dreams."

"I think I can arrange that for you." Jessie sighed and fluttered her lashes at him.

Sadie laughed and left the room. He chuckled, bent his head, and kissed her again.

She pulled away and looked at him. "I've been thinking this new group could be smuggling something. They might have found a new item to collect and sell on the black market."

"Any ideas?"

"Is it possible they're involved in gun running and illegal weapons?"

"Jess." He kissed her cheek. "Now you're thinking like a cop. If you had seen what Irwin and the others had prepared, you would understand just how realistic your theory is. Irwin knew he wasn't going to get away, so he decided to move the time frame a little." He sent off a text to Tony and Jeremy to check on a couple of things and then added Tom Maxwell to the list.

"I guess the only thing we can do now is to wait. Maybe Irwin will want to get it all off his chest." She looked skeptical. "I can hope." She stood, and he pulled her into his lap.

"You do that, sweetheart. We wait, but I have a feeling we won't have to wait too long." He held her close.

Chapter 33

Matt pulled his car up to where he could unload their bags. "Jess, Kip will pick you up at the airport. He'll meet you at baggage." He took their bags out of the trunk of the car and pulled her close.

She sighed in his arms. "I'm going to miss you."

"I'll be back as soon as the interrogation part is done." He searched her face, taking his fill. "I'll call you tonight. I'm going to miss you, too." He gave her a quick kiss. He hated goodbyes. "I need to move the car. I'll see you in a few days. Dylan promised to keep an eye out for you. If you need something, don't hesitate to call him."

"Okay," She smiled and turned to collect her belongings.

He pulled her back into his arms and kissed her one more time. "Jess, keep your eyes open. I don't think there should be any more trouble, but I don't know."

She nodded at him and walked away. Dropping her things by Sadie's feet, she ran back to him, pulled his head down, and kissed him passionately. "Goodbye, sweetheart." She strolled away, collected her things again, and turned to wave.

He stood staring at her, his mouth open, barely holding himself back from running after her. It might be nice to take things up where she had just left off.

"Hey, fella, let's move that car out of here." The

officer smiled at him.

He got in and started the car. *What was that about?* He would take it up with her again the next time he saw her. He smiled and was still smiling when he walked into the station.

The volume of Irwin's angry shouts could he heard in Tony's office. "Has he been going on like this all night?"

"Yes, sir, all night." Tony handed him a pair of earplugs. "We've issued them to everybody."

Matt grinned and put them in his ears. It made the noise manageable. "Did you have time to do some checking on the text I sent you? I sent it to a couple others, and I've gotten some replies."

"I have, and I think Jessie was in the ballpark with her guess."

"I figured she nailed it. Maxwell found some links between the new group and an old FBI agent from the Harvest Club who's in prison. Jeremy found out that Irwin traveled a lot overseas. That's how he began to dabble in the darker arts. He's into it and knows enough to scare people. We know now that he killed with it, too. Two men died in their beds, apparently both of them healthy, with expressions of terror on their faces. The autopsy said respiratory failure."

"I wonder if that's what almost happened to me." Tony rubbed his neck. "If Jessie hadn't riled him, maybe I wouldn't be here." Tony looked thoughtful. "I've never believed in this stuff, but now I'm not sure."

"From every indication of what we have right now, Irwin may have been hired to keep the recruits under control. He screwed it up because of his weakness for

Adriana."

"Did I tell you a couple of other stores that had explosives, too? One is a famous restaurant here in town. They hadn't set the timers yet. Whoever they were, they had some big plans." Tony opened the file on his desk.

"I got an email from Tom Maxwell. They confiscated Zach's computer from his prison cell." Matt noticed Tony's perplexed expression. "Zach was an FBI agent who tried to have it both ways. He gathered information from the cops and fed it to the club. It held a description of a display for the weapons buyers. It looks like it was planned to coincide with some major event in late spring. Maxwell figures it has to be something televised. An event that cable news would pick up and it could air around the world."

"It has to be our Annual Golf Tournament in the spring." Tony frowned. "That would have gotten them noticed, that's for damn sure. How did Mallory fit in?"

"He was in prison with some of the members of the old Harvest Club for a while. I think they hired him as their muscle man. Irwin was going to use and control him. They have a kind of sick history together. But, Irwin messed it up by finding and wanting Adriana." Matt handed Tony a copy of the file. "We're still piecing it all together, but we should know soon who the control person is outside of the prison. Right now, I do know that a few of the HC members in prison are getting some payouts to offshore accounts. Someone is running the operation from prison, and someone is on the outside."

"It sounds like another big case. We were able to find out who owned the trailer, but he checked out okay. He had leased it out through a leasing agency to someone out of state. Here's the information. We're checking on it now."

"I don't think I'll be surprised by anything anymore." Matt smiled crookedly. "I probably shouldn't say that. Each time there is some surprising element involved."

"What did Jessie do to rile Irwin up?"

Matt told him what Jessie had relayed to him. "That's when he came bursting through the door."

"She's one gutsy lady even though I don't understand any of it."

"The truth is, I don't think she does. She's just learned to live with it."

Tony answered his phone. "Okay, we'll be right there." Tony stood up. "They're ready for us. We have something to hold over Irwin's head. The body we found was that of his late wife, and hers was death by asphyxiation. "

"What about the other one?" Matt asked Tony.

"She was a missing coed from NYU. It looks like Irwin had a bit of a problem."

"Makes you wonder if there are any more missing girls. Let's hope Irwin is ready to talk." Matt followed Tony to the interrogation room. The closer Matt got to the room; the louder the yelling was. "This is liable to be bad." He saw Tony nod.

Chapter 34

"You haven't seen Matt much since his return from Palm Springs." Sadie carried the box of bookmarks over to the checkout counter.

"It is always that way at the end of a case. He has so much to do, including paperwork, but he calls every night." She smiled.

"Tonight's the big night, are you excited about it?" Sadie sat down on a stool at the counter. "The store looks great."

Jessie smiled at her, "I can hardly contain myself. Ever since I can remember, I wanted a bookstore. Idle Time Books is finally a reality." She turned around looking at the store with a critical eye. "I love it; I love the look of it and the smell of the books. I love that you are here and Matt will soon be to share it with me. Katie will be here too, along with Liam, Jeremy, and all my new friends. What more could I ask for?" She grinned. "Besides, Corinne Clark will be signing books. You know she's my favorite. I've read most all of her books."

"Did you say Liam Donavon is coming?" Sadie turned to look at her. "Didn't you use to have a crush on him?"

"I did many years ago. He considered me a pest, which I was." She laughed. "He always had plenty of gorgeous girls in his life." She arranged the bookmarks in a basket as she talked.

"I remember that about Liam. He always had a new girlfriend every time he came home. He was one of the biggest flirts in our small town." Sadie handed her more bookmarks from the box.

"I don't know about flirts, I do know he tortured Katie and me. But that was long ago, and we've all grown up. And now, Matt's in my life." Jessie sighed. "I hope he makes it in time."

"He said he'd be here, and he will be. Matt is worth keeping, that's for sure. I wouldn't let anyone mess it up if I were you." Sadie straightened the bookmarks in the basket.

"I know he's a keeper, Grams. He's certainly brought excitement to my life." Jessie looked at her watch. She missed him more than she had thought possible,

Katie arrived, bringing the appetizers and drinks for the night. "I wanted to get the table ready for the food. Liam should be here at any time. Jeremy is coming too." Katie blushed. "I have to look fabulous. Oh, Jessie, it looks great in here." She turned in a slow circle. "I love those pendant lights. I'll put the table right under them and back against the wall."

Jessie watched as Katie began to create her magic. Some food went into the refrigerator in the back room. The warming trays were set up. She arranged the table so it would display the appetizers to best advantage. It would be another stellar job. Jessie wrapped her arms around her friend. "I want you to know how happy I am about my two best friends being together."

"If you think you're happy, you should be me. I think I'm in love, Jessie. I mean really in love, the kind of love that poets write sonnets about." She smiled. "I'm trying to take it slow and easy so I don't scare him off."

Jessie rolled her eyes and laughed. "Still you have to be you, Katie. Don't let any man change you. You're great the way you are, and someone will love you for who you are." Jessie saw the face Katie made. "Okay, I know, I'll stop preaching. If you're happy, then I'm happy."

"I'm excited to see Liam. I haven't seen him for a while. I want him to meet Jeremy." Katie took out a serving tray for the cookies she had made. "You know my brother. I'm not sure I'll be able to control him when he gets a load of you. He'll be kicking himself for sure. Too bad you have Matt."

"I think a better way to say it is that Matt has me." Jessie sighed and gave her a dreamy look.

Katie looked at her and laughed. "I'm done with the small things. I'll be back to finish in time for your opening." Katie waved as she walked out the door.

Jessie and Sadie left after Katie. Looking at the clock, Jessie realized she had just enough time to get dressed and back to the store to make sure everything was ready. She pulled the form-fitting blue dress that Sadie had bought her out of the closet. She would wear it for Matt, she thought and smiled. He'd loved it the first time she wore it. She had some plans of her own for tonight.

"I'm so glad you wore that dress. It looks beautiful on you. Where did you get the sapphire necklace? It's perfect." Sadie held the necklace up to get a better look at it.

"Reba Thompson gave it to me. I wore it the night

of the explosion at the Yacht Club." Jessie frowned. "I've just realized how often I associate things with all the calamities that have happened since moving here. I hope this isn't going to be a trend. Reba will be there tonight, and I want you two to meet. I think the two of you will get along swimmingly." They headed back to the store. Jessie unlocked the door and turned on the first light.

"You have to admit your life has been exciting." Sadie sat down in one of the comfy chairs while Jessie turned on the rest of the lights.

"It has been." She sighed. "Although, I wonder how many times you can be chased, shot at, almost blown up, and still make it out alive." She patted Sadie's shoulder as she walked by her. "I've been lucky so far but..." The bell on her door rang, interrupting her. She turned when Katie, Jeremy, and Liam entered. Liam was just as she remembered him, tall with green eyes that always seemed to sparkle with mischief. He had the same coppery hair as Katie, but somewhere Katie had missed out on the height. He was handsome in a laid back, charming kind of way.

"Look who I brought with me. I've already told Liam he was the biggest fool to let you slip through his fingers."

Jessie rolled her eyes and blushed. "Hi, to you, too."

Katie set the box she was carrying down on the table. "Just put those on the floor, right there, boys." She pointed to the spot.

"She's always was a bossy kid, ever since I can remember." Liam winked at Jessie and ruffled Katie's hair. She slapped his hand. "She's right in your case, though. Who would have thought all of those arms and legs would grow up into you." He gave her the once over and then a big hug.

She pulled free first. He was Liam; only she was the object of his intense looks. "Nice to see you, too." She smiled and walked over to stand with Sadie, a safe distance from him.

"Didn't I tell you Liam was a big flirt?" Sadie grinned at him.

"Yes, you did, Grams, and you were right."

"Sadie, is that you, darlin?" He bent down and kissed her cheek. "Still a beauty, I see."

She patted his cheek. "You're full of blarney, but I love you."

Jessie left Katie to order her brother and Jeremy about and finished with the last minute details. She looked at her watch again. Relief filled her when Corrine Clark walked through the door. Her arrival signaled the last significant detail to be completed. Katie gushed over her; Liam rolled his eyes, and Sadie had her book signed. Finally, it was time. She removed the paper cover from the French doors that connected the store to Joe's and opened them wide. Jessie walked to the front door. She could see Reba waving at her and Molly with Kenny standing in line. All of them were waiting for her store to open. She felt all fluttery with excitement. She smiled, turned the sign over the door to *open*, and her night began.

"You've grown up quite nicely." Liam put his arm around her shoulder.

She slipped out from under it. "You're a tease."

"I'd never tease about finding you attractive." He smiled at her.

She tossed her head. "If I remember, you always found *someone* attractive, but I wasn't among them."

"You used to like me once, and followed me around as I remember it."

"I was in high school, and that was many years ago. I'm seeing someone right now that I care deeply about." She met his teasing green eyes. "I'm not in the market for a change. Excuse me, I need to talk to some folks and mingle." She walked away, feeling his eyes on her.

Sadie motioned her over. "Don't let the scallywag make you nervous. He only does it to see you blush."

"I know. I wish Matt would get here." Jessie's eyes went to the door.

"He'll be here, dear. Please try to enjoy your night." Sadie patted her hand.

"I know you're right. Look at all these people. Corrine will have significant sales from this." Jessie waved to Reba as she strolled her way. "Reba, this is my grandmother, Sadie."

"If you don't mind," she pointed to the chair, "you're just the person I wanted to chat with." Reba sat down beside her.

"I don't mind at all." Sadie smiled at Reba. "Jessie, why don't you get us some refreshments? It will give you something to do while you're waiting for him."

Jessie left them to talk. She filled two small plates with Katie's fantastic creations and put them on the table between the women along with two glasses of wine to enjoy while they chatted. She continued to greet guests and look at her watch every few minutes. She had almost given up hope when she heard the bell ring again. She knew without looking that he was there. He stood in the doorway looking at her with hunger in his eyes. She felt herself moving toward him, trying not to run.

"Hi, sweetheart. I've missed you." He put his arm around her possessively.

"Hi, yourself. I know the feeling. I was beginning to wonder if you'd make it." She glanced up through her lashes at him.

"You had to know I'd be here. I couldn't miss your big night. You look good enough to eat." He gave her his lopsided grin. "How's our Sadie?"

Jessie smiled, gazing into his eyes. "She's getting to know Reba."

"Are you sure that's a good idea. There's no telling what those two could be capable of together."

Jessie chuckled. "It should be interesting to say the least." Her face lit up. "Isn't it wonderful? Look at all these people!"

"The place is full, good for you." He smiled and looked at her. "I'm having a hard time getting past the sight of you in that dress."

"I wore it just for you." She gazed into his eyes again.

"You did?" A smile spread across his face.

She nodded. "I sure did, because you liked it on me."

"I remember." He raised an eyebrow. "Are you sure you can handle it?"

"The question is—can you?" She fluttered her eyes at him and leaned close to him. "You do know that Jeremy and Katie are an item?"

"I sure do, but not as hot as we are." He saw the familiar pink tinge on her cheeks.

She turned her face away from him, fanning her face. "Evan and Adriana are here, so are Molly and Kenny, and Liam Donavon, Katie's brother." She pointed to them in the crowd.

"Am I in danger of an old crush coming back to haunt me?" His smile faded.

"Not even a little bit." She rolled her eyes at him. "Don't you have some things you need to share with me? I want to know all about the case." She grabbed his hand.

"I'll get to all of it later, but not now. It's time to celebrate your store." He bent a little closer and whispered in her ear. "As soon as we're alone, we'll celebrate us, too."

"I'm looking forward to it." She touched his face. "I like you all scruffy like this. If I have to wait until we're alone to celebrate, then I'm holding on to you. I haven't seen you since you got back from Palm Springs, and I'm not letting you out of my sight."

"Believe me, I'm not going anywhere. You can glue me to your side. I would like nothing more than to be alone with you right now."

"Me, too. Let's get this over with, then." She took him over to meet Liam.

****

Matt loved watching Jessie work the room. She was good at it. The folks of Blue Cove had turned out in record number for her opening. She had won their hearts just as she had won his. He wanted to show her how much she meant to him. He looked at the clock on the wall. He still had thirty minutes until he would have her to himself.

He walked over to Sadie and Reba. "What have

you two been cooking up over here?"

"We're solving the world's problems." Sadie winked at him. "I was wondering when you were going to come around and talk to me." She smiled at his distraction. "I see you can hardly take your eyes off of her."

"Guilty as charged. She's good to look at, and I've missed her." He smiled when she laughed at something Molly said.

"I'll let you in on a little secret—she's missed you too." Sadie patted his hand.

"It's good you're home to guard what's yours. There's some competition brewing, and he's not keeping it secret," Reba warned him. "Don't let him move in. He's a real charmer." Reba frowned as she looked at Liam.

"Do you have plans to spend some time with her tonight?" Sadie smiled up at him.

"I do if you don't mind being alone for a little while. I promise not to keep her away too long."

"You don't even need to ask. Of course, carry out your plans with my blessing."

"Ladies, behave yourselves." He walked over to help Jessie pack up Corrine's books, as she got ready to leave.

"I'm glad she brought extra." Jessie closed one of the cartons of books. "As it was, she sold everything that I had on hand along with one of the boxes that she brought. It was a banner night for her." Jessie kept a few out of the last box. "I'll keep these twenty signed books for people who might have missed tonight."

He carried the boxes out to her van for Corinne. He laughed when he heard the way Katie was bossing her brother. He had always wondered what it would be like to have a sister. Maybe not having one wasn't such a bad thing. "Is she always like that?" He winked at Katie.

"Ever since I can remember she's bossed me around." Liam pulled a pathetic face. "Even as a little bit of thing."

"Enjoy your visit." Matt nodded. "There's always the beach if you need a little peace and quiet."

"I plan on it, along with renewing an old acquaintance." He looked at Jessie when he said it.

The challenge had been issued. Matt had seen the way Liam had looked at Jessie all night. Jessie might be over her high school crush on Liam, but he was seeing her all grown up for the first time. Liam was interested and he would be a damn nuisance. "I hope you can take the time to see the area and do a little fishing if you like it. Blue Cove is a great area for it." Matt smiled at Jessie when she walked up and grabbed his hand.

Jessie laughed. "Liam fish? That's not likely, unless, of course, a beautiful girl is the one holding the fishing rod."

"Hey, that's not fair unless you're volunteering."

She shook her head. "Not me, I'm taken. But I still think it's quite accurate. Even Sadie remembers it that way." She turned to Matt. "I'm just about ready to close up. If you guys carry those boxes out to Katie's car, we'll call it a night." She leaned close to his ear. "I think we have some catching up to do."

"Yes, ma'am, we sure do."

Matt helped Jeremy and Liam carry all of Katie's boxes out to her car. Katie and Jessie were laughing when they came back in the store.

"That's how I remember those two. They were always laughing like that." Liam gave Jessie an admiring glance. "It is amazing to me that they have managed to remain friends all these years. I hardly remember anyone from college, much less elementary school."

"They're close all right. I hope you enjoy your stay." Matt shook Liam's hand. "I'm going spend some time with my girl. I hope you don't mind." He stayed with Jessie as she locked up the store, and they walked out to the car hand in hand. "I'll be at your house in about twenty minutes. I already asked Sadie, and she's okay with it." He opened the door for Jessie and then walked Sadie over and opened her door.

Sadie looked up at Matt. "I hope you keep putting that Donavon boy in his place," she said quietly. "He was always a big flirt. I know he's interested in my Jessie, but she belongs to you. He was always chasing after anything in a skirt."

"I hate to tell you, Sadie; that's what guys do when they're young." He grinned.

"I wasn't born yesterday, I know all that." She sniffed. "The thing is, he's still like that. I wouldn't put it past him to come around, mess things up, and take off. He doesn't seem to want to settle down."

"If you're wondering if I would give up or fight for her. I can tell you right now, I would fight for her. That's how I feel about it. I missed her so much the last few weeks. Half of me was missing."

She patted his cheek. "That's all I needed to know."

Chapter 35

Matt had a few last minute details to take care of, but he still pulled up at her house right on time. She answered his knock, and he stepped in. "Sadie, here's my number. If you need anything call."

"Thank you. You two run along and have a nice time." She waved from the sofa. "I'm going to watch a show on TV."

He bent down and gave her a kiss on the cheek. "Call if you need us."

"I will, but I doubt if I'll need you," Sadie whispered in Matt's ear. "Put the roses back in her cheeks."

"I'll do my best," he whispered back.

"What are you two whispering about?" Jessie tapped her foot. "Grams, what are you up to now?"

"Nothing, dear. I just told him I wouldn't be calling him." Sadie smiled at Matt.

"Where are we headed?" Jessie took his hand after he shut the door.

"You'll see." He opened the car door for her. "I missed you." He closed the door, got in, and started the engine. "How are you processing the events of the last few weeks?"

Jessie looked pensive. "I still feel some guilt. It's hard not to feel guilty about Mallory. I had a vest on, and he didn't know it because of the jacket I was wearing. He didn't need to risk his life."

"I wondered if you were feeling guilty. I guess that answers my question." He looked at the expression on her face. "Jess, I think he did need to risk it. Reading your paper on Mallory and all that he suffered as a kid; seeing what I saw when he was dying, saving you might have saved him in some odd way. It gave him peace in his death, if nothing else. His life was not good, and he did some bad stuff. He killed people, maybe several. To find some peace at the end might have been the best he could hope for." He touched her hand and then backed out of the parking space.

"That was the nicest thing you could've said to me." She smiled at him, moisture filling her eyes.

He grinned. "You're welcome, sweetheart. All the stuff you see in this job can mess with your head. I guess that's why I keep remodeling my house. It's good therapy for me. I finished the master bedroom and bath that I started during the last case. There's nothing left for me to redo. Maybe I'll start again or better yet, restore a car."

"Running is what works for me. I've had to run on the treadmill, which isn't as therapeutic as running outdoors. It's been too cold and icy."

Matt pulled into his driveway. "I hope you don't mind coming here. I thought it would be a good place to talk. It's too cold for a stroll on the beach."

"I don't mind." She looked around and smiled. "Your house is beautiful. So much of your personality is in every room of it."

"Welcome, to my humble abode." He smiled and opened the door for her. A fire crackled in the fireplace, two wine glasses placed next to a chilling bottle of wine and a beautiful bouquet of red roses in a crystal vase were on the coffee table. The ambiance was perfect. "May I take your coat?"

"Only, if you promise to give it back." She chuckled. "I wouldn't exactly call this humble." She glanced around the room.

He draped her coat over the chair. "Mm, you smell good. Do you mind," he said putting his hands on her shoulders, "if I just hold you for a minute before we talk?"

She walked into his arms and nestled her head on his shoulder. "I'm glad you made it tonight."

"It's just how I remember it. You fit perfect." He smiled when she sighed, then led her over to the couch, and poured wine into their glasses.

"I don't know where to begin—so much has happened. I should start by telling you that the way you ended up in Evan's dream seems to have been the real deal. I can't explain it logically. Someone was obviously looking out for Adriana and wanted you involved."

"It's so weird." She took a sip of her wine.

"What do you mean?"

"I used to wonder what would happen if we were more aware of the people around us. There would be limitless possibilities to help people in need. I never thought it would happen the way it has to me, but it saved Adriana, so I'm okay with it."

"You can ask me questions. Maybe I'll be able to focus on something besides how hot you look in that dress, or the color of your eyes, and the smell of your hair."

"Let's start with Mallory."

"Mallory is a good place to start. He fell for you the first time he saw you when you interviewed the professor. I can't say that I blame him. He was already blackmailing Irwin because he knew about his problem with Adriana and several other young women. As luck would have it, Mallory ended up serving time in the same prison with Jason Cummings and Ed Jones. He was about to leave as they were coming in."

"How did they meet?"

"Mallory had read about the club from your articles. He had them all. He was obsessed with you. We found almost everything you had ever written in a scrapbook inside his house in Rocky Pointe." He glanced at the fire. "Mallory was impressed when he met Jason Cummings in the cafeteria. Jason bragged about all the money they'd made and the lifestyle they had enjoyed in the club. Mallory was hooked and introduced Irwin to Cummings when he came to visit."

"I don't understand why Irwin would visit Mallory in prison if he was blackmailing him." She sipped her wine, slipping off her heels and rubbing her foot as she did.

Matt watched her every move, taking a deep breath before he spoke again. "At some point after Irwin left the college, they became friends. I'm not sure that's the best word to use to describe them. Irwin figured out he could manipulate Mallory, and Mallory needed someone to care, however, strange that it was. They muddled along together. They lived together in Rocky Pointe." Matt sipped his wine. "Besides knowing Irwin's fascination with young college-age women and Adriana, of course, he also knew he had killed his first wife and another woman when he tried out his cultic ritual on them. Their house was a wealth of evidence."

"Strange." She sat forward and smelled the roses. "They're lovely."

"Those are for you, by the way." He gently pulled her back against him. "Where were we?"

"Irwin was introduced to Jason Cummings by Mallory, and then what happened?"

"It was during that meeting Jason found out about Irwin's extensive travels overseas and his dabbling in the occult. When he left, the club decided that Irwin could be useful, and Jason set their outside person to work on recruiting him." He took another sip of his wine. "Do you remember your first run-in with Irwin? The fear you felt before you took control and fought it?"

"I do." She reached forward for her wine glass.

"We know of two men who died when it happened to them. Irwin's wife and another woman were also victims. There might be others, as well. We're still gathering information." He felt her shiver. "Irwin is going up on murder charges along with attempt charges for what he did to Tony, Carter, and you. His efforts at mind control made the interrogation process an unholy nightmare." Matt grimaced at the thought. "He was still angry that you had rendered him powerless."

"This is starting to get interesting. Do you mind?" She tucked her legs under her when he shook his head and leaned in closer to him. He draped his arm around her shoulder. "Who was running the Collector's Club from the outside and who was doing the recruiting?"

"None other than our sweet little Southern Belle, the one you had doubts about from the beginning, Jayla Conner." He heard her intake of breath. "With the bank's president Bob Sievers help on the financial end, they were starting to build and recruit. They were all in awe of Irwin's ability to control things. He would suddenly just be there and take over."

"What do you mean" She lifted her head to look at him.

"I mean they never saw him coming. He would just appear, which might explain how Henderson was taken by surprise and Irwin got away so fast the night he killed Mallory. It also explains why Adriana never knew who her stalker was."

"A little spooky, don't you think?"

"Weird, if you ask me, and its right up there with," he frowned, "guns that don't fire. Jordon Daniels, his real name is Mike Dickerson, was involved in it all, but Randy was too afraid of Irwin or getting his hands dirty. He stayed clear of the club and had put in for a transfer."

"It looks like your feelings about Jordan panned out. I'm surprised about Bob, though, he seemed like such a nice man, and so willing to help us. Did you get to punch Jordon?" She chuckled. "You wanted to that day."

"No, but it was a pleasure to see him in handcuffs." Matt's lips twitched.

She rubbed her foot again. "Please continue."

"Irwin came into the bank all the time. The four of them would meet and make their plans. When the bank transferred Adriana from one of its other branches, the obsession started up again for him. He hatched the plan to have Mallory abduct her and take her to Palm Springs. Not because you were going there, but because they were planning something big in May. The others had no knowledge of Irwin's plan for Adriana."

He heard her take a deep breath. "So how did I find myself in the middle of it again?"

"Well, it seems that Jason and Ed were both worried about you and your keen sense for news. They decided to preempt any problems. They put the video equipment in your store and house so they could hear what you were doing. It was the perfect opportunity when you landed in Palm Springs. They figured Mallory could scare you off. I guess they didn't learn anything the first time. It didn't work then either, did it, sweetheart?" His voice took on a husky timbre.

She turned around to look at him. Their eyes met and so did their lips. He kissed her passionately then took a deep breath. "I'll never get through this if you keep looking at me like that." He gently turned her head around away from him.

She smiled. "Finish your story and I'll only interrupt you with questions. After you're done, however, all bets are off."

"Mallory was paid handsomely to scare you. That's where all the notes came in. Irwin actually wrote them. Mallory would place them in your suite using a key he had stolen. Irwin tried to put a curse on you, which you fought off." He smiled. "You gave him fits."

She shivered at the memory. "Why was Irwin there?"

"Here's where it gets interesting. Irwin was there at the same time as you to claim Adriana, which the others at that time knew nothing about. Mallory took Adriana to that old trailer leased by Jordon Daniels. The club had stored some of the munitions and parts on the site in an underground bunker as well as several other desert locations. Jordon had stolen and acquired them over a period of years from his days in the military. His specialty was explosives. The army gave him a dishonorable discharge when munitions went missing on his watch."

"No wonder you didn't like him." She reached for her wine glass.

"Jordon had changed his identity, social security number, and everything because the army was looking for him. He was able to keep one-step ahead of them. Jordon, Mallory, and Irwin went to Palm Springs every now and again, to work on the project that was going to make them rich.

"I didn't do anything to Irwin. Why did he try to kill me?"

"Irwin was angry at Mallory. He had bungled the job when Adriana escaped. The episode with Maria and Rodney didn't score him any points either. It all hit the fan when the news carried Adriana's rescue. Irwin was starting to take heat from the others in the group and was told to handle the problem, Of course, none of them knew about Radar's ability. Imagine their shock when he found the trailer, their stash of weapons, and the body of Irwin's wife." He paused when she held up her hand to stop him.

"How are Rodney and Maria doing?" Her eyes met his.

"Maria is doing well and Rodney has improved considerably. He went home from the hospital a few days ago." He turned her head gently back around again.

"You were going to tell me why Irwin wanted to kill me." She leaned her head against him.

"Irwin never intended to let Mallory have you; his plan was to kill you all along. You were the carrot Irwin dangled in front of him to manipulate him. When Mallory messed up, he threatened to kill you. He belittled Mallory to keep him under control. They had a strange relationship."

"I think that Mallory let people believe that they could control him, but he would explode when he'd had enough." She looked thoughtful.

"Exactly. When Irwin threatened Mallory, he called him some pretty awful names. It was still bothering Irwin once he calmed down. Irwin watched you the night of the street fair and got angry. He found it hard to believe he couldn't control you and blamed you for the trouble he was having with Mallory. His anger got the best of him, and he decided to kill you in one rash moment. Irwin had no clue that Mallory was watching him. After he had killed Mallory, Irwin turned his hatred on you. Mallory may have had an obsession, but it was Irwin's that brought down the group."

"Do you mean his obsession with Adriana?"

Matt nodded. "Among other things. Mallory may have suffered from mental illness from his early abuse but Irwin was a sociopath. He believed he was invincible."

"I wonder why he stayed there after Mallory's death. It was risky."

"Yes, but remember, Irwin has a big ego. He decided to stay around and finish the group's main reason for being in Palm Springs. Irwin believed he could handle it, he told the club not to worry, and remained in the area to finish the last of the three buildings. They had big plans. The timers would be coordinated to all go off within seconds of each other during the Annual Golf Tournament. With the size of the event and its popularity, the news wire would cover it globally, and their potential buyers would see on the TV news exactly what damage the weapons they purchased were capable of inflicting." He ran his hand up and down her arm and felt her shiver. "Zach's computer gave us the list of potential buyers, all contacts made by Irwin when he was in the Middle East. Your idea of weapons sales was right on. The Collector's Club was in its infant stage, so it was easy to shut it down. Left to grow, it could have become significant and dangerous. Between you and Mallory, you saved many lives."

"How so?" She glanced at him.

"Irwin had a key to the store. The club had worked there undetected for months. He honestly believed he could control the situation. Early in the morning hours, he left the store for a short time to get something to eat. He misplaced the key. That's why he was at the front of the store when the owner opened up and why he took the hostages who weren't hostages at all. He had decided to use them and a few theatrics to his advantage. He was rigging another bomb to go off inside the store so he could get away. His diversionary tactic without the club's knowledge. What is strange is he didn't need the key or the diversion. No one knew he was there. When you taunted him, his anger got the best of him. He forgot about everything else in his hatred for you."

"A stupid plan, wow! Sometimes you have to wonder about people." She took another sip of her wine.

"The main thing is Palm Springs would have been filled with celebrities the weekend that they planned to set off the explosives. I can't even imagine how many lives could have been lost."

"Did Irwin tell you all this?"

"He told us some. Jeremy found out more in his research, Zach's computer revealed a lot as did Jordan Daniels. Dylan was the one that found Jordon's record in the military. Jayla, bless her sweet little heart, became a songbird when the pressure was turned up, and she let the cat out of the bag."

"No one would have known had Irwin not seen Adriana again. Life is too strange." She sat forward to gaze into the fire. "Every action has a cause and effect." She stood and walked toward the windows. "Look at the moonlight over the water. You have such a beautiful view from here. It's simply breathtaking. You were smart to have had these windows put in."

"It's more beautiful at this moment than I've ever seen it." He heard her intake of breath as he walked up behind her, wrapping his arms around her waist and resting his chin on the top of her head. "Jess, you mean more to me than ever. I realized that watching you tonight. You're kind, intelligent, and fun. A man couldn't ask for more."

"I seem to have brought my share of trouble to this little spot in the world. I mean, how could I have known all those years ago that one interview and one angry man could impact my life and yours today." She frowned out into the night. "It makes me wonder if there are any more surprises waiting for me from my past."

"If, so we'll handle them together."

"I'm not sure it's fair to ask that of you."

"You're not asking me. I'm volunteering. I love you, Jess, but you already know that. With my declaration comes the responsibility to hang in there with you through the difficulties of sharing a life together. I'm not asking you to marry me today," he murmured. "I'll wait until you're ready. But I want to share every moment that I can with you—the good ones and the not so good."

She turned around to face him. "I want that too." She snuggled in close, pulling her head back just enough to see his face.

"Good." He gazed into her eyes. "I'm going on record right here and now that I won't put up with any shenanigans from our little Irish friend, Liam, even if he's your best friend's brother. I'm not usually the jealous type, but when it comes to you, I have a feeling all bets are off." His voice trailed off, her scent was driving him crazy.

"Hmm, that's nice..." She pulled his head down and kissed him passionately, rocking his world—and he was of a mind to let her.

A word from the author...

I live in Colorado with my husband of many years. I have three grown sons and five grandchildren. I love the whole process of writing from the first draft to the final copy.

http://www.ionamorrison.com

Thank you for purchasing
this publication of The Wild Rose Press, Inc.

If you enjoyed the story, we would appreciate your
letting others know by leaving a review.

For other wonderful stories,
please visit our on-line bookstore at
www.thewildrosepress.com.

For questions or more information
contact us at
info@thewildrosepress.com.

The Wild Rose Press, Inc.
www.thewildrosepress.com

Stay current with The Wild Rose Press, Inc.

Like us on Facebook

https://www.facebook.com/TheWildRosePress

And Follow us on Twitter
https://twitter.com/WildRosePress